"Don't you ever think about us, Clee?" he asked.

"I think about us as often as I think of cleaning the refrigerator. Having lived with me, you have an idea of how frequent that is," she retorted.

"I don't believe you." Gus moved forward another step. "I think you're imagining what it would be like if I kissed you."

"Actually," Cleo said, "I *was* thinking about cleaning the refrigerator. I bought this bunch of broccoli last week, and you know how slimy those little green leaves get—"

Gus came even closer. "It's all right, Clee," he said softly, "because I'm thinking about kissing you, too."

He was standing next to her now, so close that she could smell him again, that familiar scent that meant Gus, her lover, her husband....

Dear Reader,

Spellbinders! That's what we're striving for. The editors at Silhouette are determined to capture your imagination and win your heart with every single book we publish. Each month, six Special Editions are chosen with *you* in mind.

Our authors are our inspiration. Writers such as Nora Roberts, Tracy Sinclair, Kathleen Eagle, Carole Halston and Linda Howard—to name but a few—are masters at creating endearing characters and heartrending love stories. Their characters are everyday people—just like you and me—whose lives have been touched by love, whose dreams and desires suddenly come true!

So find a cozy, quiet place to read, and create your own special moment with a Silhouette Special Edition.

Sincerely,

The Editors
SILHOUETTE BOOKS

JUDE O'NEILL
The Midnight Hour

Silhouette Special Edition

Published by Silhouette Books New York

America's Publisher of Contemporary Romance

Again, for Neil
inspiration in all things romantic

SILHOUETTE BOOKS
300 East 42nd St., New York, N.Y. 10017

Copyright © 1987 by Judy Blundell

ISBN: 0-373-09387-X

First Silhouette Books printing June 1987

America's Publisher of Contemporary Romance

Printed in the U.S.A.

Books by Jude O'Neill

Silhouette Romance

Just One Look #464

Silhouette Special Edition

The Midnight Hour #387

JUDE O'NEILL

has written everything from radio commercials to book jackets to film reviews, but considers it all a breeze compared to teaching high school English. She tossed aside the glamorous life of an underpaid editor in Manhattan to become a full-time writer. Married to an artist, she divides her time between California and New York.

What the press said about Gus and Cleo...

Red Herrings in Cream Sauce marks the promising debut of mystery writing team Gus Creighton and Cleo Delaney. The courtship of hard-boiled Max Fast and sharp-witted Sophie, who demands time out from the case to investigate sales at Saks, is delightful....
> —*The New York Book Review*, 1983

Max and Sophie are back, and marriage hasn't slowed them down a bit. In *Murder on the Westchester Express*, the detectives are as clever as ever. Publicity notes indicate that authors Creighton and Delaney will marry later this year; let's hope that won't slow them down either....
> —*The New York Book Review*, 1984

Marriage must agree with Creighton and Delaney; *Fast Moves*, their third book, is already being hailed as a modern classic....
> —*Flash Magazine*, 1985

Best-selling page-turner *Fast Moves* heads for the screen; Gus Creighton to pen script....
> —*Hollywood Beat*, 1985

Trouble on *Fast Moves* set leads studio to take chance on Gus Creighton to direct his script....
> —*Hollywood Beat*, 1985

News around Hollywood and New York is that the trial separation of Gus Creighton and Cleo Delaney is working all too well. Word is the couple won't even talk, let alone banter.... —"Lucy Knows," *New York Daily Press*, 1986

The film *Fast Moves* showcases author Gus Creighton in his new role as director....
> —*Eye on Film*, 1986

On her own now, Cleo Delaney does not disappoint with her devilishly delicious new book, *Guilty as Sin*....
> —*The New York Book Review*, 1986

Publishing and film worlds alike are speculating about the shaky Delaney/Creighton marriage. A breakup could mean the end of Max and Sophie Fast's adventures in print or on celluloid. C'mon, Gus and Cleo, kiss and make up!
> —"Lucy Knows," *New York Daily Press*, 1987

Chapter One

Cleo was no coward. She'd been told this by her editor, her agent, her ex-husband and her mother, so it had to be true. Practically fearless, they said. She was bold, brave, perhaps even reckless, and never afraid to confront a daunting situation.

So any minute now she should be unclenching her hands from the steering wheel to start up the car again and drive off the rough shoulder of the road. She'd turn back onto the main road in that bold, brave fashion she was known for and roar down that last hundred yards to the perfectly innocuous country inn looming menacingly ahead of her.

Any minute now...

"Who am I kidding?" Cleo asked the empty car. Talking to herself had ceased to worry her several months ago, and that had started to worry her. She sighed gloomily and rested her head on the steering wheel. She felt sentimental and crazy, and she had to admit that all she really wanted to do right now was to whip the car around in a fast U-turn and leave the blazing maples of Connecticut in her dust as she sped back to the cool gray solace of Manhattan. She'd probably give in to the impulse if she wasn't positive that the old car would sputter and stall as she was impressively burning rubber. What did she know about cars? She was a New Yorker.

A sensible person would have several good reasons for pulling off the road, she knew. Take, for instance, her car. The Green Gables Inn had been recently transformed into a luxurious resort, and she supposed it might be a bit embarrassing to arrive in the lime-green '72 Valiant she'd borrowed from her brother-in-law. He called the car a classic, but it was more accurately termed a bomb.

And then there was the way she was dressed. She felt ridiculous in the nun's habit she had to wear for the weekend ahead. The thought of actually appearing in it in public was mortifying, as was the respectful and completely undeserved solicitude she'd received from the gas-station attendants and toll-booth operators on her drive up to Connecticut.

But the last and most logical reason she should have for this sudden strange cowardice would be that she really should be nervous about attending the First Annual Detective Writers (Put Your Mouth Where Your Money Is) Murder Weekend. In a matter of minutes, she would be matching wits with her more experienced peers, in front of journalists and television crews, in order to solve what promised to be an outlandish and extremely tricky murder plot.

The weekend had been touted as the most lavish ever produced, with carefully selected actors and actresses playing various "suspects" and an exorbitant fee for entrants promising that only the most dedicated mystery fans would match wits with their favorite writers. And then there were the inducements: gourmet food, lavish suites, a formal ball Saturday night—all were held out tantalizingly to attract the most famous mystery writers in the business. They'd responded in droves, all for the fun of dressing up as the famous detectives they'd created to solve the murder plot the flamboyant Denton Ballard, avid mystery fan, multimillionaire and creator of the weekend, had cooked up to stump them. The grand prize of a trip for two on the Orient Express wasn't nearly as important as the publicity that would follow the winner as the Greatest Detective in the World. It was nonsense, of course, but it was amusing nonsense, and it was all expenses paid.

Any fool would be nervous facing such an event. The only problem was that Cleo wasn't any fool. She was a very particular kind of fool, an illogical, emotional one, so none of those reasons bothered her very much. What had her paralyzed behind the wheel at the moment was the simple fact that the inn up ahead was full of memories she just couldn't face. Gus had proposed to her there. Lurking about and waiting to throw a net of sentiment over her head was the ghost of a woman she wanted to forget, a younger Cleo, a twenty-seven-year-old innocent who still believed in love.

Three years ago, after a marathon session finishing their second book together, she and Gus, in a state of exhaustion, relief and exhilaration, had finally mutually confessed their long-pent-up longing, lust and devotion to each other. To celebrate, they'd driven up to the Green Gables Inn. Gus had proposed at midnight, and they'd giddily bribed the sleepy desk clerk to raid the down-stairs cooler for the last bottle of Taittinger.

It had been a wonderful weekend. Then they'd had to go ahead and spoil it. They got married.

Cleo sighed again and lifted her gaze to stare out through the dirt-streaked windshield at the riotous colors of the glorious extravaganza that was a New England fall. The blazing leaves only made her feel worse. You couldn't even count on maple trees to stay the same. Everything changed.

The sleepy country inn had been bought by a major hotel chain and now had twenty-four-hour room service. She and Gus were no longer struggling writers; no longer were they together. They'd separated a year ago when he'd gone to Hollywood to direct his first film, and it was only a matter of time before she straightened her shoulders, accepted defeat and went to a lawyer for a divorce. But in her mind, if not legally, he was already her *ex*-husband.

Life had certainly taken on an unreal quality lately, Cleo mused. Once she'd lounged at the inn in a silk camisole, sipping champagne, warmed by love; now she would go through the weekend ahead dressed as a nun, chugging diet root beer from a can, and warmed, she was sure, by nothing more exciting than an electric blanket.

Why was it that in the movies the lives of recently separated women always turned glamorous? They explored previously undiscovered talents in fabulous new careers and were courted by sexy new suitors with none of the disagreeable habits of their ex-husbands. The only exciting emotional commitment Cleo had these days was to her computer. That took care of her days, true, but who wanted to curl up against floppy discs on a cool autumn night? She had the same career, the same apartment she'd had when she was single, and the same fierce ache in her stomach she'd developed the year before.

Gus was the one with the suddenly glamorous life-style. Just two weeks ago she'd idly scanned a copy of *Flash!* magazine left on her table in a delicatessen, and had seen Gus looking up at her with that familiar, maddening, conspiratorial grin. On his arm was an angelic-looking actress called Wendee Tolliver, looking extraordinarily pleased with herself. Cleo's vision had blurred and her stomach had turned over; she'd had to run for the small, dimly lit restroom and splash quantities of cold water on her face to prevent her from relinquishing her perfectly good corned beef on rye.

She'd been able to handle the wild success of Gus's film, but wispy platinum blondes were something else. She'd suddenly had an all-too-accurate picture of why Gus had remained in Hollywood after the film had opened, and exactly what kind of success he'd been enjoying.

But after that initial embarrassing reaction, she'd taken it all in stride. One had to be mature and accept the fact that one's ex-husband was going to take a lover sooner or later. It wasn't any big deal. No big deal at all.

Cleo looked down and was surprised to discover that she had succeeded in completely crumpling her can of root beer between her hands, and they were now sticky with syrup. She supposed she'd unconsciously had her hands around Gus's neck—or Wendee Tolliver's. She sighed. A true mystery writer, she'd take homicide over divorce any day.

She turned the ignition key resolutely. The engine coughed and sputtered, but at least it started up again. She gripped the steering wheel with her sticky hands and headed for the turnoff. It was time to get to work.

For the weekend ahead definitely was work, she reminded herself as she skidded after a van full of a camera crew from *Dateline: Entertainment*. Ellison Fink, her agent, had talked her into it so vigorously that she couldn't think of it as anything else. She'd balked when he'd told where it would be held, but Ellison had been adamant.

"You can't pay for publicity like this, Cleo. And you can't avoid every place where you and Gus have been together," he'd pointed out reasonably. "You'd never go out of your apartment." Cleo had sighed and agreed. Ellison was right; she needed the publicity for *Guilty As Sin*, the first detective novel she'd written on her own, without Gus. And besides, Ellison had been more on the money than he knew: she never *did* go out of her apartment.

She slowed when the inn came into view. It was as charming as she remembered it, long and sprawling, the various additions completed over its history giving it an appealingly awkward grace. The hotel chain had repainted it in its same weathered colors of gray and green and repaired it with careful attention to maintaining its rustic charm. Here in New England, there were profits to be made from authenticity.

The newly paved circular drive in front was crammed with all varieties of expensive foreign automobiles. Cleo inched ahead, guessing that their degree of luxury most likely depended on the royalty checks from the latest books of their detective-novelist owners. The Ferrari in front meant number one on the best-seller list and an appearance on the *Today* show; the Mercedes nestled up to its rear bumper meant the owner was hot on its heels. It was anybody's guess who was arriving in the long gray limousine that had pulled in behind her. The windows were smoked gray to conceal the stellar identity of its passenger, but Cleo would lay down a bet that this writer had sold a book to the movies or had a television series in the works at the very least.

She didn't envy whoever it was ensconced in the back seat, however. She was living proof that the dazzle of that brand of fame had a tendency to strain lives and crack marriages. It had all happened so fast—Gus's decision to direct *Fast Moves*, their huge fight after she found out he'd committed himself to the project without telling her, and later, his obvious reluctance for her to come with him. It seemed to Cleo as though one day she was bundling up her husband's sweatshirts and stuffing them in a duffel bag for the flight to California; the next, the only news she got about him was gleaned from the pages of *Variety*. Then long-distance phone lines had crackled between silences and evasions. Gus had become uncommunicative and a stranger to her, totally wrapped up in his film. Their marriage had suddenly become a drag on a rapidly rising career.

Would Gus have backed out if he'd known what the consequences would be? She doubted it. He'd finally been able to fulfill a long-held fantasy—to turn their third book and first best-seller about their battling married detective team, Max and Sophie Fast, into a movie. He'd abandoned his screenwriting four years before to collaborate with Cleo on their first book, and he'd always wanted to go back to it. The film based on *Fast Moves* had surprised both of them by catapulting him into the limelight in a way no book review in *The New York Times* had ever accomplished. No matter how many books they sold, they would never be able to equal the fame—and money—that Hollywood could offer.

The old Valiant chugged forward, spewing clouds of black smoke that barreled out of her exhaust and lingered in the crisp autumn air. It was almost like being back in Manhattan. She put the car in neutral. If the parking attendant didn't get to her soon, everyone behind her would choke to death.

She was proved right when a fit of coughing broke out behind her, and a moment later a gravelly voice greeted her. "Cleo Delaney—that's you, isn't it?" A thick-fingered hand was thrust through her window and Cleo recognized the broad features of Sidney Clott, writer of such best-sellers as *Meet My Uzi*. He was dressed in the trademark white suit of his refined former-boxer detective hero, Mickey Dance. She took his hand and their fingers adhered briefly in a handshake gummy with root-beer residue.

Sidney gave a strained smile and unobtrusively tried to wipe his hand with his handkerchief. "Uh—nice hand lotion. So, should I be calling you Sophie Fast this weekend? And is Gus Creighton playing Max?"

"Hello, Sidney. No, he's not. And I'm not playing Sophie," Cleo returned. She always felt a bit uncomfortable with Sidney. He had a velvety manner that was completely incongruous with his stocky build, and he invariably complimented her on her books. Cleo, in all honesty, couldn't return the favor. Gus had remarked after meeting Sidney, "The man's body matches his prose—he's built like a trash compactor."

Sidney looked suddenly contrite; surely he'd known, along with everyone else, that she and Gus were separated. "I'm sorry—I shouldn't have mentioned Gus, should I? What can I say—I'm a writer, not a politician. Tact somehow eludes me at the worst of times." He leaned companionably on her open window, his wide face looming into hers. "It's just that I love those books, especially *Red Herrings in Cream Sauce*. Murder in a delicatessen, I love it. And *Fast Moves*, of course—fabulous film. What are Max and Sophie doing next? I hear rumors of a television show."

Cleo stiffened. She'd thought that the battle over the rights to the characters was a private one, but this was the first she'd heard about a television show. She and Gus had been warring politely through Ellison, their agent, with Gus obstinately refusing to make any kind of settlement where Max and Sophie were concerned. No wonder, if he had a series in the works.

But she didn't want to tell Sidney Clott all that; it would spread through the weekend guests like wildfire and end up on *Dateline: Entertainment* that very evening. She shrugged and answered offhandedly, "I'm not sure yet—we've put them on ice for a little while. I've got a new detective I'm pretty fond of these days."

"Sister Mary Claire, of course. Haven't read *Guilty As Sin* yet, but I saw the review in the *Times*. Wish I could get your kind of press—'psychological complexity and fast-paced wit.' I always get 'gritty muscular prose.' You know." He straightened and glanced briefly at his watch. "Well, I can't wait to go check out this 'lavishly appointed suite' Denton has promised me. See you at the party." Sidney started to stick his hand toward her for another shake, but thought better of it. Instead, he waggled his thick fingers in a wave and headed for the inn.

The attendant signaled to Cleo and she shifted into first with a grinding of gears to pull over to the curb. She handed him her keys through the window. Trying to control her irritation over what Sidney had told her, she reached for the veil on the seat next to her. She slipped it over her unruly black hair, tucked up the stray strands and glanced at herself quickly in the rearview mirror.

The veil was a bit too large and slipped over one eye, giving her a strangely rakish look that was rather inappropriate under the circumstances. Cleo pushed the veil back on her forehead and tried to cultivate the serene look suitable to her outfit. It didn't work. She looked frazzled, annoyed, and frankly, pretty silly.

She grabbed her weekend bag from the back seat, then swung her door open vigorously. Wincing, she heard metal scrape against metal as the heavy door smacked into the side of the long gray limousine, which had unobtrusively glided up next to her.

Cleo slipped out of the door hastily. "Sorry," she hollered over at the gray-smoked passenger window, hoping whoever was inside could hear her. Heaven only knew what Pulitzer prize winner she'd managed to offend. She knocked gently on the window. "I didn't see you."

The smoked window slid slowly and ceremoniously down, Cleo's knuckles sliding along with it as she squinted into the dim back seat. The shadowy figure reclining against the soft leather cushion leaned forward. One finger pushed a pair of sunglasses down to the end of a nose, and a pair of golden eyes caught the slanting ray of October afternoon sunlight. They eyed her speculatively over the dark frames. A very familiar, very wicked grin flashed.

Gus. What was he doing here? Strength drained from her legs, and confusion sped through her in a warm, dizzy rush. She looked back at him, stunned and wary; after months of telling herself he meant nothing to her anymore, she was none too pleased to find that her pulse had accelerated from the impact of seeing him again. And it wasn't just from surprise, either; those warm eyes and the sensual twist of the long mouth still made her respond to him in the most elemental way. No matter that she knew him so long and so well. He was still the most devastating man she knew.

All shades of tawny amber, from his eyes to his hair to his skin, dancing on a tightrope of his wit and his style and his exuberance, he had alternately compelled her and driven her crazy from the first moment when he'd plopped himself down at her table in a Greenwich Village café to announce who the murderer was in the mystery she was reading. "It will be much more interesting to talk to me," he'd said with absolutely no pretense at modesty.

But Gus had lost the ability to charm her by his unexpected presence. Whatever was he doing here? Why was he riding in a limousine as long as a yacht? And where was his Hollywood tan?

Be nice, she warned herself fiercely. *Take Grace Kelly as your model. Regal, sophisticated, cool . . .* Her chin lifted, and she gave him an icy glance as she attempted to mask the upheaval going on inside her.

But she could never fool Gus. His grin merely broadened.

"Don't give me that Grace Kelly look," he said.

"What are you doing here, damn you?" she snarled.

"What kind of language is that for a woman of the cloth?" Gus took off his sunglasses and looked at her sadly, shaking his head. "Cleo—or should I say Sister Cleo—what can I say? The separation has been difficult, I know. But locking yourself away in a convent like this—such a waste. And I know you so well, Clee. How can you possibly do without—"

"Gus—"

"You've got to reconsider. Black is very becoming on you, I admit, but—"

"What are you doing here, Gus? This is a literary event," Cleo interrupted pleasantly. "You're not a writer anymore. You're a screenwriter."

"Oh, good. We're starting out on the right track. And I was afraid you'd be nasty."

"What are you doing here?"

"Don't you remember, Clee—I used to write detective novels, too. Remember that guy Gus from West Twelfth Street you used to know?"

"No."

"No?" Gus's golden eyes darkened to the color of burnt sugar. When he spoke again his voice had softened and slowed, taking on the cadences of his Tennessee origins. It was a tone that, in the past, had never failed to turn her bones liquid. "Sure you do. And I'm still that same guy, Cleo. When are you going to see that? When are you going to realize that I haven't changed?"

A tiny, shimmering shiver of heat, made up of equal parts of desire, pain and longing, edged slowly up her spine. If only it were true. If only she could believe it. If only he were the same man she'd fallen in love with so long ago.

Then Cleo looked past her ringless left hand to the long gray limousine with the smoked-glass windows and the chauffeur with the shiny black cap. She surveyed the car slowly, taking her time.

"Of course you're the same guy, Gus," she said finally. "And you're riding on the Seventh Avenue IRT right now. Now, concentrate very carefully and maybe you'll be able to answer this question: what are you doing here?"

Gus slid closer on the seat and put one hand on the door next to hers. One little finger brushed against hers, and the disturbing warmth that flicked at her insides made every muscle in Cleo's body tighten. She let her hand drop to her side.

He watched her hand fall and looked up at her as if surprised at her question. "I've come for the weekend, Cleo. I'm here to solve a murder. Aren't you?"

Chapter Two

Right now I'm more likely to commit one," Cleo answered grimly. She stepped forward to grasp the outside door handle and kept her hand steady on it. "Are you telling me that you're playing Max Fast this weekend?"

"Well, I'm certainly not playing Sophie. I didn't bring the right clothes. Are you going to let me get out of the car?" Gus asked mildly.

"No. You're not doing this to me, Gus. I don't have time to play verbal Russian roulette with you this weekend. I'm here to publicize my new book."

"Your new what?"

"My-new-book," Cleo enunciated through gritted teeth.

"You wrote a new book?" Gus asked, his voice an almost convincing mixture of amazement and a pat on the back. "Well, that's great news. I'll have to read it."

"That's okay, Gus, I know you don't read anymore," she returned sweetly. "But I'm sure you could get someone at the studio to summarize it for you."

"Ah, of course. In between my eleven o'clock orgy and my twelve o'clock polo lesson. Listen, Clee, do you mind letting me in on why you're wearing that strange outfit? Not that you don't look, uh, wonderfully inspiring. But do you know something I don't? As far as here on the earthly plane, I mean."

"Can you give me a slight hint of what's going on in that minuscule pea you call a brain?"

Gus whistled softly. "Nasty, nasty. I can tell you must have flunked charity class in nun school. I was just wondering if Sophie had a miraculous conversion on the Long Island Expressway or something. Should I have brought a clerical collar for Max?"

"Gus, I'm not playing Sophie this weekend. Surely that must have penetrated your single-minded concentration on your own point of view. I'm playing Sister Mary Claire."

"Who?"

"Sister-Mary-Claire," she said with forced calm.

"Oh—your new book, of course. I *do* have to get that summary. But, Cleo, don't you think everyone here will be expecting you to play Sophie? She's much more popular than this Sister Mary Clarissa, you know."

"Claire."

"Whatever. By the way, your veil's tilted over one eye, there. You look like you just downed a pitcher of margaritas. Very unholy of you, I must say." When she reached up, scowling, to adjust the veil, Gus seized the opportunity to slide out of the car and stand next to her.

If only he weren't so big, Cleo thought irritably. He wasn't too much taller than she was, but his broad shoulders always made her feel dwarfed in comparison. "Besides," she continued, "if I played Sophie, that would mean I'd have to work with—"

"Max." Gus smiled crookedly at her. "Exactly. Or is playing Sister Mary Claire getting to be a habit with you?"

Cleo groaned and turned away to start toward the inn. "Do you think you could make a valiant attempt to keep this conversation above the junior-high level?"

Gus ambled next to her, his hands in his pockets. "Come on, Clee, what's Max without Sophie? That's like Nick without Nora—Masters without Johnson—Moe without Larry—"

"Gus, I—"

"Admit it now—don't you feel pretty silly in that thing?"

"Not at all."

"Well, you look pretty—"

"Thank you," Cleo broke in smoothly, "you look nice, too."

Gus laughed, deepening the fine lines at the corners of his eyes. "Thanks. I thought I looked rather well, myself."

Cleo shot him a look from the corner of her eye. He did look well, she admitted grudgingly; Gus had always had his own sense of style. His tweed jacket looked expensive; it was perfectly and loosely tailored, with a beautiful multicolored weave. Underneath it Gus was wearing a faded blue pullover with a pair of even more faded jeans, but he made the combination look elegant. On his feet were an ancient pair of sneakers. As a matter of fact, they looked familiar.

"Aren't those the sneakers you used to play basketball in every Saturday at the West Third Street playground?"

"Yes, why?"

"I tried to throw them out a year ago, Gus. Don't you think they're a little shabby for Rodeo Drive?"

"Nah. They go nice with the jacket."

Cleo shook her head, then stepped up her pace. "I should have had them bronzed. Look, Gus, do you mind? I'd like to check in before dark. Let's just agree to stay out of each other's way this weekend, okay?"

"Okay," Gus said agreeably, trailing behind her toward the porch steps. "I don't want to spoil the weekend for you."

"Too late."

"What I mean is, I know this thing is a test for you—to see if you can attend one of these literary events without me."

"For heaven's sake—"

"Ah—the outfit is wearing off on you, I see. Anyway, I admire you, Cleo, I really do. You've got guts. I know you must be paralyzed with nerves, afraid you won't measure up—"

Cleo paused at the foot of the stairs and turned to face him. "Don't be ridiculous. I am not."

"You are too."

"I am not."

"Are too."

"Not."

"Too."

"Not. Gus! I'm asking you for once in your life to be mature about this. Now, if you'll excuse me—"

"Sure," he continued in the same maddeningly amiable tone. "It's better this way anyway. All these reporters and camera crews around this weekend—we don't want the world to know about our working habits.''

Cleo eyed him suspiciously. "We don't?"

"Nope. We don't want everyone to know that I came up with the plots. For your sake, Cleo."

"You *what*?"

"Cleo, Cleo," he continued mildly, "don't get upset. You were very important to the books, too. The woman's touch. That's why I let you collaborate with me in the first place. I can tell you that now that we're separated."

"You *let* me collaborate—"

"Hey, it was the least I could do. There you were, the unsuccessful novelist, trying to make that cup of cappuccino last all afternoon—"

"And you, of course, owned a coffee plantation in Brazil at the time."

"And I was on the brink of a successful career in screenwriting—"

"Writing ads for Jiffi-Cloud Toilet Tissue—"

"But I saw you needed help. Structure. Plotting. You were good at the love stuff, of course—"

"I was good at the *love stuff*? Are you crazy? What about the plot for *Red Herring in Cream Sauce*? What about—"

"Exactly." Gus nodded judiciously. He pointed to his chest. "Plot by Gus Creighton." He pointed to her. "Love stuff by Cleo Delaney."

"I don't believe this," Cleo announced to a passing parking attendant, who politely ignored her and continued up the steps to the inn. She turned back to Gus. "Did you lose the ability to think in Hollywood? You'll have to come back to Manhattan for lessons."

"You know, I sense some hostility here—"

"Hostility? Is that what you feel out in California? Try *rage*. For your information, I'm the one who structured the plots. You couldn't construct one alone to save your life! Or anybody else's, either!"

"Oh, really? Prove it."

"What?"

Gus shrugged and leaned against the porch pillar. "Give up publicizing Sister Mary Christmas. You can do a book tour like everyone else. You be Sophie. I'll be Max. We'll work together like the old days, but we'll see who solves the murder first. What do you say?"

"Forget it." Cleo felt furious but wary. Was it possible that Gus had really turned into this self-aggrandizing egotist who claimed credit for their success? Could he really be the pompous jerk he appeared to be?

Gus slipped his sunglasses back on. With those warm eyes obscured, he looked cool and dangerous. "All right—why don't we sweeten the deal a bit—have a real wager."

"What do you mean, a real wager?"

"We'll just have something at stake that we really care about."

"Like what? We already agreed I'd get custody of the computer."

"I was thinking of Sophie and Max."

Cleo's heart began to pound. "What do you mean?"

"Whoever loses the wager will give up their half of the rights to Sophie and Max—with the financial details worked out satisfactorily, of course. But we'd finally stop all this arguing about it." When she still hesitated, Gus patted her arm. "I know what's bothering you—your reputation. Don't worry, Cleo," he said grandly, "if I win, I'll share half the credit with you. No one will have to know. Like always. I've always been a charitable guy, haven't I?''

"A regular Mother Teresa." Cleo's grip tightened on her bag and she imagined the *Post* headline if she followed through on her impulse at the moment: "Director Run Over by Lime-Green Valiant: Crazed Nun Held for Questioning."

How could she have even wondered if Gus had changed? Of course he had. It wouldn't be the first time that Hollywood had turned a decently talented person into a towering mass of ruthless egotism. And in his slimy, predictable way he was now trying to maneuver her into giving up her half of Sophie and Max. But Gus was making the same mistake he always had: he was underestimating her.

"So is it a deal?" he asked, regarding her over his sunglasses. He slouched against the pillar, managing to look both monumentally bored and supremely confident.

Cleo smiled a small, chilling smile. *Poor thing,* she thought with wicked compassion. *He doesn't even have the good sense to be nervous.*

"Deal," she said. She shook his cool hand with her sticky one. Then she pushed past him and went up the stairs to the inn.

Snap! She'd taken the bait.

It wasn't exactly an auspicious beginning, however. Even he had to admit it was a little early to have her already be furious with him. But for his plan to work, she had to play Sophie this weekend, and if he had to provoke her into it deliberately, he would. It wouldn't have mattered anyway; he'd seen that cold film of ice in those extraordinary gray eyes from the first moment she'd realized who was in the car.

He knew he shouldn't have taken the limousine. Wendee had arranged it for him as one of her little "surprises." His immediate inclination had been to refuse, but his plane had landed over two hours late and Wendee had also cancelled the rental car he'd reserved. He'd had no other way to get up to Connecticut on time, and he was in a fever to see Cleo again. It was pure bad luck that she had smashed her door into the limo and discovered him. He'd definitely lost ground with that ill-timed, ostentatious entrance.

Gus leaned against the pillar, tilted his sunglasses low on his nose and watched Cleo walk up the stairs to the inn. She was the most damnably beautiful woman. Even in that somber black habit with its shapeless lines she looked sexy. He grinned as his gaze trailed down her legs to her shoes. Even from here he could see the delicate sheen of her hose and the elegant, and he'd bet expensive, lines of her pumps. Leave it to Cleo. Never had a nun been so stylishly shod. The door banged shut behind her and he pushed off the pillar to start after her, feeling something like a hunter tracking his prey—or a detective tailing his suspect.

He caught up with her in the lobby. The late-afternoon sunlight slanted through the thick glass panes of the windows, barely illuminating the interior. Cleo was almost lost in her black habit against the dark wood of the old post-office counter that served as a front desk. Gus began to move toward her but hung back when he caught the slightly disturbed note in her voice. She was holding out her room key to the obviously frazzled clerk.

"I'm sorry to trouble you, but could you possibly find me another room?"

The clerk replied in the piping, soothing tone of one who was used to such finicky behavior from guests. "But Ms. Delaney, I don't think you realize—Suite Two is one of our most popular. It has a big antique four-poster canopy bed and—"

"A fireplace, yes, I know," Cleo interrupted patiently. "But could you possibly find me another anyway?"

Somewhere inside Gus a tiny, glowing flicker of hope sprang to life. This was good news—Cleo couldn't bring herself to stay in Suite Two. When memory exerted so strong a pull, couldn't love still linger? He knew how she must feel; just walking into that room, he was sure, would cause memory to blaze into life. Love had been born in that room with an urgency and fire that time— and a major hotel chain—couldn't erase.

Suddenly he felt positively cheerful. He approached the desk briskly, nodded at Cleo and smiled at the clerk. "I'm here for the murder weekend," he told the clerk as she handed Cleo a new key. As Cleo shouldered her bag and turned away without a word, Gus signed the register with a flourish. "Is Suite Two available, by any chance?" he asked offhandedly, making sure his voice carried.

He didn't have to turn around to know that Cleo had stopped dead in her tracks. He could feel her waiting behind him, tense and still.

"Here you are, Mr. Creighton. You're in luck—the suite just became available. It's one of our finest."

"Oh, believe me, I know," Gus answered. He picked up his bag and turned quickly to catch Cleo off guard, but she was already crossing the lobby toward the stairs.

Gus decided to wait. He hungered for her so badly his hands had trembled when he'd first seen her again, but he knew better than to push her. He'd felt a loneliness these past months that was terrifying in its specificity; he couldn't risk losing her again.

For he missed one woman, and only one woman. Once he would gladly have tumbled into the silken web of a Wendee Tolliver, but that was before Cleo. Five years ago he'd found her, and the years with her and without her had never diminished her impact on him.

So how, Gus asked himself for perhaps the thousandth time, had he managed so spectacularly to lose her, when he'd thought he was doing the only thing that would ensure their life together?

Fast Moves, their third book, had been their breakthrough commercial success—a runaway best-seller from the first, surprising even the hopes of their publisher. They were the darlings of the morning talk shows, a couple who bantered as expertly as the wisecracking couple they'd created. The twisting, quirky, competitive tension between them had sent ratings soaring.

Then they had started work on their fourth book, and for the first time they had trouble working together. They had always argued, but now the arguments were strained with the pressures of success. And Gus had come to the uncomfortable realization that it was his fault. Each clever idea of Cleo's, each expert turn of phrase, ground into him how completely he was tied to her—loving her so deeply, respecting her so much, she was bone and sinew and blood to him, she was life. And suddenly, Gus had realized that somewhere along the way, he, the most independent of people, had lost himself. Everywhere he turned he saw Cleo—her all-enveloping, trusting love, her loving family, her ideas, her wit, her talent. Reeling with how completely his world was made up of her, knowing he was being unfair, terrified he would begin to resent her, Gus had withdrawn—and felt guilty for his withdrawal.

When Ellison had called them with the news that a major studio was interested in the movie rights for *Fast Moves*, he'd seen a way out. He'd held out for the contract to write the screenplay. Cleo had agreed to postpone work on the book to give him time to write it, and she began another novel that eventually became *Guilty As Sin*. After months of writing and weeks of trips to the Coast for rewrites, missing Cleo like crazy, Gus had returned to New York feeling strangely depressed. It wasn't until he got the call that asked him to step in as director that the lethargy lifted; a thrill had shot through him and he'd accepted without hesitation. Then he had hung up the phone and had to tell Cleo. Never before had he made such a decision without consulting her. But when salvation reaches out to you, you grab it like a drowning man grabs for a life preserver—he just hadn't had a choice.

Gus had realized the next day, alone on the plane, that he'd made the decision in order to save his marriage. He knew with a sudden conviction that startled him that he needed to make his own way, his own project, his own money. He'd always trusted his instinct completely; it had propelled him across the scuffed floor of the café to Cleo's table that first day; it had spoken to him with the clear tones of a bell that he should marry her and be with her forever. He would make this film, and then he could return to her, feeling like himself once more.

And he would return with a substantial amount of money. Hollywood paid well; for the first time they would be able to feel comfortable and secure. Gus knew it was insufferably masculine of him, and he would never admit it to Cleo, but it was important to him that he would have enough money now to support them for quite a while, tide them over through the difficult progress of their next novel. He wanted to give her so much.

So often in those months in Hollywood he'd been so close to asking her to come out, needing her clear-sightedness, her humor, her strength; but Gus knew as he'd known nothing else in his life that he had to do this thing alone. He was terrified of this new project and afraid of his terror, thinking that the cast could sense it, smell it, and he would lose control. Every night he crawled into bed exhausted. He'd known their phone calls and the few visits they'd managed had been unsatisfactory, strained, but still he strove on, heading like a bull toward the red flag of the film's opening. Then he could stop, turn, go and win her back. But after the film had been edited, he had flown back to his wife and discovered that he was too late.

She had slipped through his fingers. Cleo's icy demeanor, her remoteness, told him that his marriage had fallen apart. He could no longer rely on his childish belief that he could, with words, make it all right. Panicked, he had flown back to Hollywood. But he'd found no solace there. What he did find was time to plan. He'd held back on the negotiations for Sophie and Max; they were the last tie holding her to him. When Ellison had mentioned the murder weekend, he'd seen a chance to work with Cleo again. They'd always been great collaborators.

Cleo was no ordinary woman. She didn't allow herself to feel hurt, or at least she didn't admit it. She just became impossible to reach. Gus had never mastered the art of getting through her quills to the soft underbelly of emotion he knew was there. But then, he had never hurt her so deeply before.

The knowledge that he had hurt her battered him, destroyed him, made him want to run up to her room now, capture her in his arms again, cradle her against him. To feel her curl around him once more... But he knew she wouldn't. She would stiffen and withdraw, her gray eyes as cold as winter skies.

He had hurt the woman he loved. Perhaps that was unforgivable, but he couldn't let it stop him. It meant that he would have to be devious in his attempt to win her again. He'd have to be sneaky and crafty, with absolutely no regard for the rules.

Gus grinned broadly and started up the stairs, whistling. He knew he could manage that. After all, wasn't that the way he'd won her in the first place?

Cleo slammed her door with a satisfying crash and stalked through the small sitting room into the bedroom. How could he bring himself to stay in the same room they'd had three years ago? It demonstrated a lack of sentimentality that was positively chilling. She tore off her veil and hurled it on the four-poster bed. Then she threw herself on the bed after it and gazed furiously up at the ceiling.

She had a sinking feeling that, after her decision to marry Gus Creighton—if you could call such a headlong rush into matrimony a decision—playing Sophie Fast this weekend could be the worst mistake of her life. Cleo wondered idly if it was too late to get Gus selected as the intended victim in the murder plot. She would gladly offer Denton his services.

It was too late to back out now, even though she was gambling with the one thing she cared about most. She would have to be on her toes this weekend if she wanted to solve the murder first and get control of Max and Sophie. She couldn't underestimate Gus's abilities; he was a very intelligent man, and he knew his business inside and out. He was adept at figuring out the curves and switchbacks of many a complicated plot.

She glanced at her watch. She wouldn't solve anything if she didn't get down to the cocktail party; she certainly didn't want to miss any possible clues. And she didn't want Gus to get a head start.

She sprang up quickly, then sighed when she looked down at herself. Of course—she was still a nun. She was terribly fond of Mary Claire, but she had to admit that the woman's wardrobe left a little something to be desired—like some decently attractive clothing.

At least that was one problem she could solve easily. Flipping over on the bed, Cleo reached for the phone and dialed her home number. She absently fluffed out her hair into its usual wild style while she waited for the phone to be picked up. It was time to abandon chaste black cotton for chic black silk, time to gather her wits and ferret out clues, time to enjoy the supreme satisfaction of beating Gus at his own game. It might turn out to be absolute torture to get through, but her first murder weekend had begun.

The babble of voices and the familiar smell of cigarette smoke, alcohol and a blend of the three or four currently fashionable perfumes signaled that the cocktail party was in full swing. Cleo headed across the lobby, jumping suddenly when a loud crack of thunder rumbled outside in the dark night sky. Apparently the crisp blue afternoon had turned into a stormy evening. It may have been appropriate for the activities to come, but it was not exactly good news for Cleo. She was an acknowledged chicken when it came to thunderstorms.

She tugged nervously at the lapels of her black silk jacket. When she'd called her sister, Molly, who was staying at Cleo's apartment with her husband, Jeff, for the weekend—"Gives us downtown types a taste of the good life"—Molly had taken her wardrobe problems in hand, and urged her to wear her black silk suit without her white blouse. "The jacket alone with just your long strand of pearls, Clee," Molly had advised breezily. "Dressier, and very sensual. And remember to leave off the veil, will you?"

The result, Cleo thought as she caught a glimpse of herself in the mirror, was decidedly different from what she'd expected when she'd brought the suit to wear to tomorrow night's formal ball. She'd thought that with the addition of a high-necked blouse and the veil that the suit would be properly sedate for her role as Sister Mary Claire, and its elegant lines were one way to compensate for her having to look at gorgeous sleek gowns on other women all night. Now, although the jacket over bare skin was perfectly modest, it was also, Cleo admitted with a nod to Molly's fashion sense, perfectly suggestive. Tonight one thing was certain—no one would ever mistake her for a nun.

She pushed open the door to the parlor. The room looked cozy and welcoming, with a cheerful fire in the grate chasing away the gloom of the evening as the rain began to streak down the thick panes of the lace-curtained windows.

Cleo stood for a moment to scan the crowd. Most people seemed intent on sampling as much as possible of the champagne while trying unobtrusively to identify the famous writers in the room. Sidney Clott was holding forth in one corner, his short plump hand waving his champagne glass around precariously, and behind him,

Isis Gold, the grande dame of British mystery writers, charmed a circle of listeners. The two best-selling mystery-thriller writers, Bart Gregg and Telly Longfeld, were deep in conversation by a window while being surreptitiously watched by the rest of the room.

She had just decided to cross the room to speak to Denton Ballard when a champagne flute snaked over her shoulder and stopped in front of her chin. She twined her fingers around the delicate stem.

"Thanks, Gus."

He stepped around her. "How'd you know it was me?"

"The attack on my blind side. Always a dead giveaway." Cleo sipped her champagne, trying not to stare at him. He had changed his clothes as well and looked fairly devastating, she had to admit, in the same tweed jacket and a pair of loosely tailored gray trousers. He was even wearing a heavy silk tie in muted grays and violets, and had traded in his disreputable sneakers for a newer pair, as a nod to his impersonation of Max Fast, who was known for his bad feet. Now she noticed that his shaggy brown hair seemed to have lightened in California; the soft, shaded lamps picked out sun-streaked golden strands.

"Very nice," she murmured. Gus cocked his head and looked at her. "The champagne," she pointed out.

"It's Taittinger," he said. "Remind you of anything?"

"Oh—celebrations. Birthdays. New Year's Eve. Armistice Day. The usual."

Gus smiled, his laugh lines crinkling, his amber eyes warm. "Not proposals at midnight?"

"So has Denton started all this up yet?" Cleo asked quickly, instead of answering.

The smile didn't waver; as a matter of fact, it broadened. "Nope."

"I really should go tell him that I'm playing Sophie this weekend."

"I already told him—I hope you don't mind. He was delighted. It seems we're better box office as a couple. And you know Ellison wanted you to be Sophie originally, so there won't be a problem there."

"How do you know that?" Cleo asked suspiciously, and as Gus opened his mouth she broke in irritably, "Don't answer that. Ellison told you. That's what I get for having an agent named Fink," she muttered.

"By the way, may I say I prefer Sophie to Sister Mary Cordelia?"

"Claire."

"Whatever. Anyway, I like the way you wear that suit." His gaze traveled along the V of the neckline and down along her hips. "I hate to tell you, though—you forgot your blouse. Not that I'm complaining or anything."

Cleo felt uncomfortably warm at his unwavering examination, and took a sip of champagne that drained half the glass. "Molly's suggestion. She's sending me up some clothes by messenger, since I'm no longer clergy."

Gus laughed. "I can't wait to see you in a hot-pink leather miniskirt and a black lace undershirt."

"She's not allowed to send me any of her clothes. I gave her very strict instructions."

"Since when does Molly follow instructions? Especially strict ones," Gus said, bemused. "Is she still trying to get your parents to leave the bucolic paradise of Long Island and buy the loft upstairs from her and Jeff?"

"I think she's given up."

"She's probably just resting. And how's Andie?"

"Fine."

"Still living in Philadelphia?"

"Yes."

"And your parents?"

"They live on Long Island."

"Cute. I meant, how are they?"

"Fine."

"Is that all you're going to say?"

"I assumed it was an obligatory question, so I gave the obligatory answer."

"You're not fair, Cleo," Gus said quietly.

"Neither are you." She held his gaze steadily. Cleo's boisterous family had taken Gus to their hearts from the first, and it had hurt Cleo when, in those last months before the separation, Gus had suddenly begun to pull away. He had denied it, but he had. And he had sunk into his work in Hollywood and barely surfaced to keep in touch.

"I should call Molly when I get back to Manhattan," Gus said suddenly. "I do miss them, Cleo."

She swallowed. "They miss you, too."

"I'm glad to hear that," he said quietly. "I like to be missed." When Cleo looked away to examine intently the patterns of raindrops snaking down the windows, he said in a lighter tone, "So, partner, what do you think our plan of attack should be?"

"How do I know? I'm only good at the love stuff, remember?"

"Oh, I remember," Gus said, his voice dropping into its Tennessee-honey cadences. "You were always very good at the love stuff. Do you remember that weekend at the Waldorf—"

"No."

"No? The week in May in East Hampton—"

"No."

"How about the trip to Bermuda—"

"No."

"The bus kiosk on Forty-second Street?"

"Fifty-seventh."

"Gotcha."

"Gus," Cleo said, turning toward him furiously, "this is a working weekend. I am not interested in your insinuating reminders of our tawdry escapades—"

"Tawdry?" Gus put a hand to his heart. "You wound me. Mortally. *Tawdry?* They were spiritual. Romantic. A rainswept street in midtown Manhattan. Two o'clock in the morning and no cab in sight. A couple, sprinkled with spring rain—"

"Drenched to the bone—"

"Steaming the night with a kiss so profound the world dropped away—"

"That was your wallet dropping away, remember? I had to pay for the cab."

"Cleo, where did this cynicism come from? I'm talking about an earth-shattering experience."

"I thought the part when the cab broke down on Tenth Avenue especially soul stirring."

Gus grinned. "At that point, as I remember, my soul wasn't the only thing that was stirring."

Cleo expelled her breath in a sharp hiss. "Listen, you piece of primordial ooze—"

"So you want to talk about biology. That's just my point. There's the male cell, and the female cell, and—"

As Cleo opened her mouth for the devastating retort she knew she'd be thinking of any minute, Gus quickly pointed toward Denton Ballard. "Wait a second here, Clee. Looks like Denton's ready to kick this thing off, so we'd better listen. Don't want to miss any clues. Don't worry, I'll help you out if things get confusing."

Cleo just had time to shoot him a furious look when Denton began to speak. "Welcome, everyone," he said, his pale blue eyes alight as he looked around the room. Cleo turned toward him, glad of the distraction, and smiled back at Denton's pleased grin when he saw her.

It was hard not to like Denton. A fixture at literary cocktail parties in New York and a terrible gossip, he'd always backed up his obsession with talented people by giving pots of the considerable Ballard family fortune to the arts. This weekend was his special project, and he was practically rubbing his hands together with glee at the prospect of a roomful of writers to mystify.

"Tonight I've been asked to announce why we've all been invited here, and a very pleasant task it is. Ladies and gentlemen, I'm very pleased to announce the engagement of Miss Susan Scarlett-Gray to Mr. Derek Twittingham-Jones."

Several people applauded lightly, and Gus leaned over to say in a low tone, "Looks like Denton's starting off the weekend without preliminaries. He's already introducing suspects and we haven't had a murder yet. Where is this Twit fellow, anyway?"

"There." Cleo indicated a slightly overweight young man with a red face across the room. He was smiling and nodding as a few people surrounded him offering their congratulations. "But which one is Susan Scarlett-Gray?" she asked, turning to Gus. "Do you—" She stopped abruptly when she saw that Gus looked pale. He was staring across the room, his features suddenly tightening. "Gus?"

He cursed under his breath, and when she looked over to where his burning eyes were trained she felt a swift, devastating pain stab her somewhere around the ribs. For the woman standing with her small hand tucked into the arm of the red-faced man was none other than the delicate and ethereal Wendee Tolliver, who was now beaming a very soft, very private smile at Gus.

Chapter Three

Cleo wondered if her old pitching arm from years of summer softball was still accurate. Wendee couldn't be more than ten yards away. But she suspected that even the lissome Wendee couldn't be felled by a crystal champagne glass.

As she watched her receive congratulations from other guests, Cleo realized with dawning horror that Wendee must be the actress playing Susan Scarlett-Gray. That meant that she would have to deal with her all weekend. This called for some serious scrutiny.

Wendee certainly seemed typecast as the other woman. There was no denying that she was beautiful. Her ice-blue dress skimmed down a slender twenty-three-year-old body kept trim by extensive workouts with Hollywood's most dedicated aerobic instructors. Cleo had learned this, and various other press-release tidbits of Wendee's actress-on-the-brink-of-success life-style, from the magazines she devoured on the supermarket checkout line. For an actress with only one film and a canceled TV sitcom to her credit, Wendee managed to get quite a bit of publicity.

Now here she was, gleaming right in front of Cleo in all her dewy, tanned flesh. A shimmering shower of hair the color of moonlight drifted past cornflower-blue eyes and a small, perfect nose to hang straight to a small, pointed chin. She couldn't have been more opposite to Cleo's dark eyes and strong features. Cleo had never been one to worry much about her own style, but women like Wendee made it difficult. She felt like an earthenware mug next to her porcelain-teacup fragility. Men probably couldn't look at Wendee without wanting to protect her. She *did* need protection, Cleo thought dryly, carefully unclenching an unconsciously formed fist. But it was from the men's ex-wives.

She sneaked a look at Gus. He had regained control of himself and was sipping champagne coolly and watching Wendee over the rim. But Cleo knew Gus, and she knew that he was not as calm as he appeared; she would guess that he was seething with some kind of emotion. Could it be that he was in love, really in love, with Wendee Tolliver?

She put down her glass shakily and turned away. The thought actually made her feel ill. At least she hadn't just eaten a corned beef sandwich. Cleo suddenly felt an overpowering need to be alone. She'd slip up to her room unobserved, slide between cool sheets, and take a nice three-day nap...

She knew without turning that Gus was watching her. Cleo straightened her shoulders and took a deep, steadying breath. She was no coward, she repeated to herself, and she was no sentimental fool for love. She was beginning a new life without Gus, and if he wanted to fall for a narcissistically well-toned, tanned, silly, vapid, vacuous, shallow, insubstantial blonde, she wouldn't be so petty as to make any judgments.

She wrenched her attention away from Wendee to listen to an impeccably dressed, dark-haired man in wire-rimmed glasses who spoke up at Wendee/Susan's elbow. "I'd like to propose a toast," he said. "To my best friend, Derek, and his chosen bride, the very beautiful Susan. May you sail through life smoothly with the wind at your backs." He raised his glass and the others did the same.

Wendee/Susan bowed in his direction. "Thank you, Bruno."

"Hear, hear," a tall, elegant man with reddish hair said. "Well said, Mr. Haines."

"Nothing to it, uh—"

"Anthony Guy—call me Anthony."

"Of course."

"How are we ever going to remember all these names?" Gus's voice was normal and even by her ear.

"There's supposed to be character biographies in our rooms after dinner tonight," Cleo replied. "But I wouldn't worry about it. You can always get the low-down from Wendee."

"Ah, you saw her."

"She's rather hard to overlook." Cleo picked up a lobster canapé and nibbled at it savagely.

"Cleo," Gus said, turning toward her, "I had no idea—"

"Did you guys have a little lover's quarrel?"

"We're not—"

"It's no concern of mine. I'm glad that you have such a nice—friend."

"Really?"

"Really."

"Oh. In that case, let me tell you all about it. We met—"

"Spare me the delicious details, will you?"

"I thought you were glad for me."

"Oh, I am. But I can think of more fascinating topics than your friendship with Wendee Tolliver. How do you feel about aluminum siding these days?"

"Listen, Cleo, seriously, I didn't know she was going to be here. I know it must be a shock for you. After this stupid party I can explain—"

"No need to explain. Anyway, Wendee appears as though she'd be happy to."

"Gus! Are you surprised? I knew you would be." Wendee glided up next to Gus's elbow and kissed him on the cheek. The voice coming out of the angelic creature was surprising; deep and distinctive, it had a natural huskiness that Cleo had to admit was sexy. "But you spoiled everything, you sneak. I was on my way to the airport from the Pierre to meet you. I thought it would be marvelous fun to drive up in the limo together, and I even had a bottle of your favorite champagne and everything, but you left without me."

"I didn't know you were coming to the airport, Wendee," Gus said tightly. "I thought you were in L.A. And I didn't know you'd be here, either," he pointed out.

"I decided to come at the last minute."

"I can see that." Gus's hand shot out and caught Cleo's elbow just as she was slipping away. "Wendee Tolliver, I'd like you to meet Cleo Delaney."

"Cleo—" Wendee's wide blue eyes got even wider and her mouth dropped in a soft O. "How do you do," she said, recovering quickly and flashing a friendly smile. "I didn't know you were going to be here. Did you, Gus? I hope so," she said confidentially to Cleo. "Gus hates surprises."

The smile Cleo had plastered on her face grew strained. *Why are you telling me about my husband?* she asked Wendee silently. She supposed that Wendee's months with Gus in L.A. qualified her as an expert. What did Cleo know about Gus, anyway? Five years of working and loving together hadn't prepared her for the past year of estrangement, that was for sure.

"Are you here with someone, or are you on vacation this weekend?" Wendee asked her cordially, apparently forgetting—or choosing to forget—that Cleo was a writer on her own.

Cleo smiled back graciously, considering it a better alternative to kicking her. "I came to publicize my new book."

"Oh, yes, you wrote a new book. The one about the nun—what's her name again? My agent tells me it will be a great part if you sell it to the movies. Sister Mary—?"

"Christmas," Cleo supplied.

"Claire," Gus broke in quickly, with a piercing look at her. "It's the best thing I've read all year," he told Wendee.

"I thought you didn't—" Cleo began, but Wendee was already speaking.

"Maybe you should peddle the project to a few studios. And Gus could direct it! I'd be glad to get you in touch with my agent," Wendee said helpfully. "Oh, how silly of me, I'm sure you have a good agent. Not that I'm campaigning for the part or anything. I'm holding out for the part of Sophie in the television show I keep hearing Gus is going to do."

"Oh, are you?" Cleo asked politely. "I'll have to be on the lookout for that one."

He stirred beside her. "Wendee, I never—"

"So you're playing a part this weekend?" Cleo asked.

"Susan Scarlett-Gray. My agent didn't want me to do it—he called the weekend a silly publicity stunt for detective writers—oh, sorry about that. Anyway, I figured with all these writers here and all this press, it wouldn't be a bad idea. It *is* good exposure."

"Oh, I don't think you need any more exposure," Cleo said sweetly, carefully avoiding looking at the deep slash of Wendee's neckline.

"So, Wendee," Gus broke in jovially, "can you give Cleo and me any hints? We're working as Sophie and Max this weekend. Who's the guy in glasses who made the toast?"

"That's Bruno Haines. And the one with red hair is Anthony something or other." Wendee finished her champagne and looked around quickly. "Listen, I'd love to chat, but this is a job, after all—I'm supposed to mingle. I'll see you later, Gus. Nice meeting you, Cleo." She began to move away, then touched Gus's arm and smiled mischievously at him. "They don't tell the actors who the murderer is, or else—" she giggled conspiratorially "—you could probably persuade me to tell you." Then Wendee glided away again.

"She's darling, Gus," Cleo said dryly, taking a long sip of champagne. "Her charm is matched only by her ethics."

Gus emptied his glass with a gulp. "Look, let me explain about Wendee, will you? I—"

"It doesn't matter."

"Will you stop saying that! I want—"

"Gus, I'm just not interested," Cleo said, her voice low with suppressed fury. She grabbed his arm with a sharp jerk. "Let's just mingle, all right? We're supposed to be Sophie and Max. And we've got a wager riding on this weekend. After all, we don't want to let our Wendee down for her television show, do we?"

"Cleo, she got that from *Variety*, not me. I never—"

"And where did *Variety* get it from? Hedda Hopper?"

"I don't know where they—"

"It doesn't matter. This weekend should—"

"Will you let me finish a sentence please?" Gus demanded suddenly, stopping in his tracks and jerking her to a halt. "I can't finish any—"

"What are you talking about? I don't—"

"You see, you just—"

"You're the one who keeps—"

"Me? I'm trying to—"

"You just think that everything *you* have to say is so impor—"

"—get a word in edgewise here, while you—"

"Look, I don't want to talk about it, okay?"

"Talk about *what*?" Gus demanded, exasperated.

"Wendee Tolliver!" Cleo whispered angrily as she tugged Gus forward. "Come on, we're missing something over here."

She pulled him along to join the rest of the guests, who were watching the engaged couple intently as if the murder could be committed any minute. Wendee, in character as Susan Scarlett-Gray, was teasing Derek Twittingham-Jones for neglecting to bring a gold cigarette case, his engagement present from her.

"That's all right, darling, I understand," she said, her distinctive voice carrying across the room. "You don't like it. You think it's vulgar, I suppose, and I only got the ruby because you said how much you liked them."

"Don't be silly, darling. I love the case." Derek mumbled this into his champagne, obviously embarrassed at the scene his fiancée was creating. "I just forgot."

"This must be what's called a lovers' quarrel," the red-haired man spoke up. "I wouldn't know, though. I've never been in love. That doesn't mean I couldn't be persuaded, though."

"Mr. Guy has never been in love?" Wendee/Susan asked skeptically. "I don't know whether to believe that or not."

"Believe it, Miss Gray," Anthony replied, bowing slightly to her. "I have somehow managed to elude the silken noose that, once slipped over the head, makes men fools."

"A noose? Really, Mr. Guy, I don't think I like that implication," she returned, but Cleo couldn't watch her anymore and turned away.

In the early part of their relationship, when they were merely collaborators and friends, Gus used to talk to her of his romantic affairs. She had been blithe and offhand with him, while inside she'd been seething with jealousy. But that murderous feeling was nothing compared to this. This was a pounding force that built up behind her eyes and made her hands shake and her vision blur. All she wanted was for the party to end, so they could all go back up to their rooms and—

Go back up to their rooms... And would Gus and Wendee be going together to Gus's room, Suite Two, where once he'd whispered "forever" in Cleo's ear, where they'd once made love with an intensity that had shaken them, awed them by showing a dimension to their love they hadn't imagined was there?

Cleo took a shaky step backward. A buzzing began in her ears, and she was terribly afraid she would either faint or enliven the weekend with a real murder—a double one, with Gus and Wendee as the all-too-deserving victims. Instead of either action, both of which might attract a bit of attention, she tried to concentrate on something other than the beautiful Wendee. For the sake of her sanity and her pride, she had to concentrate on why she was here. She was here to detect, to gather clues about the upcoming murder, not her ex-husband's extracurricular activities. Obviously Gus had arranged the wager so that he'd be able to do his Sophie and Max television show, but it would be over her dead body. Or somebody's dead body, whenever it happened to turn up this weekend.

Cleo studiously trained her gaze on Derek. He was smiling proudly at the attention Wendee/Susan's bright remarks were receiving from the rest of his guests, but all at once he patted his jacket pocket thoughtfully and eased unobtrusively out of the room.

Cleo looked around to see if Gus had noticed, but he was still watching Wendee and Anthony. She started to speak, then stopped. If this was a competition between them, why should she tell Gus every little thing she noticed? Besides, it might not turn out to be anything at all. She could always tell him later; surely Denton had planned to ease into the murder weekend without too many dramatic events at the start.

Cleo had just consoled her conscience with that thought and had reached over to retrieve her glass when the lights suddenly and dramatically went out.

She knew it must be contrived, she knew it must be part of the show, but Cleo's heartbeat accelerated and she couldn't contain a small gasp of surprise. It was pitch-black in the room, and the only thing she could hear was a babble of voices, with Wendee complaining above the din about the wiring of old country inns. Anthony Guy interrupted several times politely to point out that the Green Gables Inn had been recently renovated, but she continued to rail in her throaty voice. All else was confusion as the storm raged outside.

Thunder crashed and Cleo suddenly felt the need for a familiar voice in all this darkness. She stepped back cautiously and felt her heel descend on a foot. She imagined she could hear the bones crunch.

"Ouch," Gus said gruffly. He reached out to steady her with one muscular arm around her shoulder. Cleo tensed but didn't move away when a particularly loud crash of thunder resounded through the room. It wouldn't do any harm to relax for a moment, just until her heart stopped beating so fast.

"You okay?" Gus asked softly.

"I'm fine. The lights just went out. No big deal."

"Mmmm. This is Gus behind you, remember? I know how you are about power failures."

It was true. Gus knew her fears all too well. Once they'd been house-sitting on a stormy weekend for her parents on Long Island. The power had gone out suddenly and when Gus had appeared, a dark shadow at her elbow, she had uttered a piercing scream and jumped straight back into a three-foot cactus. She'd screamed again from the pain, blasting Gus just as he was feeling his way toward her. He'd claimed for weeks that he had a hearing loss in his right ear.

Now she heard a low chuckle behind her. "Just don't scream," he said. "I think I'm finally getting the hearing back in that ear. Fortunately there isn't a southwestern theme to the decor here, or you might be picking spines out of your—"

"You picked them out," she muttered. "I couldn't reach. By the way, you can let go of me now."

"I think I'll hang on for a little while. I just want to make sure you're not the murderer."

"There hasn't even been a murder yet."

"I'm just being prepared."

"Gee, what a Boy Scout," she growled.

The blaze of lights suddenly returned. Everyone blinked and looked around. Gus dropped his arm from around her shoulder.

"Thanks," Cleo said. "And could you come around from behind me? I feel like I'm being followed."

"You didn't mind my being behind you after your encounter with the cactus," Gus pointed out. He appeared again in front of her and sipped at his champagne, raising his eyebrows at her over the rim.

Cleo tried to ignore him and scanned the room in search of Derek, but he hadn't returned. She noticed Guy and Bruno in the corner having an animated conversation.

"Hey, Max," she said to Gus, "why don't you make yourself useful and go gather some evidence." She jerked her chin at the two men across the room. "I'll go mingle without you."

"Okay, boss." Gus grinned and obediently moved across the room to smoothly maneuver himself into the two men's conversation.

Heaving a long sigh of relief, Cleo backed away into a convenient corner. She stared out the rain-streaked window with unseeing eyes and took several long, deep breaths. It was a very simple situation, really, she told herself, trying to be calm. I'm trapped here for the weekend with my ex-husband and his girlfriend. And all three of us have to play out a mystery-weekend charade.

The parts are all assigned, so all I have to do is play Sophie Fast. What would the spoiled but blunt and sardonic Sophie do?

Cleo stared at the reflection of the room in the windowpane. The scene looked bright and blurred and slightly unreal. I'm not Cleo Delaney, she told herself firmly. I don't feel like murdering that tawny-haired man across the room, nor his husky-voiced sweetheart now traipsing toward the door. I'm Sophie Fast, and therefore I am in control. I'm not Cleo, I'm Sophie.

"I'm not Cleo," she said under her breath.

"Then who have I been talking to all evening?" Gus asked.

"Will you stop coming up behind me!"

"You used to like it when I—"

"So, did you discover anything interesting?"

"You have this little run in the back of your left stocking—"

"I meant about the weekend."

"We're having oysters at dinner."

"I meant something important."

Gus looked wounded. "It is important. I'm upset. You know how much I hate oysters. And we're having pâté, too. Yuck. How come I never get served what I like at these elegant dinner parties?"

"Somehow I don't think Frosted Mini-Snaps would be appropriate for the evening."

"I like Cheerios now." Gus was suddenly interrupted by a loud crash. Everyone in the room tensed, then looked around at one another speculatively.

And then came the scream. It started as a wail, then intensified into a piercing cry of anguish and fear, reverberating through the antique-filled parlor with all the incongruous savagery of a wild animal prowling outside their door in the Connecticut countryside. Slowly, it died away.

"Do you think somebody else found out about the oysters?" Gus asked.

"The library," someone said, and everyone took off.

They streamed across the lobby and down the carpeted hall. Cleo was the first to push open the heavy door to the oak-paneled room, Gus directly behind her. She stopped dead and he bumped into her as they took in the scene before them.

Susan Scarlett-Gray sat weeping over the body of her fiancé, Derek Twittingham-Jones, in the middle of the room. A sudden bolt of lightning lit the macabre scene eerily, and thunder boomed as if on cue.

Denton couldn't have engineered a more convincing scene. The blood looked very real, as did Wendee's white-faced shock. And the bloody-handled knife that seemed to be imbedded in Derek Twittingham-Jones's broad back looked real as well. Then Cleo saw Derek's nose twitch almost imperceptibly, and she relaxed.

"Horribly realistic," someone muttered behind her.

"Denton does put on a good show," someone else added.

"I wonder what the crash was," Cleo murmured.

"The curtains must have knocked over that table," Gus answered. The heavy green-velvet drapes were lying on the carpet next to the body, the blood stains on them obviously attesting to the fact that Derek had clutched on to them as he fell.

"I saw him when I came into the room," Wendee said hoarsely. "He was reaching out to me, he couldn't speak—he grabbed the curtains as he fell." She covered her face in her hands. "It was awful."

Denton Ballard stepped over and felt for a pulse. "I'm afraid he's quite dead," he announced soberly. Then he looked up and scanned their faces. "By Jove, I wonder who did it." He waggled his eyebrows at them. "Don't you?"

The tension broke, and everyone dissolved into relieved laughter. Denton stood up and dusted his hands on his trousers. "All right then," he said. "Tonight when you return to your rooms you'll get a list of all the characters, and a copy of the contents of Derek's pockets to start you out. Now, let me remind you of the rules. Remember, since you're all such murder experts, you're only getting three clues—the contents of the dead man's pockets and two more verbal clues sometime during the weekend. Now, you've already received one verbal clue, but I won't say any more about that. You have to figure out what it is. The rest depends on your powers of observation. No questioning of subjects allowed, but keep your ears and eyes open. You have five minutes to go over the scene. After that, what do you say we go in and have some dinner?"

The guests began gingerly to walk around the body to look for clues. Isis Gold took notes authoritatively while Sidney Clott peeked over her shoulder at them.

Gus peered at the bloody knife. "Remind me not to walk around this place alone, will you?" he whispered to Cleo.

"At least not with Wendee around."

"Susan," he corrected.

She shrugged. "Whatever."

Cleo savagely pulled on knee socks and an oversize T-shirt. She scrubbed her face and vigorously brushed her teeth. Then she dragged a brush through her hair energetically, making her scalp tingle. Finally, with a muffled curse, she threw the brush across the room, where it hit the fireplace grate with a gratifying clang. Her toothbrush followed with a smaller, less satisfying, ping.

Dinner, she reflected, had been something of a strain.

In fact, it must have been a kind of torture devised by the vengeful Furies who presided over the debris of failed marriages. For how could anyone remain cool and collected while sitting in a candlelit dining room that had once been a magic place where vows of undying devotion had been exchanged over glasses of perfectly chilled champagne, when that same room was now presided over by the giggly but stunning mistress of your ex-husband? Especially when your ex-husband sat, unexpectedly grave and silent, across the table, unwilling to venture a word or a gesture that might make the evening a touch more bearable.

Cleo flopped down on the bed with a sigh. To be fair, there really was no way to make the situation bearable. Certainly not for her, at any rate. Wendee seemed to be having a fine time. She had chattered through dinner and thoroughly enjoyed every morsel of her meal.

The best thing to do was to pack up tomorrow and leave, and think of some explanation for Denton and Ellison later. She could slip away in the Valiant early in the morning, and providing her luck changed once she left this place, the car would cruise back to Manhattan without incident and she could be in her apartment by midday.

But there was still a long, stormy night to get through. She glanced at the clock. It was midnight, and the hotel had quieted down. At dinner and suddenly unable to carry on the charade of being the bright and witty Sophie Fast, Cleo had left the table while others were still lingering over their desserts. She wasn't Sophie Fast; she was Cleo Delaney, and she was miserable.

Sleep would be hard to come by, she knew. If only she had stayed long enough for a warm brandy. It was a luxury she loved to indulge in when she was feeling restless. Tonight she was more than restless; she was jumping out of her skin. Her entire attention was focused on what was probably happening behind Gus's closed door, and the thought was terrifying and painful and absolutely wrenching.

The knock was soft but it startled her. Thunder boomed as Cleo bounded off the bed and to the door.

"Who is it?"

"Room service. Complimentary brandy before retiring."

She eased open the door and peeked around it. Gus was balancing a small tray with a glass of brandy on it and trying to look casual.

"I don't want any," she said.

"Yes, you do. Come on, Cleo, this is a peace offering. I know you're upset."

"I'm not upset," Cleo said, reaching for the brandy. "Thank you, and good night."

Gus leaned against the frame so she couldn't close the door. He eyed her T-shirt and socks. "You look cute— like a teenager at a slumber party."

"Should be right up your alley."

He raised his eyebrows. "You are upset. You can't fool me. You weren't yourself at dinner."

"Oh? Who was I? Queen Elizabeth?"

"Grace Kelly. Again."

"And I was trying to be Sandra Dee."

"Clee, I know that look so well. Cool, disinterested, regal—that uplifted chin, that tilt of the head—your nose was pointing toward Canada all night long."

"Don't be ridiculous. Look, Gus, this is the eighties. I'm a modern woman, I can be in the same room with my ex-husband and his—"

"I'm not your ex-husband." Gus held up his left hand. His wedding ring glinted in the soft light of the hall. "I'm still married to you, remember?"

Cleo held up her own ringless hand. "That depends on your point of view," she said airily, taking a swig of brandy. "As I was saying, I can be in the same room with my *ex*-husband and his mistress without—"

"Cleo," Gus said steadily, "Wendee and I are not sleeping together. She's not my mistress."

"On to greener pastures?"

"She never was my mistress. She never *will* be my mistress. Where did you get that word, anyway? Nineteenth-century financiers who smoked cigars had mistresses."

"Oh, excuse me—is she your 'lady,' then? Your main squeeze, your significant other, your primary relationship, your steady, your ball and chain?"

He sighed. "She's my friend."

"Do you really expect me to believe that?"

"Yes."

Cleo looked at Gus. One thing she never doubted was his honesty. His constancy, yes. His honesty, never. "Then why is she here, Gus?"

"For publicity, like she said. Look, Cleo, Wendee is a nice person, and I like her. Underneath, she's very shy. Her career isn't really as important to her as security and love, and that's hard to find in Hollywood. She needed a friend."

Cleo raised an eyebrow. "What about the picture in *Flash!* magazine?"

"You saw that? I just saw it yesterday, in Wendee's apartment—she'd just seen it too."

The eyebrow raised higher. "In her apartment?"

"Relax, Clee. I only went there to pick up my clean laundry—"

The eyebrow raised to an impossible height.

"Well," Gus said, feeling suddenly defensive, "I get so busy, and we go to the same place, so she offers to pick it up for me sometimes. She likes to do things for people. Anyway, she was just as shocked as I was by the implication of that picture. As a matter of fact, she was worried about your reaction." Skepticism still marked Cleo's face, and Gus was uncomfortably aware of the fact that he was bombing. Everything had seemed so innocent with Wendee in California—as a matter of fact, he hadn't thought much about her at all. She was just so friendly, so yielding, so... *nice.* And so unlike the complexities—and the exhilarations—of his relationship with Cleo. He hadn't been attracted to Wendee at all. He'd been too desperately involved in trying to save his film before his marriage fell apart. And now he was in the impossible position of trying to defend a casual friendship with an admittedly beautiful but basically boring young actress to an estranged wife who could indicate volumes by the lift of an eyebrow.

Gus sighed again. "Actually, she kind of reminds me of my sister, Laura. Or what Laura would have been like."

"Oh." That stopped Cleo dead in her tracks. When he was twelve, Gus had lost his parents and his younger sister in a small-plane crash. Gus, sick with the flu, had been planning to follow to the family vacation cabin with his grandparents. He'd ended up being raised by them. In some indefinable sense, he had never gotten over that loss. Cleo didn't know how anyone could. So even though Laura had been a tomboyish brunette and Wendee was fair-haired and delicate, she understood Gus's weakness for a young woman who looked up to him. To a point. And it was a very short, very tense, distance to that point.

"So, you can see that the situation this weekend isn't ideal, but I'm sure we can all be friends," Gus finished. The look in Cleo's frosty gray eyes made him backpedal hastily. "Well, maybe she's not your type. But I just wanted to explain, so you'd understand."

"Don't worry about it, Gus. It doesn't matter."

"Would you stop saying that! Of course it matters—we're married, aren't we?"

Despite her relief at discovering that Wendee wasn't Gus's mistress, Cleo found that, for some reason, she was still furious with him. "Would you stop saying *that*? You live in Los Angeles. You have freshly squeezed orange juice and your bowl of Mini-Snaps for breakfast every morning by a swimming pool. I live in New York. I have a fried egg on a roll in the Greek diner on the corner. You call that togetherness?"

"Cleo, you're all wrong."

"I am?"

"I switched to Cheerios for breakfast. I told you already."

Cleo put her brandy down carefully on the small pine table by the door. Despite the forced light tone of the conversation, she saw that her hand was shaking.

"Gus, it's late," she said, beginning to close the door. "We should really—"

"We should." Gus didn't move. He was studying her intently. "Cleo," he said finally, "if you still want to leave tomorrow—"

"What makes you think I want to leave tomorrow?"

"Well, I thought after tonight—you still seem disturbed, and—"

"I'm not disturbed in the least," Cleo said coolly. "I wouldn't dream of leaving. I made a commitment to Denton, not to mention my wager with you. I'm looking forward to getting the rights to Sophie and Max."

Gus took a step forward. "I don't believe that you're as cool as you look," he said.

Cleo backed away a step but kept her hand on the doorknob. She recognized the deliberate tone in Gus's voice, and it unnerved her.

"Don't you ever think about us, Clee?" he asked, his voice soft and insistent.

She cleared her throat nervously. "I think about us about as often as I think about cleaning the refrigerator. Having lived with me, you have an idea of how frequent that is."

"I don't believe you." Gus moved forward another step. "I think you're thinking about us right now. I think you're imagining what it would be like if I kissed you."

"Actually," Cleo said, cursing the strained quality she heard in her voice, "I *was* thinking about cleaning the refrigerator. I bought this bunch of broccoli last week, and you know how slimy those little green leaves can get—"

Gus came even closer, a whisper away. "It's all right, Clee," he said softly, his voice as warm and sweet as the brandy she could still taste in her mouth, "because I'm thinking about kissing you, too." His eyes looked dark, the firelight behind her catching glints of green in them.

He was standing close to her now, so close that she could smell him again, that familiar scent that meant Gus, her lover, her husband...

Her husband. His every feature was as familiar to her as her own. She knew without touching him how his thick, shaggy hair would feel underneath her fingertips, how his skin would feel, his mouth, the muscles of his back, his arms. And, Cleo admitted, shuddering, the familiarity of him only made her desire more profound and more impossible to fight.

Perhaps if they kissed, just once, she'd find out that the magic had truly disappeared. If they kissed, just once, she finally might be free of him.

Cleo's lips parted as she watched him, as if in a dream, bend his head to hers. Lightning flashed as the shock of the first tentative, warm contact of his mouth sent her blood pounding in her ears and her heartbeat racing.

For the first time in a year their lips met, gentle in their hunger, cautious in their need.

Stop now, Cleo, she told herself wildly as her body began to sing with swift, shocking arousal. *You've got to stop. Immediately.*

Any minute now...

Chapter Four

It was too much. The simple sensations of the roughness of his cheek, the softness of his mouth, the sweet taste of his questing tongue, were all too dizzying familiar, too well remembered. Like a Victorian heroine, Cleo felt faint, but the slow, deep kiss went on, and she found that she hadn't the will to stop it.

A tiny sound of need and desire escaped from her mouth into his, and he echoed it, his low groan vibrating a call that seemed to distill every sensual memory she'd ever had of him into this one heady moment. Her bones turned to water, but somehow she managed to keep standing; the force of her desire kept her there, her need to keep his mouth against her own.

How could she have lived without his hands? His touch could bring tears to her eyes, with its possessiveness and its indescribable tenderness. His hands couldn't seem to get enough of her now, as they skimmed down her body hungrily, always returning to range over her hair, her face, tracing her features with strong sure fingers.

And how those same hands had once known every secret part of her, had luxuriated, tantalized, teased, inflamed...

An ache rose up from the very depths of her, an ache so sharp it pulled Cleo up short. Her throat constricted with fear. What was she doing? She wrenched herself away from Gus, her heart pounding, and she looked at him gravely while she searched for words.

Gus's gaze was as serious as hers; his face showed the same struggle to find the words to break the tension between them, to answer the questions that such a kiss had suddenly flung into their faces, flaunting their attempts to lighten the atmosphere between them.

Quickly, before he could speak, she turned away and slipped back inside her room. She gently closed the door against him.

Gus dragged his head out from underneath the pillow. The hands of the clock were nudging six-fifteen. He flopped back against the pillows and groaned. He *had* finally managed to fall asleep, true, but the last thing he remembered was watching the hands hit five o'clock.

Might as well hit the shower; he knew he wouldn't be able to sleep any more. The kiss at Cleo's door had knocked him senseless, and returning to this suite had pushed him completely over the edge, rocketing him into a sleepless night spent burning up with a fever he could only blame on the power of Cleo's kiss. He'd never wanted a woman so much in his life.

Gus headed for the shower. The steamy water invigorated him, and he began to feel more cheerful. She *had* kissed him last night, and kissed him with every bit of the passion he remembered, that he ached for. He had felt her mouth open against his again, had felt the textures of her skin and her hair and the smooth curve of her waist, and her breasts, so soft and full, pressing against his chest. He could feel how smoothly they would fit against his palm...

This wasn't helping any. Gus quickly reached over to turn the cold water up and gave a muffled shout at the shock. But it helped.

Back to the kiss. She *had* to be warming up to him again. He had felt her hands skimming over him, and there was desire, hot and forceful, in her touch...

Gus turned the cold water up some more. The problem was, he admitted, that even though he knew now that she still could lose her head over a kiss, it wasn't enough. There would always be an electric, galvanizing current running between them, but Cleo was a strong woman, and she could resist it if she wanted. Only with love in her heart would she make love to him again. Since that was the only way he wanted her, he couldn't object—provided, of course, she still loved him, and against all odds, he'd bet on that. Gus was a stubborn optimist.

Everyone in the film industry had told Gus it would be impossible for him to direct the first picture he wrote. They told him to forget it; they told him to take the money for his screenwriting and run. But he hadn't listened. He'd always been stubborn when it came to what he felt was right for him. Perhaps that stubbornness could now get him something more important than film and book contracts. It could get him back his wife. He couldn't consider any other possibility. He loved her too much.

Gus turned off the water. It was just, he told himself, a matter of time.

* * *

"Never in a million years will I allow that to happen again," Cleo said to herself in the mirror. She finger-combed her wet hair into place and decided she needed makeup today. Despite her authoritative words, she looked pale and uncertain, and she needed all the help she could get.

She chose a black turtleneck bodysuit and jeans, and added her man's tank watch as her only jewelry. With her dark glasses and leather bomber jacket, she would look cool, no-nonsense, unapproachable—more Garbo than Grace Kelly today.

Over the rushing water of her shower she'd given herself a strict talking to. She'd have to channel all of her anger and her confused emotions about Gus straight into a compulsion about her work, just as she'd been doing all along. He was determined to beat her still, she was sure. What if the kiss at her door had been part of the plan to unbalance her, to get control of Sophie and Max so that he could continue with his Hollywood life-style? And consummate his friendship with Wendee?

Gus may have been sincere when he said that Wendee reminded him of Laura, but Cleo had an intuition that sisterly devotion wasn't what Wendee had in mind. She'd definitely been territorial last night. She had been about as shy and insecure as a bulldozer.

She shouldn't care, of course—she and Gus were estranged. But Cleo had to be honest and admit to a raging, ridiculous jealousy where Wendee was concerned. She seemed to embody every delectable woman Gus had told her about dating years ago, when they'd been writing partners.

What she had to do, Cleo told herself, brushing out her hair vigorously, was to accept her jealousy as a normal phenomenon aggravated by a past experience with blondes in Gus's life, and then do her best to ignore it. No problem. She'd just try and stay out of Wendee's way. As long as Wendee's way wasn't in Gus's way. Or Cleo's way.

It's going to be a very confusing weekend, she told herself wearily. *Stay on your toes.*

By the time she'd finished dressing, Cleo was ready for battle. She gave herself one last look in the mirror, nodded in approval of her no-nonsense look and, as a last touch, slipped into the leather jacket for armor. She marched down the stairs to the breakfast room.

The room was crowded and it took a moment before she spied Gus, who was packing away a huge breakfast. Straightening her shoulders, she crossed the room briskly and stood at his table.

Gus looked up and scrutinized her black turtleneck, dark glasses and the leather bomber jacket. "Don't tell me—Grace Kelly has been edged out by Rambo, right?"

"How's your breakfast?" Cleo asked sweetly, sitting down.

"It's great. Let me get the waitress and you can order—"

"I'm not hungry. We should get started. Did you look at the materials Denton left in our rooms?"

Gus nodded, his mouth full.

"The love letter that was in Derek's pocket was strange," Cleo mused. "Are you going to eat all those pancakes?"

"I guess not."

Cleo cut a generous piece and absentmindedly chewed on it. "It just didn't sound like Derek."

"This is based on your intimate knowledge of his character, I suppose."

She nodded and forked up a bit of scrambled egg. "I know we only know him from last night and that biography we got, but you have to admit that all of the suspects were really characterized last night. Derek was the bumbling type, Bruno was the aristocratic snob type, that redheaded guy Anthony the devil-may-care bachelor, Susan the dim-witted floozy—"

"I thought she was more the femme-fatale type."

"Mmmm—I guess that it's always difficult to separate the actor from his part—are those blueberry muffins in that basket?"

"There's only one left," Gus said pointedly.

"Thanks." Cleo crumbled the muffin and began to butter a piece. "Now, where was I?"

"Insulting Wendee, I think."

"I was talking about the letter. The language was so stiff. And those nautical references—" Cleo fished in her big leather pouch and came out with her copy of the letter. "'My darling Susan,'" she read. "'Last night overwhelmed me. You are determined to break it off and yet you grant me this one last weekend at The Gables. Darling Susan, as you pointed out, I'll never be free, but you are unmoored and always will be. But though I am forever anchored to another, I plot my course by your steadfast star.'"

"The guy needs some help with his style, no doubt about it," Gus said, stirring his coffee.

"But which guy?"

"Bruno. You agree?"

"Absolutely. Sounds just like him. Did you read in the bio that he's a sailor? He toasted Derek and Susan with 'smooth sailing.' And he's married to that mousy-looking woman, so he *is* 'anchored to another.' Are you going to finish your eggs?"

Gus pushed his plate closer to her, then quickly snatched back a piece of muffin. "All right, so possibly Bruno and Susan were having an affair. Let's go over the sequence of events last night and see what we come up with."

"Okay. First, Derek and Susan's engagement is announced. Bruno makes a toast. Then, Susan makes a fuss about her engagement present. She and Anthony have a polite but nasty argument about marriage. Derek pats his pocket like he's missing something and slips away—"

"That's when he left? You didn't tell me."

"I'm telling you now. We can bet he left to get the cigarette case because it was found on his body. Anyway, then, the lights went out—"

"You got scared—"

"I wasn't scared."

"You were, too."

"I was not. The lights were out for about four or five minutes, right?"

"Right."

"The fuse box is right outside the door to the parlor, so just about anyone could have done it."

"I know. I checked this morning, along with about fifteen other people."

"Then the lights came back on, and you went to talk to Bruno and Anthony—"

"Bruno suddenly said he needed some air and left the room to go out on the terrace. Everyone saw him, too. He knocked over a tray of glasses on the way."

"You didn't tell me that."

"I'm telling you now."

"Then Susan left the room. You and I spoke for maybe two minutes, and then we heard the scream. There was no way that Susan had time to get to the library and stab Derek three times, right?''

"Right. That lets out Wendee as the murderer."

"Breaks my heart," Cleo said around her muffin.

"I'll bet. So, since Derek was still alive when Susan found him, and he pulled down the curtains and knocked over the table and everything, the murder must have been committed after the lights came back on but right before Susan left the room. You know what puzzles me—"

"What?" Cleo asked as delicately as was possible with a mouthful of eggs.

"First, that your charming mother never taught you to swallow your food before you talk, and secondly, that the lights went out. Since the murder was committed after that, what was the point?''

"Maybe so the murderer could slip away and get the murder weapon for later. Or maybe it's just a red her ring. Speaking of herring, I could really go for some lox. Do you think they have any?''

"I'm glad you weren't hungry. Have the rest of my pancakes. So, leaving that question aside for the moment, who are our suspects? It could have been Bruno or his wife or a half dozen other people who left to freshen up for dinner. Anthony's date, that brunette—"

"Or Derek's parents, the Twittingham-Joneses."

"Or the butler."

"Oh, Gus, come on."

"Really. He looks sneaky. And I don't trust anyone named Ripper. We can just bet what his first name is.''

"Just Denton's idea of a joke. Actually, Denton was out of the room, too—it could have been him. The only people we can eliminate are ourselves and the ones who we agree stayed in the parlor." Cleo thoughtfully polished off the rest of Gus's pancakes. "Now, what about that other slip of paper that was in Derek's pocket? Do you have it with you?''

Gus smoothed out a crumpled piece of paper. On the top was printed ROCKS. A few lines down was handwritten 18kgdbt. At the very bottom was simply 800. Gus frowned. ''Do you think Denton's cooked up some kind of spy ring and this is in code?''

''Anything is possible. Where do you think the verbal clue fits in?'' Cleo put down her fork and recited, ''If a boy's best friend is his dog, what's a girl's best friend?''

''I have no idea,'' Gus said absently. He was busy admiring the light in Cleo's eyes, a special light he hadn't seen in a long while—since they'd worked together last, in fact. He'd always found her mind the sexiest part about her. Well, maybe not the sexiest, he amended, a smile quirking the ends of his mouth. But it was true that though it had been her legs that had led him over to her table that first time, it had been collaborating with her and seeing her mind work that had led him to fall in love so completely.

Cleo frowned down at the paper. ''I've got it,'' she said.

''Well?''

She looked over her shoulder at the rest of the diners. ''I'll tell you outside, okay? Let's let everyone enjoy their breakfast—we want to get a good head start. Come on, you've had enough breakfast, haven't you?''

''I've hardly had *any* breakfast. You had all of it.''

Just then the frazzled waitress finally appeared. ''Can I get you something?'' she asked Cleo.

''No, thanks, I'm not hungry this morning.'' Cleo stood up, grabbing the last half of the muffin. ''Come on, Gus, don't just stand there. Every second counts, and it's going to take me at least ten minutes to start that Valiant."

"You mean I have to ride in that lima bean?"

"If you want a ride, you do."

The town of Beech Corners had sometime in the last three years gritted its sturdy Yankee teeth and devoted itself to the rich urbanite overflow from the Green Gables resort. Outposts of chic Manhattan delis, boutiques and chocolate-chip cookie stores lined the tree-shaded Main Street. The local stores kept up with clever names, bleached-wood floors, and Italian lighting mixing with New England antiques. It didn't take Cleo and Gus very long to find the jewelry store called Rocks.

"Aha!" Cleo crowed when she saw it. "Diamonds are a girl's best friend, all right. Now we just have to find out who bought an eighteen-karat gold bracelet for eight hundred dollars."

The proprietor looked as if he'd be more at home behind a fishing pole than a sleek high-tech counter showcasing antique jewelry. He dropped his L. L. Bean catalog when they showed him the receipt.

"You're from that mystery weekend up at Green Gables," he said, beaming. "I didn't think anybody'd be in so early. You're the first. Yes, I sold the bracelet a few days ago to a man with a blond lady. She was a looker." He looked at them carefully. "Say, haven't I seen the two of you before?"

"I don't think so," Cleo said. "Can you tell us something about the man who was here?"

"He had one of those lockjaw accents. I couldn't see his hair—he was wearing a cap. You know, one of those Greek-fisherman-type things."

"Was he overweight?"

"Can't say that he was."

"That let's out Derek," Cleo said, nodding to herself. The owner peered at Gus. "You look familiar."

"I'm Gus Creighton."

"John Barnes. You sure do look familiar, Mr. Creighton."

"I directed *Fast Moves*. You might know me from that."

"Don't think so. Never heard of it."

Cleo suppressed a giggle at Gus's crestfallen look. She turned back to the owner. "Can you tell us anything about the man? Any distinguishing characteristic? Color of his eyes?"

"Well, I can only tell you what I've been told to tell you, can't I. And I already told you that. He was wearing a cap, the lady giggled a lot, and he wore those tinted glasses so I couldn't see his eyes."

"Thanks for your help," Cleo said, disappointed. It didn't seem like very much to go on, though the description certainly sounded like Bruno—glasses, lockjaw accent and all. But maybe it was just *supposed* to sound like Bruno. She looked down gloomily at the display case. A garnet and diamond ring in an old-fashioned setting winked up at her. "What a pretty ring," she said slowly, distracted.

When she looked up, John Barnes was grinning at her. "I just remembered where I've seen you folks before—it was a couple of years ago—you came in looking at a ring very much like that one. I remember because you'd just gotten engaged the night before. You folks remember that?"

"Here? But the shop looks so much bigger and lighter," Gus said, looking around. "This can't be the same place."

"Sure it can, when the tourists pour in from New York City like they do. Got to change with the times. Say, I'm glad to see that you two are still together. Did you ever get that ring?"

"No," Cleo said uncomfortably, sliding her left hand into her pocket. She didn't want to tell this nice man that she and Gus were separated. "We didn't have time, so we just got wedding rings—we weren't engaged very long. We got married as soon as we could. We didn't even have a honeymoon. Had to make a deadline on a book."

"Too bad. That's the way to do it, though. Never believed in long engagements, myself. Well, you enjoy yourself on that mystery thing up there. Good luck to you."

"Thank you," Cleo and Gus said together, then turned quickly and left the store. They stopped outside under a tree. There was an awkward pause.

Gus looked over the top of her head and squinted into the distance. "I'm sorry I never got you that ring," he said.

Cleo slipped on her dark glasses. "Water under the bridge," she said. "Where should we go now?"

Gus slipped on his glasses as well, the black lenses hiding some emotion she'd seen in his eyes that she couldn't quite decipher.

"I think we should dig into that gourmet picnic lunch the hotel packed for us," he said.

"You just had breakfast an hour ago."

"Correction—*you* just had breakfast an hour ago. I'm starved. Come on, Clee, let's find some sunny green field and have a picnic."

Just then thunder rumbled distantly, and they noticed that dark clouds had blown across the sky, darkening the sunny morning. A blazing orange leaf spiraled down on a gust of wind and landed on Gus's shoe.

He stared down at it while a pattern of raindrops plastered it to the leather. Then he looked up again. "Well, how about a muddy brown field, then?" he asked.

"I'm glad you capitulated on that muddy field," Cleo said, stretching her slightly damp socks toward the fire. She reached over to dab hot mustard on a slice of turkey, then wrapped it around a gherkin and slipped it into her mouth. She was trying hard to appear completely at her ease, and she was succeeding pretty well, she thought. Gus had no idea that his suggestion to eat on the floor of the living room of his suite had completely knocked her off balance. Her only defense had been to pretend it was the most normal suggestion in the world.

But as she avoided Gus's eyes and stared into the fire, she couldn't help remembering the last time she'd stretched out beside him on this rug in front of the fire. It had been the night they'd arrived at the inn three years ago. The tension had been unbearable, the months of yearning building up into this one long night. They had made love for hours on the rug, locked together, straining, slick with the dampness of sweat and tears, tasting each other's salty skin, their bodies velvety and supple and agonizingly sensitized to every touch. The wood had crackled and spit and sizzled as firelight had burnished Gus's golden tone, highlighting his shoulder, his beautiful back, his hands...

"Cleo?" Gus's voice was soft but it cut through her recollection, tearing it into the shreds that their marriage had become. "What are you thinking about?"

"I'm thinking about the case," she answered, leaning back on her elbows and keeping her face averted.

"Liar."

"Obviously the man who bought the bracelet was—"

"You're thinking about the last time you were in this room."

"—Bruno, and he bought it for Susan Scarlett-Gray—how do you know what I was thinking about?"

"You blushed. You always do."

"It's the fire. Now, I was thinking—"

"Cleo, I've thought about that weekend a hundred times since I've been here. It's torture, staying in this room, knowing you're down the hall—"

"Gus," Cleo said evenly, "I don't want to talk about this. I want to talk about the case. You seduced me into coming here—"

"Honey, I haven't begun to seduce you," Gus said, his voice low, curling around her ear. "Yet."

"Wrong choice of word, I see. Gus, if you brought me here to—"

"Relax, Clee. We can talk about the case. I just brought you here because I think better on my own turf."

"Now, there's one statement of yours I can wholeheartedly agree with."

"I know I shouldn't ask you this, but what exactly do you mean by that?"

"Gus, you know how you are about your 'turf'—like the Jets and the Sharks. For heaven's sake, you've stayed in one apartment for ten years because you can't face finding another neighborhood deli. You were so reluctant to pry yourself away that after we got married we had to sublet my co-op and live in *your* overcrowded apartment—"

"Hey, I built a loft for the bed."

"—that was freezing in winter and boiling in summer and had a constantly running toilet—"

"The super fixed the toilet. Remember, after you chased him for three blocks with the plunger?"

"It had a kitchen the size of a postage stamp—"

"I thought it was a perfect size. Remember that night right before Alan and Patti were due for dinner, and I kept bumping into you, and we ended up—"

"And the bathroom! Hunks of plaster fell into the tub—"

"Hey, they only *grazed* you. And they missed me completely."

A delicate snort came from Cleo's lips. She bent her head forward so her hair hid her face. A series of strange, muffled grunts came from underneath the black waves, and Gus grinned; he recognized the strangled sounds of his wife's reluctantly giving in to her sense of the ridiculous in the middle of an argument.

Cleo looked up to meet Gus's grin. Memory had washed over her so unexpectedly; that horrified look on Gus's face as a particularly large chunk of plaster fell between his legs, barely missing a very vital organ and sending a small tidal wave through the tub. How they had laughed then, almost upsetting the champagne perched precariously on the low wooden stool next to the tub.

Now, looking over at Gus, the memory flashed from his eyes to hers and they burst out laughing. They gave themselves up to it, weakly flopping back on the rug. Gus quieted first and admired the line of Cleo's throat as she threw her head back in the full-fledged enjoyment that he loved to watch. When she wiped the tears from her eyes and looked over at Gus, she found his expression had sobered.

"We were so good together, Clee," he said, his voice rough. It sent a thrill skittering up her spine; it raised the hairs on the back of her neck. "So good." He leaned toward her.

Cleo closed her eyes as his finger circled around her clenched hand. It insinuated itself inside to nestle into her warm closed fist.

She felt him move closer to her, felt his breath against her cheek. Cleo sucked in her own breath as she was suddenly hit with desire, a force so acute it was painful. How could she have ever believed that she had exorcised him, that love so irrevocably given could dissipate and die? How could she have imagined that desire this shattering could be tamed by just one kiss in a deserted hallway?

She opened her eyes. If his gaze held the faintest trace of mockery, she would die. But there was uncertainty in those honey-colored eyes, and longing, and desire, and somewhere, a shadow of pain. Perhaps his expression mirrored her own.

With a soft moan of surrender, she leaned toward him for the kiss she was terrified of, yet wanted so desperately.

This time, there was no caution. Instantly, the kiss flamed into something incandescent; they were swept into a roaring, spinning vortex that annihilated everything but each other. Surely, Cleo thought dizzily, her body wouldn't be able to contain this feeling; surely she would explode from it. His mouth was hot and hungry; she could feel his teeth and his tongue and his breath as their hands moved over each other's bodies with a skittering, desperate compulsion to feel everything, to omit nothing.

His hands were on her breasts again, on her thighs, cradling her face, tracing her ears. His mouth was on her neck, his voice, hoarse and deep, capable only of saying her name. They spurred her on as she clutched him and moaned his name in return.

And how ravenous she was for him, too. She was swept back into the passion of that first weekend they'd made love; they had begun just as tentatively, and had lost control so soon. They had loved the firelight because it had allowed them to watch each other's faces as they pleased and tantalized each other, exulting in their power.

But this time they kept their eyes closed. Cleo was afraid to look again; she blocked out everything but the feel of his lips and his hands. The red firelight burned behind her eyelids as she gave herself up to the annihilating sensations. She was half-wild, unable to think or to reason, when he picked her up in his arms and carried her to bed. But as her hot limbs felt the cool sheet beneath her, she had a brief instant of absolute clarity.

She saw the canopy above her, the rose-shaded light on the small oak stand, the old-fashioned wallpaper with the tiny violets printed on it, and Gus there, next to her.

It was all so familiar, so right—her husband, and the bed where they had made love for the first, unforgettable time.

Cleo stayed the hand that was fiercely roaming down her body. She gently brought it to her lips while her eyes held his.

"So good," she whispered. An answering flame lit Gus's gaze and his fingertips turned gentle as they outlined the sweet curve of her mouth. Slowly, reverently, Cleo brought his face down to hers, cradling it. She opened her mouth to his.

She wanted to linger, to savor, to concentrate on each individual moment of their lovemaking, since in the back of her mind she hadn't dispelled the knowledge that this passion would undoubtedly leave a legacy of guilt and regret. But she pushed the thoughts away and clung to Gus, burying her nose in his flesh to smell him again, devouring him with her eyes, her hands.

Though they had gone over the edge of their control, they hadn't abandoned tenderness. There was delicacy in Gus's fingertips, there was knowledge, exquisite and gentle, in his touch. They kept their mouths together in a deep kiss throughout their joining, needing the contact of lips and teeth and tongue to tell them what the other was feeling.

Desire gathered strength as they kissed, building until it swept away everything, carrying them away, heedless of anything but the straining tension between them. As they moved together, Cleo closed around Gus with a fierce possessiveness that no longer had the power to surprise her. With a soft cry, she gave herself up to him completely.

When it was over, they lay quietly together. Cleo found it impossible to speak; she had been so moved that she was terrified of being the one to say the first word to set the tone. Their intimacy had the delicate balance of a house of cards; one strong wind would blow it away.

As she curled against Gus in an agony of indecision, she felt his chest rise and fall in the regular rhythm of sleep. Relieved, she eased herself off him to dress quietly and quickly. Holding her boots in her hand, she allowed herself one last, long look at his sleeping face.

He lay on his back, sprawled across the rumpled covers, naked, one arm still flung outward to hold her against him. His mouth looked full and sensuous, his five o'clock stubble accentuating its softness. Dark lashes covered the warm honey gaze of those eyes, and the thick brown hair usually brushed off his forehead was tousled and messy. He'd never looked so sensually appealing, or more vulnerable. It was the Gus she'd fallen in love with, and the Gus she was unable to trust again.

Strangely disturbed, unbearably moved, she reached over for the comforter at the foot of the bed and covered him gently. As she drew it up across his chest, Cleo was surprised to see a solitary tear drip off her chin and make a dark, lonely spot on the downy material.

Chapter Five

Gus sneaked a peek at Cleo through his eyelashes as she turned and headed for the door. He kept his breathing regular and even. If she knew he was awake, he'd have to speak, and what would he say? He couldn't even think, let alone talk; he'd probably have to restrain himself from throwing himself at her pink-stockinged feet.

He'd felt her there, seemingly relaxed against him, yet coiled with tension. Her soft, pliant body had stiffened within moments after their lovemaking. Gus hadn't been sure how to react, but knowing Cleo as he did, he knew she needed time alone to absorb what had happened before she could discuss it. So he had obligingly feigned sleep.

He heard the door to his suite close with a soft click, and Gus sighed deeply and propped himself up on the pillows. His body still felt warm and alive from her hands, and he could smell her scent on his sheets. The fact that she had made love to him with such heart-breaking beauty, such possessiveness, was enough to content him for a time, for it gave him hope. Better to have that hope than to speak and to risk hearing her stammer, deny, evade, withdraw.

Tonight there would be time enough to talk. And tonight, come hell or high water, she would end up in his bed again. He wouldn't let her call this afternoon a mistake, never to be repeated. He wouldn't let her deny it had happened.

It was a mistake. A horrible, stupid, unfortunate mistake. And she would never repeat it, Cleo told herself, slamming her door. At least she could gain some consolation from that. She might be an idiot, but she wasn't stupid.

Maybe all ex-wives go through this, she decided, stomping into the bathroom to run hot water into the tub. They go to bed with their ex-husbands one last time, just to learn that it was really, truly, over. That the magic was really gone.

And that was what she'd just learned. She *had*.

She left her wrinkled clothes in a heap on the floor and climbed gratefully in the tub as it filled with the steaming water. Her thighs felt taut, her breasts were sensitive, and her insides had the consistency of pudding. It had been a long time since she'd felt this hot, languid tenderness in her body, and underneath it, like a buzz of interference impossible to ignore, a not unpleasant but entirely unwanted sensual urge for more.

Cleo filled her hands with water and splashed her face, over and over until her eyes burned. She soaped her hands and her legs and her stomach and chest, and vigorously shampooed her hair. But no matter how hard she rubbed and massaged and scrubbed, she couldn't get rid of the feel of his hands on her again. Maybe, she thought, closing her eyes, running her hands along her slick skin, because she didn't want to.

The thought propelled her out of the tub. She dried herself briskly, as penance. She had an hour and a half to get ready. Too long. Cleo dug into the suitcase that her sister Molly had sent up for her. She'd asked Molly to send her floor-length blue velvet dress for tonight; it was elegant and simple, and she always felt right in it. Maybe not gorgeous, but perfectly acceptable. Molly, when she'd heard Gus was there, had made numerous and enthusiastic alternate suggestions. But who would trust a woman who had worn a pink leather miniskirt to a cocktail party at her husband's law firm?

Cleo dug into the bag, past a jumble of tweed and suede and cashmere—one thing she had been sure of was that Molly would pick the best of her wardrobe— searching for the cobalt blue of the material. It was nowhere to be found. Instead, her fingers slid along the seductive luxury of heavy satin. Cleo drew out the material slowly and discovered, to her horror, a red satin gown.

She should have never trusted her wild and wily sister, that was for sure. She shook out the dress slowly, hardly daring to look. It was beautiful, and it even seemed as though it would cover her decently enough. But this wasn't a dress of a woman running away from her sensuality. No, the woman who would wear this dress was asking for trouble.

Cleo spied a note pinned to the protective layer of tissue paper and snatched it up.

Dear Cleo
Don't be angry. The blue velvet is nice, but when it

comes to ex-husbands like Gus (and you'll forgive
me, dear sister, if I point out that there are no ex-
husbands like Gus, being that most women wouldn't
be crazy enough to let him go . . .) nice just doesn't
cut it. You've got to at least look your sexiest while
you're telling him to get lost. You'll be smashing.
Trust me. Anyway, you're supposed to be Sophie
Fast, and she has guts, even if you don't.

"I do have guts," Cleo said irritably to the absent
Molly. Suddenly the phone shrilled at her bedside, and
Cleo snatched it up.

"Hello?"

"Hi, Cleo, it's Wendee. Listen, I just called to make
sure you're doing okay with the clues, if you got all the
bios last night and such. I'm helping Denton out a bit."

"I got them, Wendee, thanks."

"Sure." A throaty giggle sailed over the wire. "I just
called Gus—was he grumpy. He gets like that if you wake
him up. Well, I guess I'll see you at the ball tonight.
We're going to have a drink beforehand, so don't panic
if you don't see Gus for a bit."

"I'll take a couple of tranquilizers. Thanks for the call,
Wendee."

"Oh, don't mention it. Bye now."

Instead of throwing the receiver across the room, Cleo
summoned up a mature attitude and replaced it gently.
Rather a flimsy excuse for Wendee to call, but now Cleo
knew that she was having cocktails with Gus before the
party. She'd certainly managed to get across that piece of
vital information. In her shy, insecure way.

"Men are idiots," Cleo growled. She wondered if
Wendee was, at that moment, picking up Gus's laundry
from the valet with her very own fragile, narrow hands.

"I never picked up his laundry, and I was *married* to him," she announced to the empty room.

She regarded the dress again with a new perspective. Shaking it out in front of her, she saw with a woman's eye how the material would drape against her body, how it would move when she moved. Then she held it up against her and looked in the mirror. After a shower she usually sported her drowned-rat look in her wrapper with her wet hair, but now, with the scarlet cloth against her, she saw a chic and devastating woman looking back. The dress definitely had—possibilities.

Cleo thought of Wendee Tolliver, and a surge of her usual feistiness surfaced again. Molly was right. Even if she was giving up Gus for good, it didn't mean she was going to hand him over on a demure, blue velvet platter trimmed with lace. She needed all the scarlet satin ammunition she could get.

Gus deftly avoided the waiter bearing down on him and hunted for a quiet corner. It was hard to locate one. A TV crew was busily shooting chattering groups of men in tuxedos and women in glittering gowns who were enthusiastically downing champagne and admiring the "ballroom"—created that afternoon by opening the French doors between the drawing room and the parlor, to make one long room. Except for a few chairs along the wall, the furniture had all been cleared away and the two huge fireplaces at either end had been lit; the room glowed with their light and that of what seemed to be a hundred candles.

A small orchestra was tuning up in one corner, and Gus went to the opposite side of the room, dodging a group of writers earnestly discussing how successful the mystery weekend was turning out. Gus grinned as he passed by; he didn't hear anything about clues or suspects or hunches. Just raves about the tarragon chicken packed in the picnic lunch and the excellent vintages of the various wines.

He never thought he could possibly get tired of expensive champagne, but this weekend was proving that anything was possible. If he saw another champagne bottle, he'd throw a tantrum. Wendee had surprised him at his door with a bottle of it earlier, which he'd refused to drink, and now everywhere he turned, someone was offering him a glass. Denton was certainly fond of the stuff. Gus found himself longing for a cold, uncomplicated bottle of beer—no glass.

He scowled and avoided Wendee's eye. She was making him uncomfortable this evening, acting oddly proprietary all of a sudden. As if they were lovers who'd had a falling out. Under pale brows she was sending him smoldering glances that he didn't understand in the least. Her mysterious behavior and her sudden puzzling bids for his attention were almost comically opposed to his own obvious concerns. All he could think about was Cleo. Looking at his watch every few seconds was getting to be a habit, for she still hadn't shown up.

Cleo... Gus felt his stomach tighten as she walked in. He actually had to lean back against the wall for support.

Cleo. *Where did she get that dress?*

She stood poised in the doorway, the clean line of her chin lifted challengingly. One gleaming shoulder was bare in a stunning dress he'd never seen before. The sensual fall of red satin was somehow draped so cunningly around her body that he had no idea how it could be fastened. He would certainly like to find out. It fell from one shoulder and sheathed her breasts and waist and hips in the same loving way he had caressed them earlier; underneath the rich material he could make out the line of her long, elegant legs.

Her chin-length wavy black hair was swept up with some sort of rhinestone clips into a froth piled on top of her head. Her eyes looked dark and enormous. Small diamonds were in her ears, but she wore no other jewelry. She needed no flash and fire other than herself.

Wendee moved into his line of vision, and he looked past her, barely caught by the white blur of her dress. She seemed as shallow and insubstantial as the first snowfall next to the raging storm that was his wife. Wendee had never even been in the running with Cleo, no woman ever had, and that was the problem, that was why he was mooning at his wife across a crowded room as if she were a strange, exotic woman he'd never seen before but was irrevocably destined for.

The room faded as she approached him, and when their eyes met, his heart seemed to cry out to hers that this night was theirs; it could go on forever with longing and love and desires met and satisfied...

"Hi," Cleo greeted him, her eyes scanning the room. "I think we've wasted enough time already today—what do you say we get to work?" The cheerful professionalism was so incongruous with the erotic vision before him that Gus took a moment to recover and remember that Cleo had no idea she was causing various compelling fantasies inside his head. Or perhaps, Gus thought with a wry twist to his mouth, she did indeed.

He should have known better than to formulate lovestruck rhapsodies around Cleo. She would unbalance him every time. But he could unbalance her as well.

"Let's talk about this afternoon," he said.

"Okay," she said agreeably, snatching a glass of champagne from a passing waiter's tray. "Gosh, I'm sick of this stuff. What I wouldn't give for a beer. Anyway, so far all the evidence points to Bruno, which worries me—it's too easy. We're supposed to think that Derek found that love letter and the receipt, and then either Bruno had an argument with Derek or he just decided to knock him off so he could have the lovely Susan all to himself. Right?"

"Cleo, I wasn't talking about the case."

"I know you weren't; I was. It seems to me that I'm doing most of the brain work around here. I've been checking around, and just about everybody figured out the jewelry-store clue—and you can bet they all suspect Bruno, too. It's all too dull and predictable. Something wild has to happen tonight."

"That's for sure," Gus agreed. "Why don't you meet me in my room around midnight and I'll see what I can do?" Cleo grimaced and turned away slightly to scan the crowd, giving Gus a glimpse of the back of the dress. It wrapped and draped and left delicious inches of her back bare. There were no zippers or buttons that he could see, but he could easily spend the whole night looking. As long as he found them eventually.

"And there's something else that's been bothering me," Cleo continued, turning around again.

"Me, too," Gus said. "How did you get into that dress?"

"Bruno's letter," she went on, ignoring him. "The tone is strange. When I read it again, I realized that the references Bruno makes to the fact that they can't be together all have to do with his wife. But what about Susan? She was engaged to Derek, after all."

"I guess he didn't take it that seriously. Is there an invisible zipper back there, or something?"

"Maybe," Cleo mused.

"*Maybe* there's a zipper? Is that a challenge?"

"I'm going to keep my eye on Bruno and Susan tonight, that's for sure."

"Because if there is, I think I'm man enough to handle it."

"I think you'd better handle Susan Scarlett-Gray first."

Gus stiffened when he felt a small hand slide down his arm.

"I see you finally found the champagne, Gus," Wendee said. "Hello, Cleo."

"Hi, Wendee."

"Glad you finally made it. I thought our Gus was going to burst with anticipation."

Our Gus? She hadn't realized they were sharing him. Cleo summoned up a polite smile; she felt a surge of relief when she saw that Gus looked very annoyed.

Wendee smiled back. "This hasn't been much of a vacation for any of us, has it? I mean, it's so lovely up here, and all I've been able to do is trail after Denton as he orders the actors around. He's worse than a director. That's a gorgeous dress, Cleo," Wendee went on, switching gears easily. "I'm just like you," she said matter-of-factly. "I don't care if it *is* last year's dress; I wear it anyway."

"I can see that." A giggle started deep in Cleo's chest; she felt slightly hysterical, and she wondered whether to inform Wendee that she'd seen the same B movies, so they could go on like this all night.

"Wendee," Gus broke in brusquely, "Denton's looking for you."

"He is? Again?" She sighed. "The man is too much. He hasn't left me alone all weekend."

"He's heading for the library. You'd better hurry and catch him."

"All right. Save me a place at dinner, will you?" Wendee pouted at Gus.

"Sure," Gus said agreeably. "Do you get to eat at the grown-up table this year?"

Already moving away, Wendee threw Gus another pout over her shoulder but continued on.

"I don't know what's gotten into her," Gus said, looking after her.

"I think it's marvelous that Wendee can overcome her handicap and be so relentlessly social if she has to," Cleo said virtuously.

"I'm sorry about this—"

"That's all right. I must say I've been trained to have your various admirers being flaunted in my face."

"What do you mean? I don't have any admirers. Except for you, of course. And the guy who owns the jewelry store in town."

"I don't mean now. Before we were engaged, while we were writing *Murder on the Westchester Express*. You used to give me blow-by-blow accounts of your dates the night before over coffee in the mornings. I'd have to pass the cream and hear about Bunny or Fawn or Bambi—"

"Come on, Clee, you make it sound like *Wild Kingdom*."

"No, sweetie, *you* made it sound like *Wild Kingdom*. Anyway, I was the one who had to watch you drool into your Danish every morning."

"Don't be ridiculous," Gus returned huffily. "I never drool. You have a handkerchief handy? I think there's a spot on my tie." He raised his eyebrows at her and grinned. "It's not like we were involved at the time. Anyway, I was desperate."

"That was obvious."

"I mean for you. You were so damn *sisterly*. I was hoping to drive you crazy with jealousy so you'd realize how much you craved my body."

Cleo froze. "Do you mean that you told me about all those women just to get a *reaction* from me? Detail after detail, woman after woman—"

"Actually, Cleo, to be honest, there perhaps weren't, well, quite so many as I made out—"

"What?"

"I might have embellished a bit."

"What?"

"All in a good cause, Clee. After all, you did marry me eventually, so—"

"Of all the devious, sneaky, underhanded "

"Thanks," Gus said modestly. "Don't mention it—"

"Childish, immature—"

"Now wait a second here—"

"—idiotic, cheap tricks—"

"Hey! It worked, didn't it?"

"Oh, yes," Cleo said sardonically, "we lived happily ever after, didn't we?"

Gus ignored the remark. "I remember that time I told the story about Bambi and the Staten Island Ferry. You dumped yogurt into your coffee instead of cream and then took a sip. You spit it out all over my sweater. And that green rug of mine was never the same."

"Not exactly a loss to the world of interior design. I really don't believe this. Four years after the fact, my ex-husband announces that to get me into his bed he made up a pack of lies about his prowess with various women who had the cumulative IQs of a couple of fleas—"

"Hey—I didn't say they were *all* lies. I had to have some experiences to draw from, after all." At Cleo's look, he finished, "Though, of course, I didn't enjoy any of them in the least."

Cleo's expression was stony. "You're not upset, are you?" Gus asked. "It was four years ago. It's actually kind of funny, in a way. Remember the banana yogurt all over my sweater? Talk to me, Cleo."

"You," Cleo said distinctly, "are a piece of sludge. It's so typical of you—instead of confronting an issue, you resort to some underhanded stratagem—"

"Look who's talking about confronting issues. What about this afternoon, Cleo?"

Cleo stiffened. "What about it?"

"Why have you refused to acknowledge it?"

"I have not."

Gus drew closer, his eyes glittering. "You have."

"I have not."

"Then why are you backing away from me?"

"I'm not." Just as she forcefully announced this, Cleo's heel hit the wall behind her. She stopped. Gus was so close. She watched one brown wrist emerge from a snowy cuff as he reached his hand out to lean against the wall. Their faces were very close.

She gave up. "I am," she admitted. "Gus, I don't want—"

"Oh, you do want." That damned slow Nashville cadence was in his voice again, coursing through her like a shot of good Tennessee bourbon—smooth, fiery, flushing her face and her neck, making her fingers and toes tingle. "And I'll tell you what you want. You want—"

"Here you are! Listen, we need a shot of you two talking, okay?" Suddenly they were surrounded by the crew from *Dateline: Entertainment*. A short, bald man directed the crew to set up the shot. "We don't have sound here, so just look like you're busy detecting. Okay, ready, set, detect!"

Cleo and Gus obediently turned toward each other as the camera clicked on.

"Come on, guys, help me out, will you? Say something," the bald man demanded.

"You snake," Cleo said softly, "you're still trying the same technique to divert my attention. That's why we never finished an argument. As long as we 'ended up horizontal,' as you so elegantly put it—"

"It doesn't have to be horizontal," Gus said, keeping a bland expression on his face for the cameras. "I would never be so limited in my thinking. You can be very inventive in the vertical position—"

"Would you just stop! Stop, stop, stop!" Her voice ended on a high note of hysteria, and the film crew looked over at her.

She smiled back uneasily at them and whirled back to Gus. "You might stop and consider," she said through clenched teeth, "that your methods have only been successful in the short term. We *are* separated, remember?"

"Only by a few inches, love. And I can take care of that later—"

They both jumped as Gus was interrupted by the bald man, who bellowed, "Okay, thanks!"

They waited, tense and silent, while the crew adjusted the equipment. One slender young woman said, "Boy, I'll be glad when we head back to the city. I could go for a margarita right now."

"I'll take you out for one when we get back," an equally slender young man said.

"Yeah, I like the way you take me out," the young woman snorted. "I waited an hour for you at the Red Parrot last Wednesday."

"I told you to meet me at the Parrot. That's on the East Side. I can't help it if you misunderstood."

"I just thought you were such a regular that you abbreviated it. Give me a break," she muttered. "Who knew there were two different places? Who goes to the Parrot, anyway?"

Gus turned back to Cleo with a grin. "Maybe I should give them some tips on the Gus Creighton Horizontal Treaty Plan," he said.

"Wait a second," Cleo said slowly. "The Parrot. The Red Parrot. Two different places, right?"

"That's what seemed to have caused the difficulty."

"Of course!" She pounded on his arm. "That's what caused the difficulty. Come on."

"Finally you see the light," Gus said, allowing her to discreetly steer him from the room. "Speaking of which, the fire's already laid in my room, and—"

"Gus, do shut up and listen. Remember in Bruno's letter when he talks about meeting Susan at The Gables for that last weekend? Two things have always bothered me—one, Bruno is so formal. Wouldn't he refer to Green Gables by its full name?"

"Maybe," Gus said doubtfully. "But I'd call that pretty slim reasoning."

"Call it a hunch. But I've heard him mention the name of the inn at least a half-dozen times, and he always calls it The Green Gables Inn, as if it's Buckingham Palace or something. But the important thing is what's been bothering me all along—there is no mention of her engagement to Derek in the letter. He calls her 'unmoored,' remember?"

"So? I wouldn't say Derek would be stiff competition for anyone. Do we have to keep going over this? I'm getting a headache."

"But he was rich. She was going to marry him, wasn't she?"

When she reached the safety of the lobby, Cleo flew across it, dragging Gus along with her. Upon reaching the front desk, she tapped on the bell impatiently.

The desk clerk poked his head from behind a wooden screen. "Hi. Can I help you?"

"Got any aspirin?" Gus asked.

"I was wondering," Cleo broke in, "if you could tell us—is there another Connecticut inn called The Gables?"

The desk clerk beamed a smile similar to the jewelry store owner at Rocks. "Yep, matter of fact, there is. And here's the clue—that inn burned down three years ago."

"Three years ago," Cleo mused. She turned to Gus. "That means that it's possible that Bruno and Susan *did* have an affair. But it ended at least three years ago! Remember, in the letter he said that she granted him one last weekend. So who was the man in the jewelry store with Susan, then?"

The desk clerk nodded. "Good question. You got it— and you're only the second person to get the clue so far. Whoops, I don't think I was supposed to mention that. You won't tell Mr. Ballard, will you?"

"No, of course not," Cleo assured him. "Thanks for your help."

"Sure," the man replied. "Anything for Max and Sophie Fast." He grinned appreciatively at Cleo. "Always did think Sophie was the smartest of the two."

"Smarter," Gus corrected, aggrieved.

"You think so, too, huh?"

Cleo giggled as Gus turned away with a pained expression. He tugged on her arm, and they started back toward the drawing room.

"Don't you want your aspirin, Max?" the clerk called after Gus. "You sure look like you could use it."

As the evening wore on, it was increasingly obvious that the atmosphere was undergoing a definite change. Perhaps because of the presence of camera crews and reporters from the weekly newsmagazines, the writers and fans had all buckled down and begun to get serious about the weekend. There were complicated strategies, bold advances, and subtle manipulations practiced in order to get to dance with the principal suspects. The consumption of champagne was definitely down; everyone was gunning for that extravagant voyage on the Orient Express and the silly inflated title of Greatest Detective in the World.

And Cleo was gunning for the rights to Sophie and Max and her own self-respect. She deftly avoided Gus and concentrated on milling through the crowd, trying to pick up clues that would indicate what the chain of relationships among the suspects could be.

From what Cleo could see, it appeared that Anthony Guy was avoiding Bruno, Bruno was avoiding Susan, and Susan was avoiding the participants eager to dance with her in order to pursue Gus. Gus was busy avoiding Susan. The various other suspects were dispersed around the room, chatting with the entrants and sprinkling teasing little clues throughout their conversation.

Cleo didn't worry too much about missing something in individual conversations; she knew that a clue would have to appear while everyone was aware and could interpret it. So she hung back and ignored the subtleties in favor of the obvious.

It was clear that as the night wore on Bruno was becoming more and more agitated. It wasn't until everyone was beginning to think longingly of the midnight supper and to wonder when the call to the dining room would come that he finally broke.

The orchestra was taking a break when he began the argument with Anthony in a high-pitched voice unlike his usual suave tones. Gus had sidled over to Cleo, ready to compare notes on the evening, when the tone in Bruno's voice made her, and everyone else in the vicinity, stop and listen intently while appearing to be studiously admiring the crowd.

"Yes, I heard about the letter in Derek's pocket," he was saying to Anthony "Funny that it should appear now, isn't it?"

"Rather," Anthony said offhandedly, but there was menace in his voice, a warning.

"I can't for the life of me think why a letter written three years before should turn up—"

"Yes, I agree," Anthony cut in, his voice still a honeyed thrust. "But it's old news now, isn't it, Bruno? I'd much prefer to discuss current events—so much more topical and significant. Shall we make small talk, then? You're the expert on sailing. Did you hear about that horrible accident this weekend? Out on the Sound, it was. Funny, how an experienced sailor could lose control of his craft in an average gale. They just can't figure it out. I mean, speaking of strange things, as you were, this really becomes intriguing . . ."

Bruno backed up a step, his agitation obvious though he tried to conceal it. Anthony took his arm easily.

"I'd say it's time to find the champagne, wouldn't you, old man?"

As Anthony and Bruno headed for the bar, there was a flurry of activity. Sidney Clott trundled after them, trying to look inconspicuous, but he was trailed by several other participants. Isis Gold slipped away into a corner, and Cleo saw her take a small notebook out of her pocket.

"Obviously a clue," she said to Gus. "What do you think it means, Max?"

"Hard to say, Sophie," Gus answered. "Looks like Anthony has something on Bruno. He's making him squirm with that sailing story."

"Didn't it say in the character bio that Anthony's father died in a sailing accident four years ago? That's how he inherited his fortune."

"But what would that have to do with Bruno?" Gus wondered. "He didn't have anything to gain by Anthony's father's death. The two of them just met this weekend." The orchestra suddenly swung into a lilting Cole Porter melody. "Now you've avoided me long enough," Gus said firmly, taking her arm. "We can dance and detect at the same time, you know."

"I don't want to dance. I want to go to the library."

"You want to read?"

"I want to look at the scene of the crime again. Come on."

"All right, but let's be quick about it. I don't want to miss supper. We have to keep our priorities straight, you know."

Chapter Six

No one noticed them as they crossed the hall quickly and slipped into the library. They paused for a moment; the room was dark, the heavy curtains shutting out the moonlight.

"Wait here," Gus said softly, a hand on her arm. "I'll find the light." Cleo heard a bump and a muffled curse.

"Run into any cactuses out there?" she asked into the darkness.

"Wouldn't you love it. Ah—I found it." Gus was suddenly illuminated by the light of a green-glass-shaded lamp, its soft glow seeming somehow to intensify the dead quiet of the room.

The library looked unused, neglected. Though it was generously proportioned, the paneling, bookcases, and heavy rugs and curtains gave it a claustrophobic feeling. Even though the murder had been a fake, the weekend participants had tended to avoid the dark paneled room as if some unpleasantness had lingered in the air. Cleo shivered and rubbed her hands along her bare arms.

"I don't know why, but this place gives me the creeps. I don't think I'd make a very good detective."

Gus came back across the room to her. "That's why I'm here, darling. Now, what do you expect to find here?"

"I don't know. Clues, hunches, new developments, maybe a little inspiration."

He drew closer. "How about a kiss to start? That usually inspires me."

"I thought I was the one who specialized in the love stuff," Cleo said. She crossed to the middle of the room and looked around, trying to ignore the note in Gus's voice and concentrate on finding something she'd missed. Something was nagging at her. "Now, Susan said that when she entered, Derek was already starting to topple. He reached out for her, grabbed the curtains for balance, and boom." She pointed to the spot on the carpet where Derek had fallen. "We know he went upstairs to his room to get the cigarette case. That means that after we were all congratulating ourselves at still being alive after the lights came back on, somebody left the room, lured him into the library, and stabbed him while his back was turned. Then the person had time to slip out before Susan came in."

"Fascinating. Now, as I was saying—"

"At this point, I'm betting that the murderer concealed the weapon in the library while the lights went out. He or she had already asked Derek to meet them in the library, alone."

"Why couldn't they have concealed the weapon earlier?"

"Because early arrivals were having cocktails in the library in front of the fire. I asked."

"Okay, now that we have that settled—" Gus headed toward her with a very familiar gleam in his eye.

She moved a few steps back. "Susan said that she went into the library because she'd heard a strange noise as she was heading for the stairs. It's possible, I suppose." Gus reached her side, and Cleo looked past him to the door. "The door was closed when we got to the library last night, wasn't it?"

"Yes, Sophie. Now, do you mind letting Cleo come back for a minute?"

"Don't you think it strange that, coming in and seeing her fiancé fatally stabbed in the back and reaching for her, she would take the time to—"

"Close the door. Good point." Gus's expression became thoughtful as he considered the problem. "Could have been reflex, though. People do strange things under pressure. The door is always—"

"Kept closed. I noticed that. But Susan didn't know that. We'd all only just arrived."

"Maybe it was closed when she approached in the first place."

"Then how could she have—"

"Heard the noise? I see what you mean. That door is solid oak."

"So maybe Susan Scarlett-Gray isn't the bereaved innocent she seems to be. But that still doesn't mean she killed him—she just didn't have time. She couldn't have left the parlor, stabbed him and then been sure he'd be dead by the time everyone came to look." Cleo crossed to the green velvet curtains and fingered them. Suddenly she gave them a sharp jerk.

"You doing your Scarlett O'Hara impersonation again? Somehow I don't think the inn would let you make a dress out of those."

"Gus," Cleo said slowly, "if I just used all my strength to try and pull them down and they stayed up, how could a dying man do it?"

Gus came over behind her and inspected the curtains. He shrugged. "Think you might be off base here, Soph. He was falling at the time; his whole weight was behind them. And a considerable weight it was, you remember." His breath stirred her hair; she felt it caress her bare shoulder. "Maybe," he said, "we're getting tired. It's past midnight, after all. Why don't we—"

She eased away from him. "I just have the feeling we're missing an important clue."

Gus remained in the same place, now staring at the curtains instead of Cleo's lovely back and shoulders. He addressed his remark to the window. "I have the feeling you're trying to avoid me, Cleo."

"You know, you just might make a detective, after all. Must be my influence."

"It's midnight, I have Taittinger on ice in my room, and you're avoiding me. I can't—hey, wait a second."

The note in Gus's voice made the hairs go up on the back of Cleo's neck. She watched him touch the curtains hesitantly and then reach out to grab fistfuls of the material.

He turned around and grinned at her. "Too bad they don't give a title for the Lousiest Detective in the World this weekend. We could split the honor."

"Speak for yourself. What are you talking about?"

"Derek was stabbed in the back, right?"

"Right."

Gus turned Cleo around so that her back was to him. His finger came down lightly in the middle of her shoulder blades. "About here?"

"I'd say so."

He lifted a letter opener off the desk and held it there. "Try and touch that."

Cleo squirmed and reached behind her. Her fingers wagged at empty air. "I can't."

"Of course you can't. And neither could Derek. Remember those short arms and legs? That's why there was no blood on his hands. I saw that, but it didn't register before."

"So?"

He cocked an eyebrow at her. *"So why were there bloody handprints on the curtains?"*

Cleo turned around slowly with wide eyes. "Of course. How stupid of us. The others must have noticed it."

"Some of them, maybe. I saw Isis Gold scrutinizing the curtains that night. But that means that Susan lied about Derek pulling down the curtains."

"Why would she?" Cleo wondered. "And doesn't that mean it must have been *she* who pulled them down—"

"First getting Derek's blood on her hands—"

"But why?" Cleo asked again. "She must have wanted everyone to think that Derek was still alive."

"Exactly. Which means that Derek could have been already—"

"Dead when she found him."

"Which means that the time of death could be moved up considerably. He could have been killed while the lights were out."

"But it still couldn't have been Susan," Cleo said slowly. "Remember, she was complaining about the wiring of the inn the entire time. I remember thinking how long she was going on about it."

"Maybe she was establishing an alibi."

"Maybe. But that means she *knew* that the murder was being committed—"

"And that means she knew the murderer." Gus whistled softly. "Good work, Clee."

"Did you hear Bruno talking when the lights went out?"

"I'm not sure."

"Me neither. So he could have slipped out to the library." Cleo dropped into an armchair and rested her chin in her hands. "He's still our number-one suspect, but now it looks like Susan is in on it with him. I remember hearing Anthony talking to Susan, so it couldn't be him. But it could be a half dozen other people, too. Including the butler."

Gus sank into the matching armchair. "So we're a little bit ahead, but not much. Susan's in on it, but she didn't do it. Which leaves us with the same puzzle of who was with her in the jewelry store. And the solution still seems to be Bruno."

"So maybe it *was* Bruno. Maybe the most obvious suspect is the killer. Oh, I don't know." Cleo reached over to the desk next to her and plucked a piece of hotel stationery off the top of it. She leaned on a book and began scribbling furiously.

"I'd credit Denton with a bit more ingenuity. Seems like a lazy way to construct a plot, to me. What are you doing?"

"I'm writing out a list of the suspects. Sometimes it's easier when you see it in black and white."

"But honey, with your handwriting, you'll never be able to figure anything out."

"Oh, do be quiet a minute, Gus." Cleo concentrated on the names in front of her. She stared at the paper until the letters of two names swam in front of her eyes.

Bruno Haines.

Anthony Guy.

"Haines and Guy," she murmured. "Bruno and Anthony." Why did the names sound so familiar to her?

Gus yawned and looked at his watch. "Maybe this will all make sense in the morning. Why don't we head upstairs?" He looked over at Cleo, who was still scowling over her paper. "Cleo? Bedtime? I'd be glad to escort you to my room."

Cleo stood up slowly, the paper sliding from her lap onto the carpet.

"Cleo?"

"Strangers on a Train," she said, staring in front of her.

"Great movie," Gus said. "Is it on cable tonight? Might be nice to get into bed and—"

She leaned her hands on his knees and looked into his face. *"Strangers on a Train,"* she repeated fiercely. "Do you remember the plot?"

"Are you kidding? You know what a Hitchcock fan I am. Two men meet on a train, and one tells the other that the perfect murder would be if each of them agreed to kill the person the other wanted dead more than anything in the world. It would be impossible to prove who did it— the men had no connections, so there would be no motive. Chilling."

"Do you remember the characters' names?"

"That's a tough one. Let's see...one was called Guy— wait a second—do you think—"

"Guy Haines. And the other was—"

"Bruno Anthony."

Cleo straightened up. "Bruno, Anthony, Guy, Haines. Same names, just in a different combination."

"Holy cow," Gus said wonderingly. "Of course. Denton's such a film buff, too. So, knowing Denton, that must be the verbal clue we got the first night, the one we couldn't figure out. The two men had a conspiracy going. *That's* what Anthony has on Bruno—"

"Exactly. Remember the sailing accident Anthony taunted Bruno with? Maybe Bruno killed Anthony's father for him."

"And then Anthony inherited a fortune." Gus nodded. "It just might be it. Say Bruno was still in love with Susan, even though their affair had been over for years. Maybe he asked Anthony to pay him back on his end of the deal—"

"For Anthony to kill Derek." Cleo whirled around the room excitedly. "We figured it out!"

"Not exactly. There are enough loose ends to tie up the Queen Mary. First of all, Anthony never left the parlor that night. Susan lied about Derek's still being alive, but she never left the parlor either. The only one that did was Bruno. Remember, he said he needed air and left right after the lights came on again."

"So we're back to Bruno again. Then why the whole play on the names, then?"

Gus shrugged. "It gives us a motive. And it still could be another one of Denton's red herrings. We get a clue tomorrow morning—maybe that will help. We don't have enough on Bruno yet, but we're closer to the solution, anyway." He went over to Cleo and slipped his arms around her. His hands glided over her bare shoulders and down her back. "Time to call it a night," he said huskily.

Cleo's body leaned in toward him of its own accord; surely she wasn't directing it. His hands were warm as they ran over her back, and she rested against his chest to allow him freer rein. It felt so good, so right, just as the kiss last night had felt and the lovemaking this afternoon. Just the way it always felt when Gus touched her.

She heard a low chuckle by her ear. "I can't wait to get aboard the Orient Express," Gus murmured. "After we win tomorrow—"

A chill started down Cleo's spine. She came back to reality with a bump; Gus was still only thinking about winning the prize. She stepped back slightly. "That reminds me. How are we going to settle our wager?"

Gus's hands stopped their caressing motion. A small line appeared between his brows. "What do you mean?"

"It seems that I've come up with the major breakthrough in the case. The solution is really close now."

"Wait a second. Just a minute ago you were crowing about solving the case until I pointed out all the holes in your theory. And who figured out that Derek was already dead when Susan found him?"

"And who figured out the jewelry-store clue yesterday?"

Gus stopped and looked at the beautiful woman in front of him who just a moment ago he'd been fantasizing about seducing on the Orient Express. Was he crazy? He should have remembered her killer instinct, her competitive compulsion to be the best at everything she tried. Here he'd been totally intent on Cleo, and she'd been obsessed, not with the long-lost husband who adored her, but with getting control of Max and Sophie!

His plan had been to solve the case, then show her how uncompetitive he was and share the credit with her, never mentioning it again. He'd prove he was above petty concerns like who got credit for what. Meanwhile, she'd been coolly keeping score.

Well, he couldn't let her get away with it. If she was throwing down the gauntlet, he wouldn't let it lie there, ignored.

Cleo watched Gus's eyes darken and flash as he scrutinized her silently. She felt uneasy, and she leaned against the desk behind her for support. She was hanging on to her professionalism by her fingernails at this point, and she had to keep reminding herself to keep an eye on her own interests or she'd be lost. "Look, Gus, it's not like I'm keeping score or anything," she argued. "But you have to admit that we didn't really think this wager through. How are we going to tell who deserves the credit if we win? We'll just get into another one of those arguments we'll never be able to solve. I mean, already I've figured out most of the clues—"

"But who's counting?"

"So considering the circumstances, maybe we should split up after the final clue tomorrow morning and continue on our own."

"Well," Gus said, his voice carefully neutral, "I don't know, Cleo. This is all new to you. If you're sure you can handle it—"

"I think," Cleo answered furiously, "what I can't handle is hearing just one more of your patronizing remarks. I never realized what a sexist, overbearing boor you are."

The stale air now seemed electrified. They stood facing each other, glaring each other down. Finally, Gus spoke.

"Cleo? One last thing."

"What?" she snapped.

"Does this mean you won't come to my room to-night?"

With a muffled exclamation, she spun on one silver heel and stalked toward the door. She flung it open, banging it against the wall. Red satin flashed as she whipped through the opening. The heavy door slammed with a resounding crash.

Gus shook his head. Frustration and irritation were, as usual, battling with admiration for the woman he had married.

He sighed. "What a woman," he said.

One may be lonely, and two may be true,
but three is unlucky and can be a clue.
When solemn records do show
that laughs can mean woe
when darkness makes one into two.

Cleo scowled at the words again. She'd been staring at the paper all morning, and she was starting to get sleepy. She'd refused the ubiquitous champagne at brunch earlier so she could keep her wits about her, but the lack of sleep from last night made her long for a nap. She'd tossed and turned all night.

Denton had passed out the last clue after brunch, and so far she'd drawn a blank. Gus had taken off like a shot after he read it, leaving a grumpy Wendee in his wake, and now anxiety was eating away at her. She'd finally ended up cowering in the backyard underneath an oak tree while she secretly tried to puzzle the verse out. While the minutes ticked away, she imagined that Gus was even then triumphantly revealing the murderer to Denton.

Any minute he would be sauntering out here to tell her that Max and Sophie now belonged to him. She had to beat him, and she had to stop floundering around like a fool, chasing dead ends all morning.

Who could figure out these one-two-threes, anyway? She had a feeling it referred to the chain of relationships between Anthony, Bruno, and Susan—or perhaps Derek was one of the three. One of her suppositions this morning was that perhaps Anthony was having an affair with Susan, not Bruno. But how could she prove a vague hunch? Perhaps he was trying to pin the murder on Bruno, and had planted the letter in Derek's pocket. That would explain who'd been in the jewelry store with Susan—and why the man had been wearing a cap. It would have been Anthony, trying to disguise his red hair, and putting on an aristocratic accent in order to sound like Bruno.

But her theory fell apart when she had to return to the same problem. While the lights were out, she heard Anthony, and she didn't hear Bruno. So even though her hunch said Anthony wasn't who he appeared to be, she had no basis for it.

Unfortunately, her first brilliant idea had fallen flat. Sure that the "solemn records" would indicate a marriage between Anthony and Susan, "making one into two," she'd scurried off first to the church, then to the town hall. At each place she'd met a smirking townsperson who informed her that no marriage had taken place between any of the characters, and would she mind autographing a copy of *Red Herrings in Cream Sauce*?

She was stuck, all right. Cleo groaned and threw her head back, banging it on the tree behind her and sending a shower of bark into her hair. She rubbed her head ruefully. So now not only was she stuck, she was in pain.

Who else would have solemn records? she wondered, fingering the rapidly rising bump on her scalp. She couldn't drive all the way to the state capital, for heaven's sake. But where else were records kept?

Suddenly, Cleo sat up. Then she burst into a peal of laughter. Looking around quickly, she stuffed the verse into the pocket of her tweed pants. There was no sense alerting anyone else to where she was going, and if this turned out to be another wild-goose chase, there was no sense in letting anyone know that, either—especially a certain amber-eyed detective with an obnoxious style and an overabundance of self-confidence. How satisfying it would be to burst that fragile balloon of masculine superiority.

Gus shut the door of the small shop behind him. Humming a tune underneath his breath, he headed down the sidewalk toward the moped he'd borrowed from the inn. The sooner he got to Denton, the better. No one else had been to the store yet—the loquacious clerk was delighted to inform him of that—but there was no telling how close the rest of the group was behind him. Cleo, he felt sure, must be leading the pack.

Out of the corner of his eye, Gus glimpsed a flash of the most hideous shade of lime-green he'd ever seen. Quickly, he leaped over a bench, clipping his shin on the way, and scurried behind a convenient maple tree.

Sure enough, it was Cleo, zooming by in that horrible car. He watched with a sinking heart as she pulled up directly in front of the shop he'd just come out of. Gus waited until she was safely inside, then shot out from behind the tree and headed for his moped. He just might make it. It would take her from five to ten minutes in the shop, if she made the same mistake he did. And even a moped could outstrip that car.

Gus leaped onto the moped like a true detective, and the engine clattered into life. As he sat poised to zoom out onto Main Street, he found himself suddenly paralyzed. A pickup truck waited for him to pull out, but Gus waved it ahead. Then he reached down and turned off the motor.

For once in his life, Gus told himself, he was going to be smart. He'd won Cleo through blind luck and lost her through stupidity, and he wouldn't jeopardize the tenuous connection they'd established this weekend—that is, before they'd blown up at each other last night. But Gus wasn't too worried about last night; they'd survived many a similar argument over the years. He was still optimistic, but he'd have to rethink his game plan.

He hadn't really considered the implications of his win, he admitted now. He'd been fooling himself if he'd thought that beating her would make her soften toward him. It would only drive her away further, no matter how unassuming and generous he would be about the win.

And, he realized suddenly, berating himself for his obtuseness, if he won, that meant he would have Sophie and Max. He would have taken everything from her.

Somewhere inside, Gus felt the last flash of his competitive edge flicker and die. Cleo was more important to him than his professional pride. Letting her win would give her a psychological edge that he knew she needed in order to trust herself with him again. Being the fierce, feisty, determined, irritating, aggravating, bewitching woman that she was, Cleo would never return to him from what she considered to be an inferior position.

Gus looked down at the key in the ignition of the moped. He could still make it, if he left now. Wasn't he being a little *too* unselfish, even for him? He was letting Max and Sophie go, a million-dollar deal, for a wife who had made it clear she wanted nothing whatsoever to do with him anymore.

"What the hell," Gus growled. He swung off the moped and headed for the nearest coffee shop.

"Excuse me," Cleo said to the clerk, "I wonder if you can help me."

"Certainly." The clerk turned down the Beethoven blasting from the speakers and looked expectantly over heavy black-framed glasses at her. "Is there a particular record you're looking for?"

"Yes . . . but I'm not quite sure what it is. Do you have a section for church music, or inspirational music?"

"Of course. Down that aisle at the end." He turned up the Beethoven again.

Either he's a terrific actor, or I'm on another wild-goose chase, Cleo thought nervously. She flipped through a bin of church music carefully, reading the jackets and scrutinizing the pictures. There was nothing she could connect with any of the suspects.

Sighing, she smoothed out the now wrinkled paper from her pocket. "When solemn records do show that laughs can mean woe," she recited under her breath. She flipped through to the last record in the stack, "Divine Light Records Presents Little Chuckie Lee Jones." She stared ruefully at the young boy in robes on the cover, looking especially small underneath a huge, domed roof. She didn't know what this possibly could have to do with the murder of Derek Twittingham-Jones.

She looked at the title of the record again and somewhere divine light did flood her brain as she suddenly saw another possibility. "Not a *kind* of record," she said, amazed. "A record label!"

She headed for the front again, where the clerk was busy conducting the Ninth Symphony. She shouted at him over the music. "Do you know of a label called Solemn Records?"

He nodded and pointed with his baton to a bin directly behind her.

Cleo spun around and saw that the bin was labeled "Comedy." "A comedy label called Solemn Records?" she wondered aloud. Then she shrugged. "Why not?"

She flipped through most of the bin before she found it. Somehow Denton had gotten a record jacket made up with the smiling face of Anthony Guy on the cover. The title of the album was "Just Another Guy." Flipping it over, Cleo saw that the urbane, red-haired Anthony had, before he'd inherited millions from his dead father, supported himself being an impersonator. The cuts on the back indicated that Anthony did comedy routines in the voices of Cary Grant, Spiro Agnew, Bette Davis, and a host of other personalities.

And then it all made sense. Cleo remembered Wendee/Susan's deep distinctive voice talking continuously with Anthony when the lights had gone out. But it hadn't been Susan at all—it had been Anthony impersonating her voice. Susan had been busy murdering Derek while her lover gave her the perfect alibi. Solemn records had shown that laughs could mean woe, when the darkness turned one—Anthony—into two—Susan and Anthony, having a discussion about the inadequate wiring of the inn.

All the rest of the pieces fell into place. As part of their bargain, Bruno had asked Anthony to murder Derek, but he didn't realize that Susan and Anthony were having an affair. Anthony would be perfectly agreeable to helping out Bruno—but he would pin the murder on him, with

Susan's help. They would just have to pick a time when they both had alibis, and Bruno did not.

First they'd conspicuously gone to the jewelry store, with Anthony impersonating Bruno, and bought an expensive gift. The night of the murder Anthony had slipped outside the door of the parlor, thrown the fusebox switch, and then eased back inside the room and calmly gone off into a corner and carried on a conversation, in Susan's distinctively deep voice, with himself. Meanwhile, Susan had gone to the library, having already asked Derek to meet her there secretly, and killed him, slipping the three-year-old love letter Bruno had written her and the jewelry-store receipt inside his pocket. Then she'd thrown the fuse up again, and had time to slip directly inside the door where Anthony was waiting. When everyone blinked and turned around, they were standing there together—as if they'd been together the whole time.

Then Susan had privately asked Bruno to meet her upstairs, in order to establish his disappearance. Giving him enough time to theoretically murder Derek, she'd left the parlor and headed for the library. She'd bloodied her hands, pulled down the curtains and screamed.

They'd had nothing to lose—suspicion would be thrown on Bruno, and he could hardly point the finger at Anthony, since he had sabotaged Anthony's father's sailboat years before and caused his death. Bruno might be convicted, and he might not, but in any case, Anthony and Susan would go free.

Now all the words to the verse made sense. Three is certainly unlucky when love triangles are involved.

Exhilaration raced through her. She replaced the record, spun around and started toward the door.

The booming music abruptly ceased. "You found what you were looking for, did you?" the clerk asked, still bland-faced.

"Yes, thanks."

Finally, the clerk winked. "I'll give you one last tip," he said.

Cleo wondered what the other tips had been. "Yes?"

"There was one guy in before you, but you could probably still beat him, if you drive fast enough. He was riding a moped."

"Thanks," Cleo answered, dashing out. It was Gus, she knew. She'd seen him on the moped earlier, speeding away from the town hall. He'd been one step ahead of her all day.

She jumped down the last three steps of the shop and ran toward the car. She just might make it if she broke a couple of speed laws. She swung in behind the steering wheel and yanked the creaking door shut. But she didn't turn the key in the ignition.

Why did she feel so depressed? She should be jubilant. She'd solved the case, and if she drove fast enough, she'd surely beat Gus to Denton. Then Max and Sophie would be hers. So why did she feel so depressed? If she hesitated, Gus would win, and he'd turn her beloved characters into *The Max and Sophie Show*, starring Cleo's favorite actress, Wendee Tolliver. Cleo would have to spend her time surreptitiously scouring *Variety* for the weekly ratings and taping the show in order to torture herself by watching it over and over again. Or else she'd blithely ignore its existence and have to listen to everyone praise it at dinner parties. Either way, it would be a slow death by torture.

So why was she sitting here behind the wheel? Whatever the reason, she had exactly thirty seconds to figure it out. Cleo thought hard. Maybe this time she *didn't* want to beat Gus by inches; she didn't want to plunge back into that endless, insane competition. She wanted to leave her marriage with dignity, not descending into the petty squabbles she and Gus were capable of. She didn't want to continue this war of wits anymore. One of them would always be a winner; one would always lose. What difference did it make?

Perhaps if she let Gus win this one, it would break the chain that had strangled their marriage. She would be free of this compulsion to prove herself a match for him. She would be free of the past. Ever since the very first day she'd met him, she'd been so dazzled by his style and his intelligence that she felt she had to work twice as hard to keep up. She was tired of dancing beside him, matching quip for quip, plot idea for plot idea.

Cleo rested her elbows on the steering wheel and dropped her chin in her hands. She was stunned. For the first time since Gus had left for Hollywood, she realized an essential truth: she was exhausted.

Madeleines, meringues, muffins, caviar sandwiches, goat-cheese popovers, dilled cream cheese with smoked salmon: Denton's version of high tea was certainly impressive. If only she could eat. She'd packed her bags, bid a reluctant goodbye to her suite with its enviable endless supply of hot water, and made her way downstairs to the library, and she still hadn't caught sight of Gus.

It was just like him to wait until the last minute. Denton would announce him as the winner, and he'd saunter in to claim the trip and the title, as if it had all been a breeze.

Wendee was flitting around being charming, but her baby blue eyes were constantly sliding to the doorway along with Cleo's. At least she didn't know where Gus was either. Homicidal jealousy had flared again early this morning when Gus and Wendee had walked in to brunch together; Cleo had choked on her coffee, which had provoked an extremely irritating grin by Gus.

She had just reached for a goat-cheese popover when Gus walked in. He looked casual and offhand, as if he attended high tea every afternoon at four. He gave no hint that he was about to be named the Greatest Detective in the World. No matter how silly the title, Cleo reflected, couldn't he show just a little excitement?

Gus nodded a hello at her across the room and turned to pour tea from the silver urn into a fragile porcelain cup. Wendee immediately went over to add cream for him, and Cleo turned away. Had her action this afternoon pushed Wendee into Gus's arms as the new Sophie Fast?

"All right, ladies and gentlemen, sleuths, gumshoes, and p.i.'s, it's time for the big announcement." Denton had positioned himself by the huge fireplace. There were video cameras and still cameras grouped around him, ready to be trained on the winner.

Cleo sneaked a look at Gus and found him looking intently at her with an unreadable expression in his eyes. She slid her glance away and returned her attention to Denton.

"I must confess to rather enjoying this afternoon," Denton said, blinking at them genially behind his tortoiseshell glasses. "I became the most popular person in the inn, with all of you knocking at my suite to regale me with your theories. I must say, this has been an entertaining bunch—I do believe every single suspect was denounced as the murderer. Including, I admit, me." Everyone chuckled politely, as Denton proudly patted his navy-blue blazer, obviously delighted at being thought of as a passionate killer.

"But only a few people got the whole plot down perfectly, and I have to award the title to the person who got to me first with it. Ladies and gentlemen, I give you the Greatest Detective in the World—Micky Dance, also known as Sidney Clott."

Cleo dropped her popover and stepped forward. Goat cheese scrunched under her suede pump. Involuntarily, she turned to look at Gus, who was staring at her. Simultaneously, their eyes dropped.

While Sidney Clott modestly went over how the murder had taken place, with Bruno and Anthony's murder pact and Anthony's impersonation of Susan's voice, Cleo cleaned the goat cheese off her now ruined pumps and tried to figure out how Sidney could possibly have beaten Gus.

She knew it had been Gus who'd been at the record shop before her, since he was the only one on the moped, and no one else had been there this morning. Was it possible that Sidney had come to the shop right after her and somehow beaten Gus back to the inn?

It had to be possible—there was no other explanation. Perhaps Gus had thought he had plenty of time, and had meandered back to the inn instead of riding there directly. Never before had his casual attitude been more infuriating.

"Don't look so glum, chum. You can't win them all." The usual teasing light was back in Gus's eyes.

"I know," Cleo said. For some reason, her decision of this morning had served to eliminate her antagonism. She felt almost friendly. She grinned. "I just can't believe that Sidney Clott gets to go on the Orient Express."

"Me neither." That was an understatement. Gus had never been more shocked when Denton had announced the winner. Did that bomb of Cleo's break down or something? "How's your car?" he asked casually.

"Fine. Still an eyesore, but fine. Why? Are you angling for a ride to the city?" Her heart betrayed her and began to speed up.

"No, I—well, as a matter of fact, I *am* staying in my old apartment for a couple of weeks. You could just drop me at the train station in town, though. I'm sure a train will come through in a couple of hours. I don't mind waiting."

Cleo laughed. "Okay, I give. You can ride with me— oh, Gus, I forgot. I'm driving to Long Island first. I'm going to take the ferry over. It's my parents' anniversary today, and Molly and Jeff and Andie are coming out, too."

"Oh, well, in that case—"

A ridiculous impulse seized Cleo. "You're welcome to come with me. You know the family would love to see you. And we'd be back in Manhattan by midnight." Suddenly shy, Cleo tried to backtrack. Why would Gus want to spend time with her family, when he'd spent the past year avoiding them as well as her? "Or I can drop you at the train in town. I'm sure they run frequently on Sunday afternoons."

Gus hesitated. It had seemed as though she'd meant the invitation, but then she'd just about withdrawn it. Well, he didn't care. He didn't know if he was ready to face all the Delaneys when things between him and Cleo fluctuated so widely, but he couldn't pass up the opportunity to be with her. "Actually," he began, "that sounds—"

"Mr. Creighton?"

Gus turned to see the gray-uniformed chauffeur at his elbow. "Ms. Tolliver wanted you to know that the limousine is waiting."

"Tell Ms. Tolliver—" Gus began, but Wendee came up to him before he had a chance to finish. In her winter-white suit she looked deceptively demure, her bright hair drawn back into a sophisticated French twist.

"Tell me what, Gus? Are you ready to go? I'm actually all packed, can you believe it?"

"Wendee, I—"

"Hi, Cleo. Let me tell you, I'll be glad to leave Susan Scarlett-Gray behind. I had no idea she murdered Derek—Denton didn't tell us anything, just the bare bones of the plot. He was afraid we'd overact—I mean, can you believe it? I don't know what to do with that man! Oh, I *am* sorry you didn't win, Cleo. I'm sure it would have been a real boost to your career. Now Gus here, it seemed like he couldn't care less if he won or not. We had coffee together in town this morning, and he was so relaxed! He didn't move for *hours*, which was just fine by me."

So that's why he didn't beat Sidney. He couldn't tear himself away from Wendee. A searing dagger of incredulity pierced Cleo. Gus must be in love if he could forgo his competitive pride to sit around drinking coffee instead of racing to the inn to claim victory. How stupid she'd been all along.

"Well, I'd better get going." Cleo thought she pulled off the bright, pleasant tone very well. "My parents are expecting me, and your chauffeur is expecting you."

Damn Wendee! "Cleo, I was just about to accept your invitation," Gus said quickly. "Hang on while I get my bag."

A small line appeared between Wendee's perfectly waxed eyebrows. "It's in the trunk, Gus, and I'm not sure where Robert is with the keys. I suppose I could go look for him—"

Cleo broke in. "Don't bother, Wendee. Another time, Gus? I really have to get going, and I'd take a limousine over a lima bean any day if I were you. Bye now."

Gus watched as she swept out without a backward glance, her back proud and erect despite the suitcase in her hand. His eyes hungrily lingered on her hips in the long, soft cashmere sweater, the suede skirt showing off her legs, as she strode purposefully out the door. He'd botched up this weekend from start to finish. If only there had been more time. He was sure that she would have realized from working together that they belonged together.

It was obvious, Gus decided, that the time had come for a new plan.

Wendee smiled up at him. The small line in her forehead had disappeared. "Ready, darling?"

Gus smiled a murderous smile back down at her. "Sure am, honey. Drop me at the train station, will you?"

Chapter Seven

I don't know whether you know this or not, Ellison," Cleo said, shading her eyes from the bright sunlight, "but there's this thing that agents do with their clients. It's called taking them to lunch—at a very expensive restaurant—and letting them order whatever they want. I don't think it's quite the same thing to invite them to watch you play softball. Who still plays softball in October, anyway?"

"Agents," Ellison said succinctly, squinting at the players on the field. "It's that killer instinct. Besides, this unexpected warm weather prompted the publishing-house team to invite us for a rematch after we beat the pants off them this summer, so how could we refuse? You know agents can't resist torturing editors. We could go on like this for months, if only the weather would cooperate."

"I wouldn't hold my breath. It may not seem like it, but I hear November is just around the corner." Cleo leaned back against the bleachers and tilted her head back to catch the sun full on her face. She was just teasing Ellison about having to meet him in Central Park this afternoon; it was a glorious Indian-summer day, the temperature zooming up into the midsixties, and she'd been delighted to have an excuse to leave her apartment and head for Central Park. It seemed as though all of Manhattan was here today, enjoying the unusual weather. Cleo felt lazy and comfortable in her white cotton shirt and oversize navy blazer bequeathed to her by Gus, who had claimed she looked better in it than he did. As a matter of fact, she felt better than she had in weeks. Two weeks, to be exact.

She'd been struggling with an idea for her next book, and it hadn't been going well. Morning after morning she headed for the computer with greater and greater quantities of coffee that failed to fuel her inspiration. She was getting nowhere. All she could think about was that about sixty short blocks south and three long blocks west Gus was sitting in his old apartment, *their* old apartment, doing whatever Gus did when he was in New York and not working—going to meetings, playing basketball, cruising art galleries and seeing old movies...and not calling her—not that she wanted him to.

Over the past two weeks she'd realized how much easier it had been for her when Gus had lived three thousand miles away. If he decided to come back to Manhattan for good, she'd really be in trouble.

But today she felt freer than she'd felt in a long time. Hadn't Gus said he'd only be staying in New York for a couple of weeks? Well, it had been a couple of weeks to the day, so he just might be winging his way to the Coast at this very moment. She wouldn't have to think about him or hear his name for a long time.

Ellison didn't take his eyes from the field, but he cleared his throat. "The reason I wanted to talk with you," he said, "is that I heard from Gus yesterday."

Cleo sighed. So much for not having to hear his name. "So? You're his agent. I assume you talk now and then. Perfectly okay with me, Ellison."

"I appreciate that," Ellison said dryly. "Remind me to give you a list of my other clients to see if you approve of them, too."

She grinned and watched as the batter hit a long fly out to left field. It thudded into the fielder's glove. "Any time." She knew Ellison too well to think that he'd brought Gus's name up casually, but she could wait him out. He liked to tell things in his own way, and his seeming casualness was usually a careful maneuver to disarm her. He knew it and she knew it; the galling thing was that it always worked.

She and Gus had found Ellison five years before when no other agent would take them on and he was a baby-faced unknown. Somehow they had managed to luck into what they were convinced was the shrewdest mind in Manhattan. He was now one of the most powerful literary agents in New York, but he still looked as though he worked in the mail room. His tie usually had a spot in it, when he remembered to wear one, and Gus swore that his obligatory tweed jacket had been with him since his years at Erasmus High in Brooklyn. His round face and look of perpetual mild surprise were his best assets; they had misled many a publishing executive to underestimate him. Ellison claimed that the pressure of the business and the rich food he had to consume at business lunches were going to force him into retirement any day now; he was barely thirty-five.

Ellison kept his eyes on the field. "He's decided to stay in New York. And he's got an idea for a new project."

"Oh?" The batter hit a line drive and made it to first.

"Another book."

"Oh?" The next batter, one of the many agents who had turned down Cleo and Gus five years before, strolled to the plate confidently, despite the paunch that spoke of too many rich business lunches with publishers. "Does that mean he's not going back to L.A.?"

"Sounds like it."

Strike one. "I see. What does this have to do with me?"

"He wants to write another Max and Sophie book."

Strike two. "And he needs my permission. Well, you can tell him—"

"He wants to write it with you, Cleo."

Strike three. Cleo gave up trying to be nonchalant and whipped her gaze to Ellison. "He wants to *what*?"

"That's the third out. I have to play. Wait till the next inning and I'll explain it to you, okay?" Ellison pulled on his cap, shot her a quick smile, and trotted off toward second base.

Cleo frowned after him. She had a sneaking suspicion that it was no accident that Ellison had chosen to tell her the news during his softball game. He had just effectively silenced her automatic no and given her time to digest the startling information. He was incorrigible, but she couldn't stay irritated at him; she couldn't help but applaud when he executed a diving catch for a fast line drive and whipped it to first for a quick out. She settled back to watch the rest of the inning; there was no sense getting upset until she found out what Gus was proposing. There was no harm in hearing Ellison out before she said no.

So Gus wanted to collaborate again. He'd probably suggested to Ellison that they work in their own apartments and communicate by mail, considering the rocky state of their relations. It was a foolish idea; the success of the books had everything to do with their explosive connection, the ideas they sparked off each other when they worked. What a bloodless, bland book they would turn out if they tried to collaborate any other way! Cleo smiled, and until Ellison returned, she entertained herself with the comforting thought that Gus's idea, whatever it was, couldn't possibly work.

"Nice catch out there," she complimented him as he plopped down next to her again. "Now, what's all this about Gus?"

"Thanks. You know, I was sure I wouldn't be able to make that one. Could be I'm in better shape than I thought." Ellison patted his stomach, and his round brown eyes grew wistful. "Sure miss that Danish in the morning, though."

"Ellison, do you want to elaborate on Gus's proposal or do you want to talk about Danish?"

He sighed. "Gus said he realizes your first impulse will be to say no, and you'll just hear me out to be polite. But he wants you to really think about it. He's got a fantastic plot idea—"

"Oh? What is it?"

"It needs a lot of work, which is why he needs you."

"To write the love stuff?"

"Huh?"

"Nothing. Go ahead."

"He'll have to tell you about it, but the nitty-gritty of it is that while Max and Sophie are solving their latest case, they'll also be getting a divorce."

"A divorce?" Cleo asked weakly. For some reason, she felt grieved, as if Max and Sophie were real people. Perhaps they were, to her. How could Gus split them up?

"It really offers some juicy dramatic possibilities, I think. My turn at bat. Hold on."

Cleo watched, feeling numb, as Ellison waited out balls and took two strikes before sending a pop fly into center field. She was relieved when the fielder caught it easily and Ellison trotted back to her in the bleachers.

She continued the conversation as though they hadn't been interrupted. "How could Gus think that we could possibly work together? We couldn't even get along for two days at the murder weekend."

"He said that there was one afternoon there that you really got along well together. Good communication— like the old days, he said."

"You might say that," Cleo said, hiding her flushed cheeks by shading her eyes to look out at the field.

"Anyway, he thinks it's a great idea."

"Does he want to work by mail?"

Ellison mopped his face with a handkerchief. "No, he realizes that you have to bounce everything off each other. He wants it to be a good book."

Cleo shook her head. "Ellison, I can't work with Gus. I can't even be in the same room with him. It's impossible."

He put a hand on her arm. "Look, Cleo, I'm not asking you to tell me yes or no. Why don't you have lunch with him? You two can talk about it, and then you can decide. He's expecting your call."

"I don't know."

With a sigh, Ellison stood up. "I have to get back on the field. Cleo, you know I rarely pull my agent role on you—you always pick and choose your own projects—but this could be good for you. You know we had a bit of trouble selling the Mary Claire idea. The book's doing well, but it's not the best-seller that Sophie and Max can be. Now, I don't want you to do it if you think it would be too difficult for you, but I do want you to consider it carefully. Okay?"

"Okay."

"Want to stick around for the end of the game? I'll buy you that meal. How about a pizza?"

"I can't. I'm having dinner with Molly. Pizza sounds great, though—I think she's making tofu casserole or something."

He grimaced. "Maybe you should pick up a pie with pepperoni before you go downtown. Well, they're waiting for me out there. Give Gus a call, will you? Try having lunch. Thousands of New Yorkers do it every day. It can't be that dangerous."

Cleo sighed. "I can tell you haven't had lunch with Gus Creighton in a while."

Creighton/Delaney. Cleo stared at the plate over the buzzer. She wondered why Gus hadn't removed her name. She hadn't stepped foot in the apartment since her co-op tenant had conveniently decided to move back to Minneapolis and Cleo had moved back into her old apartment with relief. She'd packed up her clothes and moved back uptown and had never returned to West Twelfth Street. Or even East Twelfth Street, for that matter. She avoided the street entirely; she was too afraid she would forget the pain and only remember how happy she had been there.

And now here she was, putting herself through the torturous experience she had gone blocks out of her way to avoid. Not only was she on West Twelfth Street, she was actually entering the building and having lunch in her ex-apartment. Not to mention with her ex-husband.

Yesterday, after fifteen minutes of arguing back and forth on the phone over which restaurant to eat in, Gus had finally suggested she come down and he would run out for sandwiches to the corner deli. "Let's not make a big deal out of this," he had said. Cleo had agreed, to prove she was treating it as casually as he. That was before she realized that having lunch alone with Gus in their old apartment was definitely more of a big deal than an impersonal restaurant would be.

But it was too late for retreat. Cleo pressed the bell and pushed open the door at the sound of the buzzer. The very smell of the hallway, the look of the paint, made her feel weak with sentiment. Her heart sank all the way down to the new boots she'd bought a week before to take her mind off Gus.

She had five flights of stairs to navigate, and it felt like fifty. With each step came a memory. The mornings she'd trudged up the stairs to work with a bag of croissants or doughnuts in her hand, dreading hearing about Gus's romantic exploits of the night before. The rainy day she'd moved into his apartment when Gus, balancing an oversize load of her books, her plants and her beloved antique lamp, slipped on the slick stairs, grabbed at the falling lamp, and then watched her asparagus fern tumble down to the landing below, dumping a cloud of potting soil on Cleo's head. The night of his thirty-fourth birthday, when he'd insisted he could carry her up the final three flights. They'd collapsed on the top landing in a heap, giggling. Cleo had assured him that despite his advanced age he was still the handsomest man she knew. They they'd sobered and their mouths had met, their searching hands had been unable to stop roaming over each other...they'd barely made it to the door of the apartment, where they'd ended up making love on the living-room floor. Afterward, Gus had smiled down at her, his tawny hair mussed, and said, "Just wait until *your* birthday."

Cleo stopped and hung on to the banister for a moment. She felt light-headed and breathless, a feeling she blamed on putting off her daily jog this past week. She was getting out of shape. Once she'd been able to run up these stairs without pause. She frowned. Once she'd eagerly run up these stairs because she'd been running *toward* something.

And what was she trudging so reluctantly toward today?

A shrill whistle interrupted her thoughts. She looked up. Gus was leaning over the top railing, looking down at her.

"You going to make it up here any time today?" He tossed down one end of a clothesline, which dangled a good three feet above her head. "Want me to pull you up?"

She was trudging toward a madman, that's what she was doing. "Keep your shirt on," she grumbled, mounting the stairs again.

A gray sweatshirt tumbled onto her head. "Too late," Gus called down. Then he reeled up the clothesline and disappeared.

Cleo balled up the sweatshirt and clumped up the rest of the stairs frowning; she should have known that this wouldn't turn out to be any ordinary business meeting. She reached the top apartment and leaned on the bell.

Gus opened the door, his chest bare, looking magnificently fit in a pair of faded jeans. "Why didn't you use your key?"

Cleo swallowed and avoided looking at him. She tossed the sweatshirt at him and walked into the room. "Because I threw it in the East River six months ago."

Gus's voice was muffled by the sweatshirt, which he was pulling over his head. "Should be still floating there, then. We could take a Circle Line cruise and look for it." His head emerged, and he grinned. "Or I can always make you another one. You'll need it when we work together again."

"*When* we work together?"

"You want pastrami or roast beef?" he asked, placidly avoiding the issue and turning toward the kitchen.

"Tuna fish," Cleo answered. She tossed her jacket onto a chair and walked farther into the apartment. She didn't know what she'd expected—Gus had always been alarmed by the prospect of change, and the place looked exactly the same as when she'd left it, if a good deal messier.

It was one huge high-ceilinged room, which Gus had partitioned with the help of bookcases and strategically placed furniture. One wall was exposed brick, and the kitchen was separated by a long, light-wood counter that Gus had built. Everything looked well-worn but well chosen. Gus's one extravagance had always been a weakness for very good Oriental rugs, and in the past couple of years he'd also made a few careful purchases of modern art. Books were everywhere, spilling out of bookshelves and piled on tables and the incongruously beautiful carpets.

Cleo studied everything but carefully avoided looking at the stairs to the loft he had built before she moved in.

It had effectively created a separate bedroom for them, and she'd grown to love waking up beneath the skylight, above the quiet apartment, nestled into Gus's hard shoulder and his soft neck, fragrant with his morning scent, deliciously rough with his new stubble.

"The place looks the same," she said, walking into the living area. She pushed aside a mass of papers and books to clear a space on the couch. "And you keep it so nice, too."

"Well I did a special cleanup, since you were coming over," Gus said modestly. He placed the sandwiches on the long, low table in front of the couch. "No tuna, so you get roast beef. Watch out for the mustard; it's a killer."

"Thanks." Cleo shifted over a bit to give Gus more room on the couch. She felt too nervous to eat, but she took a sip of tea from the mug Gus handed her.

"So you talked to Ellison," he said. "What do you think?"

"I think it's the most ridiculous idea I've ever heard, but I promised him I'd at least listen to you."

"Glad to see you're keeping an open mind. You know, Clee, I can understand why you'd hesitate, but I think we could do it. I was really encouraged by how we worked together in Connecticut."

"Are you kidding? We argued constantly. And then we had to split up. Sound familiar?"

"Well, Connecticut always makes me nervous. You know how I feel about the suburbs."

"Gus, you consider anything above Fourteenth Street the suburbs." Cleo remembered the panicked look on Gus's face when once she'd dreamily proposed moving out of the city and raising a family. His terror of having a family was something she'd thought would abate eventually, but it didn't. The loss of his family had been devastating. Even though his upbringing with his grandparents in Nashville had been happy, he'd never gotten over that sudden, heartbreaking shifting of his world.

Once she'd thought that love meant you could fill up the empty spaces in another person's life. So much love could surely push away the demons. But she knew better now.

"Tell me about your plot idea," she said crisply. As Gus sketched the outline, she avoided his eyes and concentrated her gaze on his hands. Strong and brown, his fingers square, he gesticulated and formed ideas and waved away objections with a graceful but wholly masculine style.

And dammit, his idea was good. She liked it. She more than liked it; she itched to work on it. Already her mind was working to thrash out the plot, fill in the holes, and when she figured out a whole new angle to the story, she knew she had already made her decision.

When he finished, she said cautiously, "It sounds good, Gus, but there's one thing I don't agree with. I don't think Max and Sophie should get a divorce."

"Why not? It adds so much emotion to the plot."

"Can't they just have problems? Or separate for a time?"

"But then you'd have to throw out that last third of the book. Cleo, if you go along with the rest, you have to go along with the divorce." Gus ducked his head so that Cleo couldn't glimpse his satisfaction. Not only was she going to work with him—whether she knew it yet or not—but she was bothered by the thought of Max and Sophie divorcing. He had hoped she would balk at that. They were their alter egos; surely if she wanted them to stay together, it must indicate how she felt about her own marriage.

"Well, we have a little time to decide on that anyway," he conceded, trying to sound grumpy. "When do you want to start? I can set up our old work space by the window, and—"

"Wait a second—what do you think of my apartment?"

"It's very nice, Cleo," Gus said politely.

"You know what I mean. Why don't we work there? After all, the computer is there now."

"It would be simple to move it down here. We can just put it in a cab."

Cleo looked at him irritably. "It would be equally simple to put yourself in a cab. Do you think you'll get a nosebleed if you come up to Central Park West?"

"I just think it might be better if we worked in the same space we've written all our books in. Why change a good thing? I know what it is, Clee—you're nervous about being with me alone in this apartment. Don't worry, I'll remain fully clothed at all times. And I could block off the stairs to the loft so you wouldn't be tempted."

"Tempted? Are you crazy?"

"You were tempted in Connecticut."

"But I always learn from my mistakes."

Gus stood up abruptly and went to the window to look out at the sidewalk traffic. He didn't want Cleo to see how much her remark bothered him. Even sitting in the same room with her could inflame him, make him unreasonable with his desire for her.

How could she think of that afternoon they'd loved each other again a mistake?

Now he knew for certain that he should have gone more slowly in Connecticut. Cleo was not going to give him an inch. On the contrary, she was going to regain any ground she had lost, and then some.

He would be foolish to press her, he knew. He would have to win her slowly, even more slowly than he'd imagined, and at a snail's pace compared to what he wanted. It would take more than an afternoon to capture that courageous, stubborn heart of hers. He had to buy some time. Good old Max and Sophie would come to his rescue again.

Besides, he had learned his lesson in Connecticut, Gus reminded himself. He had let go of his competitive nature there; even though Cleo hadn't gotten to Denton before Sidney Clott, he had sincerely expected her to win. Now his plan was to show her, using infinite patience, that they could build a new working relationship without banter and battles. He had gotten off to a bad start already, he chided himself. He had to keep reminding himself to be nice, polite, professional.

He turned. "You're right. This book is too important to jeopardize by setting ourselves up for emotional complications. Besides, Cleo," he said, "we started out friends. We might have to practice a bit, but we can get that back again. Can't we?"

Cleo felt bitter laughter choke her, but she smothered it. Friends? Friendship had nothing to do with the feelings aroused by the man in front of her.

She was letting herself in for heartbreak. She was putting her emotions to a test they might not be able to stand.

But she was no coward. And she had changed since Connecticut. There she had come face-to-face with the fact that she could no longer keep up this desperate war of quips and cleverness with Gus, this need to win to prove she was as good as he was. She had realized there that being that bright, witty woman hadn't kept her from losing him.

If Gus could do it, if he could retain his distance while they would be at such close quarters, working together for months, then she could, too. No problem.

She nodded, looking him straight in the eyes, willing herself not to falter. "All right, Gus. You got yourself a partner."

"Great." He grinned and crossed back to the rug in front of her. Her heart raced as his arm shot out—was he going to touch her? But he reached for his pastrami instead.

The spasm of heat that had already begun to curl inside her died slowly away. Cleo chewed reflectively on her roast beef and noticed how Gus's jeans strained across his thighs as he sat cross-legged on the rug, cheerfully demolishing his sandwich.

No problem, Cleo, she told herself grimly. *You just can't keep your eyes off him. But it's no problem at all.*

How they managed it she didn't know, but they did. They worked long hours, they ate breakfast and lunch sitting in Gus's living room staring at pages of words and the amber screen of the computer, they paced, they improvised dialogue, they politely passed the cream for the coffee, they congratulated each other on a clever line, and they rarely exchanged one personal word.

The line of professional behavior was adhered to with scrupulous rigidity. It was as though just one casual touch, one brushing of hands, would undo them. So they edged around each other carefully. Gus no longer leaned over her when she was at the keyboard. She no longer absentmindedly put her hand on his shoulder as they pored over the pages they had written that day. She no longer stretched out on the floor and did leg lifts when she was feeling restless. She didn't even take off her shoes and work in her stocking feet, unless it was a particularly nasty day and she had to for the sake of Gus's carpets. But at this point, even being in her socks was a casual, intimate gesture she felt uncomfortable making.

No longer did they hoot with laughter at their own words, or argue fiercely about a favorite line. They both conceded politely if the other made a point of objecting, just as politely, to an idea. And when the long day was over, Cleo left as quickly as she dared.

She would always feel awkward at that time, when suddenly she would get up from the table and become, instead of a writer, a woman. Gus would stretch and get up to wash his hands. It was a familiar ritual, his way of stopping the workday and beginning the evening. While he was in the bathroom, she gathered her things quickly. Then when he came out, rubbing his hands on a towel, she would say an amiable good-night and head for the door. She'd jolt uptown on the subway and tell herself how wonderfully professional and mature she was being.

The book was going well, but Cleo had to admit that she felt the absence of the rush of joy she usually felt when working with Gus. Adrenaline had pumped through her when they had battled their way through a book, and the conflict had been worth it for the days of pure exhilaration when they would grin at each other, feeling very pleased with themselves at their genius.

But their working method on this book was different. It wasn't bad, Cleo told herself, just different. It made for solid, competent, professional writing. The plotting was tight and expert. The dialogue was crisp. They did the same number of pages every day. Every evening they would politely tell each other that the book was going very well. And they almost believed it.

The only problem they had was that they couldn't agree on the ending for the book. Gus courteously affirmed that Max and Sophie had to divorce; Cleo just as civilly suggested that they separate, but reconcile in the end. Since the decision had little to do with the actual murder plot, they were able to deal with the disagreement quite easily. They ignored its existence and trusted time to resolve it. In other words, Gus figured that Cleo would see the light and come around to his point of view. And Cleo felt the same.

November passed swiftly. Dusk came earlier and earlier as time passed, and Gus would light the lamps one by one as they worked on. They took time out to admire the first snowfall, even taking a break to walk out together to pick up sandwiches for lunch, and shivered through a cold snap that lasted a week, with temperatures going down to zero. They suffered through a head cold together. And then, suddenly, it was Christmas.

"Don't move. Just keep your head tilted just for a— Cleo! You moved."

"I didn't."

"Yes, you did. Now, hold still."

Cleo kept her head in the same position. She looked out at the snow mixed with sleet falling on Long Island Sound. Whitecaps ruffled the iron-gray water, and ice was beginning to melt along the beach. Large, ugly patches of mud poked through the slick yellowed grass of the long sloping lawn that led from the porch down to the water. It was a cheerless sight for Christmas morning, and Cleo, wrapped in a huge white terrycloth robe her mother had brought her back from some fancy hotel in London, had been perversely enjoying its ugliness and her solitude.

But then her mother had appeared with her camera. Oohing and aahing over Cleo's profile and the symphony of white and gray and silver in the scene, she'd begun clicking away behind her.

Kit Delaney had been an obstetrician all her life and then had discovered photography on her retirement. She'd started with snapshots of the changing scene outside her home on the Long Island Sound, moved on to portraits of her husband and three daughters, and was currently embarked on a lucrative business photographing beaming parents with their newborn infants. It had turned into more than a hobby; even the three sisters had to admit that their mother had an eye. Unfortunately, she chose to exercise her talent at the most inconvenient times, when one was trying to read a book or cook an omelet or wake up properly.

And now, just when Cleo had been peacefully wallowing in her gloom, she had to hold still and feel like a cliché—Woman and Stormy Landscape: Study in Melancholy. She stirred restlessly.

"You moved." Kit came out from behind her camera and shot her an accusing glare.

"Mom, have you ever considered taxidermy?"

Kit laughed and put down the camera, then plopped down next to her daughter. "Whew—I'm exhausted."

"It's only eight o'clock."

"All those presents tired me out. Your father is whipping up some delectable breakfast. It seems to involve lots of banging of pans and whistling—sounds like one of those experimental music pieces. Anyway, I'd guess it should be ready by tomorrow morning sometime."

Cleo started to get up. "I should go help."

Kit pushed her down again. "Don't be silly. He enjoys it. He just kicked me out of the kitchen. Besides, I want to talk to you."

Cleo sipped at her coffee and looked down into the cup. "What about?" she asked. She knew very well what about.

"You know very well what about. What's going on with you? You tell me the book is going fine, you and Gus are getting along fine, *Guilty As Sin* is doing fine, everything is fine..."

"So?"

"So why don't you look fine? You look terrible. You've been dragging around the house all weekend—"

"I have not."

"You've been dragging around the house," Kit repeated firmly, "saying everything is fine. It's very disconcerting. Not to mention repetitive."

"I guess I'm just tired. I've been working pretty hard. I'm sorry I've been dragging. Molly and Jeff and Andrea will snap me out of it today."

Kit gave her a hard look, the kind of look Cleo had dreaded when she'd been a feckless teenager. It was maternally knowing and very irritating. Cleo had never been able to fool her mother.

"Mom, I'm fine."

Kit winced. "Just don't use that word again, and I promise I'll leave you alone." She reached over for Cleo's coffee and took a sip. "So where is Gus this Christmas?" she asked offhandedly.

"He went to Nashville to be with his grandmother. We thought it would be a good idea to take a week's break.

The book is ahead of schedule, we can afford to take the time, and sometimes it's good to leave it for a while to get some perspective..." Cleo wound down, realizing that she was chattering, always a tip-off to her mother that she was avoiding the question.

Kit gave her another hard look, sighed, handed her back the coffee cup and stood up. "I'm going to leave you alone now," she announced. "I'm making a very difficult decision—I'm not going to badger you. And you know how much I love to do that. Consider it a Christmas present."

"Thanks." Cleo smiled as she watched her mother give her one last worried look and head for the stairs. She was grateful to Kit for not pressing her. She just couldn't look at her strange mood too closely; the very thought filled her with terror. She knew, of course, that it had everything to do with Gus, and she just didn't want to know why. She was determined to hold on childishly to the flimsy fact that since she was being so mature, she couldn't possibly be making a mistake.

She returned her gaze to the bleak landscape outside the sliding glass doors. The snow that had started so promisingly early this morning had now completely changed to sleet, and it was washing away the delicate dusting that had coated the landscape.

"What's wrong with this picture?" Cleo asked herself under her breath. It was Christmas morning. She was an adult woman with only her parents for comfort, and she was currently brooding because her ex-husband, over the past month and a half, had demonstrated graphically how little her nearness affected him. She was staring out at a gray and cheerless morning—no snow. Even the Christmas tree, which the busy Delaneys had neglected to buy until late last night, was small and pitiful. The scene wouldn't exactly inspire Norman Rockwell.

Cleo sighed and, her eyes still trained on the comfortingly depressing scene outside the windows, reached over to put her coffee cup on the table at her elbow. She missed, and the cup tipped over, spilling its brown liquid all over her new snowy-white robe. The thick material soaked up the dark stain.

She closed her eyes and willed her screaming nerves under control. "It's going to be a long winter," she said.

Chapter Eight

So how was your Christmas?"

"Fine. Yours?"

"Fine."

"How's your family doing?"

"Fine. And your grandmother?"

"Fine. How was your New Year's?"

"Terrific. Yours?"

"Great."

"Have a good flight back from Nashville?"

"Fine," Gus said.

A pause stretched out into long seconds. "Well," Cleo said awkwardly, "I guess we should get back to work. That is, if you're ready."

"If you are."

"Sure. As I remember, you wanted to talk over the last scene we did."

"Right. But if you'd rather go on—"

"No, no. Why don't we look it over together?"

"Fine."

Cleo leafed back through several manuscript pages. "It's the scene after the funeral, where they get into an argument about their lack of communication. You thought it was unrealistic."

"Right."

"And I said that Sophie's point was that they were never honest with each other, they were always keeping up a front. You want to read over these last pages?"

"Sure." Gus frowned as he read the pages she handed him. "Really, this dialogue is stupid. Remind me never to write anything before I have my coffee in the morning. Plus that two-week break has broken my concentration. But you had a good Christmas, right?"

"Fine. And you did, too, right?"

"Oh, yes." Gus looked back down at the pages in his hand. He'd had a horrible Christmas. He had missed her so much. It was hard to spend that holiday away from the woman he loved, but it had been impossible to suggest they spend it together. It was too meaningful a step, it was fraught with too much significance, and he'd known Cleo wasn't ready for that. Over the past weeks he'd begun to wonder if she ever would be.

So they'd avoided the subject as best they could. They hadn't exchanged anything more than the formal greetings of the season. How could they exchange the normal gifts of collaborators—a bottle of perfume, a scarf, a tie—when once the holiday had been the excuse to pamper each other with presents, to plan surprises, to splurge, to wait, breathless with excitement, for the other to open the perfect gift? Gus remembered too many joyous Christmases to pretend that this one could be anywhere near the same.

He remembered tramping all up and down the avenues together, the air fragrant with the scent of the Christmas trees stacked up on the sidewalks. They would spend an evening looking for the perfect one, then struggle homeward with it, out of breath from laughter and exertion. Christmas was the one time of the year when Cleo would exercise the baking skills she'd perfected as a teenager. Out of sentiment and love, cakes and breads and cookies would pour out of the tiny kitchen in a constant stream. They spent Christmas Eve picnicking alone in front of the fire with a bottle of champagne and whatever they craved, no holds barred, from the gourmet deli. At midnight, they would exchange one gift. The next day, laden with packages and bags of Cleo's baked goods, they would pile into the car with Molly and Jeff and ride out to the Delaneys on Long Island. The heater would never work, and their laughter would be punctuated by clouds of vapor across the car seats. Later, after presents and turkey, he and Cleo would hold gloved hands as they went for a solitary walk through the snow.

But this year he'd gone to Nashville, thinking he would get pleasure out of keeping his grandmother company. Usually she went to the Islands for Christmas, then flew up to spend time with them in January. She'd been delighted to see him, of course, but she'd never been the type to hover around him, mending his shirts and baking cookies. She was busy with her golf and her friends, and Gus found himself, for the first time in his life, sulky about it. Finally she'd confronted him on New Year's Day, telling him brutally in her soft Nashville twang to get his behind back up to New York and straighten things out with Cleo before he drove his beloved grandmother crazy. How he'd ever let her get away in the first place was beyond her.

So he'd skulked back up to Manhattan to find that Cleo was in no better shape than he was. So far, she'd been so distant, so removed, so touchy. Frustration was beginning to ball up in his stomach, making him dread the winter ahead.

But hell, Gus thought, January always made him depressed. He'd have to keep all his resolve to make it through, he knew; even when she'd had that terrible cold last month, with a red and constantly running nose, he'd found her devastatingly sexy and had longed to take care of her, keep her warm, fix her chicken soup. Well, maybe send out to the deli for some.

He looked at her now, poring over the manuscript. Her dark hair was drawn back off her face and anchored with a bright plastic clip he found endearing. Those perfectly arched dark eyebrows and the full red mouth were arresting in her pale creamy winter complexion. She was wearing a soft, oversize beige wool sweater with matching soft, slim pants in the same material. She'd kicked off her boots immediately after she'd arrived this morning. He smiled at her bright yellow socks. He loved when she was in her stocking feet. *God, I really must be desperate,* Gus thought crazily. *I'm mooning about her socks.*

"Gus?"

He looked up, startled, hoping his face hadn't betrayed him.

"Yes?"

"Uh, do you want to get started, then?"

"Right." He watched as Cleo reached back to sweep her hair up more securely in the clip, her unconscious habit before getting down to work. He ached to press his mouth against the wispy hairs on the back of her neck. Instead, he whirled around and walked quickly over to the window. She tossed off the first line of dialogue to start, and he answered. But all the while his mind was consumed with the pleasure of simply being in the same room with her again.

Gus closed his eyes for a fraction of an instant and fought for control. It was going to be a long winter.

Cleo hung her coat in the closet and shivered. "Maybe I should keep my coat on today," she said. "What happened to your heat? Doesn't your super know it's February out there?"

"It went off last night. Supposed to be fixed later today."

"The coldest day yet this winter, and no heat. Do you think we'll be able to work? Maybe we should take the day off."

"Let's see how it goes. I bought lots of firewood this morning, so that will help. Here, I brought this down for you." Gus handed Cleo one of his sweaters, and she slipped into it gratefully. It hung loosely to the middle of her thighs, but she looked great. The soft cornflower-blue did wonderful things for her dark gray eyes.

Rubbing her cold hands together, Cleo went over to warm up by the fire. "Well, I guess we should get started." She tried to sound normal, but she was nervous about today. They had finally reached the point in the outline where Max and Sophie reminisce about their first meeting and wind up in bed together. Though they usually let their love scenes fade out at a discreet point and left most of what followed to the reader's imagination, Cleo was still reluctant to write the tender scene with Gus.

"Right, let's begin," Gus said.

"I thought yesterday went well."

"Yes."

"Well—"

"I guess we should block out the scene first," Gus suggested. Cleo looked up warily. "I mean verbally, of course."

"Of course. Okay, after the second body is discovered, it reminds them of their first meeting. They talk about it—"

Gus drew closer to the fire. "Right. But I'm worried about the transition from the polite facade they've been keeping up to this warmth that suddenly springs up again."

"Moods can change abruptly sometimes."

"But what triggers it for Max and Sophie?"

"Finding the drowned body—just like in the first book. Remember? It would be the same situation if we went back to the café where we met." She drew back a little from the fire. "I mean, I assume it would."

Gus nodded. "So let's talk for a minute about what they'd be feeling. At this point in the story, Max is still intent on keeping the marriage together. He's keeping his distance a little bit because of Sophie's attitude. But he's really still crazy about her. He's dying to make love to her. And Sophie feels the same."

"Right."

"So they're working closely on this case, and they're just keyed up with frustration. Being near each other is torture."

"Right. Do you think it's getting any warmer in here?"

"A bit. Now, all we have to do is figure out that word or that gesture that will break the dam and let all that pent-up sensuality just gush out—"

"Right. Gus, do you want some coffee?"

"Oh. Sure. I just made a pot. I'll go warm it up."

"I'll do it." Before he could protest, Cleo walked quickly into the kitchen. The slightly cooler air there was a relief. Standing so near that fire had made her face very hot. She turned on the flame under the pot and searched for the thermal coffeepot they used when they were working. "Gus, where's the thermal pot?" she yelled.

"It might be in the dishwasher. Or in the cupboard over the sink," Gus said, his voice getting closer.

"That's okay, you don't have to come—" Cleo backed up and landed on Gus's foot "—in," she finished lamely.

He quickly stepped back again as if he'd received a shock. "Sorry. Here it is."

"I'll get the cups." Cleo reached toward the cupboard and wished Gus would return to the living room. His kitchen was way too small to accommodate two people comfortably. Even though one memorable evening they'd managed to do quite well...

She found the cups and rinsed them out briskly.

"Cleo, they're already clean."

"Oh. We should get to work. I'll bring the coffee," she suggested pointedly.

Gus didn't move. "That's okay, I'll wait. Now, as I was saying, all it will take is just a tiny suggestive push, and they'll fall into each other's arms like they've been starved."

"Oh, yes."

"So they're alone in the apartment together, and that's all they're both thinking about, but they continue talking about the case." Gus reached around her to get the dish towel. His arm brushed against her breast. He immediately backed off. "Sorry."

Cleo moved over a few inches, bumping up against the refrigerator. "Can you hand me that tray? And they have to discuss the clue they found on the body. Not exactly a prelude to seduction."

Gus handed her the tray, careful not to touch her. "Here. No, it's not. But when two people are dying for each other they don't need candlelight and music—any situation will do."

"That's true." Cleo put the cream on the tray along with the cups.

"I don't see how they can hold out anymore."

"I don't either."

"We've really been building up that sexual tension."

"I know. We're good at that."

They smiled faintly, and their eyes held. The kitchen seemed very small. The pause seemed to stretch out forever as they stood suspended, unable to move.

"I guess the coffee's ready."

"I guess."

"I'll check it." Her heart thumping, her palms damp, Cleo finally leaned over to inspect the pot. She bumped up against a part of Gus she was, at that moment, desperately trying not to think about. "Sorry," she said quickly, straightening as Gus backed up at the same time.

"Maybe I should wait in the living room," he said gruffly.

"Okay. I'll be right in with the tray." She poured the hot coffee into the thermal pot.

"Let me take it."

"No, I'm fine. Go ahead."

"Come on, Cleo, I know from experience that that tray weighs a ton."

She hoisted the tray off the counter. "I'm fine. Go ahead."

"Here, you take the coffeepot and I'll take the tray." Gus reached out to grab the tray, and his fingers brushed against Cleo's. Simultaneously, they jerked their hands off it. Between them, the tray fell with a crash to the floor. The two china cups knocked into the cream pitcher and all three broke with a tinkling of glass and china. Miraculously, the coffee stayed in the thermal pot. Stupefied, they stared down at the tray and the broken china and glass.

This is ridiculous, Cleo thought. *How much longer can we go on being so polite that we act like idiots?*

If this goes on much longer, Gus thought, *we'll destroy the apartment.*

Sighing simultaneously, they each bent down to retrieve the mess. Their heads met with a sharp crack.

Gus backed up hastily, holding his throbbing forehead. "You okay?"

"Fine. You?"

"Fine. Maybe you should take the pot and I'll clean up the mess and bring in the cups. Then we can go on with the scene."

"Fine," Cleo said. She walked out, put the coffeepot on the worktable in the living room, and went directly to the bathroom to splash her face and neck with cold water. Funny how much the fire had warmed up the apartment. Maybe the super had fixed the heat after all.

For the next few weeks, Cleo and Gus tacitly avoided being in the kitchen at the same time. In fact, Cleo had begun to notice that the longer February wore on, the farther away they got from each other. If this kept on, soon she'd be shouting new plot twists up to Gus in the loft.

Keeping their distance should have helped their concentration, but it didn't. The pages were stacking up slower and slower. Even so, by the third week of February they had reached the point in the book where the decision about the divorce would have to be made soon.

Cleo watched Gus as he adjusted the tortoiseshell glasses that he was vaguely embarrassed about wearing and that she privately thought were incredibly sexy. He had announced when she'd arrived this morning that they needed to talk about whether Max or Sophie would stay together, and she was waiting for him to begin.

Gus frowned as he gazed out the window to a few flakes drifting down against a pale winter sky. He couldn't seem to gather his thoughts this morning; he hadn't been able to concentrate in quite a while, as a matter of fact. Both of them had been moody, abstracted, and cranky under a mask of excruciating politeness. The work was suffering, he knew, and he knew he was. But he didn't know what he could do about it; he couldn't give in to his longing to take her into his arms and kiss her, long and hard. He just had to keep going.

"I know you feel strongly about Max and Sophie staying together," he said in a polite tone, "so I don't want to press you on it, but sooner or later we'll have to come to a decision."

"I know, Gus, and I understand why you're bringing it up now," she replied carefully from the couch. "But I think we have at least another month until the scene in the courtroom. We agreed that that would be the climactic scene for the relationship, and they'll go through with the divorce or not there. So we could still put it off. Unless you want to talk about it, that is."

"I do like to have an idea of where I'm headed in this last third of the book. I understand you have a different way of working, of course, and that's fine. But maybe we could just kick it around a bit."

"If you want to, of course."

"If you don't mind—"

"Not at all. If you think we have to. Go ahead."

"What I was going to say was," he said, "that perhaps your emotional tie to Max and Sophie is getting in the way of your objectivity. Not that I think that's a bad thing necessarily."

"I see. I don't really think you're on the right track there, Gus, though I suppose it would be an interesting point, were I a different kind of writer," Cleo said smoothly despite the jolt of irritation she felt. "I'm thinking about what's best for the book. Perhaps your own emotional state has something to do with this compulsion you have to cut all ties between them."

Gus's hand tightened on the windowsill, but his voice was even and carefully judicial. "That's an interesting point, Cleo, but I think you're just a bit off base. I've always kept a certain emotional distance from my work. I realize, of course, that you work differently. But the mature writer—"

"Thank you for explaining your method of working, Gus. Incredible that I've spent five years underestimating your emotional objectivity."

"I didn't mean to upset you."

"Not at all. I'm perfectly fine. As I was about to say, I've always been of the opinion that the writer has a hard time understanding his emotional motivations in a work until some time after the work is completed."

"Excellent point, Cleo. You do have a way of summing things up. So when the writer in question writes from her emotions—and I use 'her' in a hypothetical sense, of course—it can be difficult for her to understand a writer who primarily works from the intellect—"

"Intellect!" Cleo finally exploded, leaping up off the couch. "You wouldn't know an intellect if it came up and bit you on the—"

"Is this how you prove to me that you're not emotional about the issue?" Gus snarled back. But the irritation he felt was nothing to the exhilarating sight of Cleo jumping off the couch, her lovely face flushed with the heat of battle. His blood felt as though it hadn't been pumping in months. He controlled himself as best he could. "If we want to decide about Max and Sophie's divorce, we have to approach it in a mature way."

"Then maybe you should leave the room and let me decide," Cleo shot back furiously.

"Oh, really?" Gus asked menacingly, taking a step toward her. "So we could have hearts and flowers for the ending? How sweet."

She advanced toward him angrily. "No, we'd have a realistic scene of two adults working through their problems instead of giving up like two infatuated teenagers. Of course, if we're talking about an adult solution, I'll be happy to take you step-by-step through it so you can understand how it works."

Gus reached the middle of the room and glared at her. "I'm the one who manages to keep things on an adult level around here."

"You think so? I'm the one who maintains the professionalism of this so-called mature partnership."

"Hah!" He spit the word out, now only inches from her face.

"Hah, hah!" Cleo returned, her eyes blazing.

"Well, hah, hah—" Gus stopped abruptly as the comical side of the situation started to assert itself. "Hah," he said weakly. They both grinned, then laughed sheepishly.

Gus sat down wearily on the couch. "I'm thirty-six years old, and you make me act like an idiot," he said.

Cleo sat down next to him. "I make you?"

"Okay, okay. But it felt good to yell at each other, didn't it?"

"Yes." Cleo giggled. "We're in bad shape."

"Cleo, I don't want to yell at you, I really don't. But I just can't tiptoe around you anymore." Obviously agitated, Gus stood up and began to pace. "I can't concentrate on the book anymore, I can't sleep, I can't eat—it's like I'm sixteen again, and you're the pretty girl in math class."

"Are you trying to tell me that you *are* an immature teenager?"

"I'm trying to tell you that I'm being driven stark raving mad by you," Gus said, seriously. "I can't be polite and professional anymore. I have to tell you how I feel. I can't keep working with you and keep my distance." He stopped and turned to her. The light of amusement had faded out of his golden eyes, and something she didn't want to face had taken its place. She saw his hands ball up into fists and his eyes sweep her body hungrily.

Cleo tensed, knowing that finally, finally, the unspeakable was about to be spoken. When serious, Gus was dangerous. He wasn't going to change the subject with a quip or a brisk return to work. Moistening her dry lips, she desperately searched for words to lighten the moment, to forestall what she knew was coming. *Dear Lord, give me the strength to resist him,* she prayed.

Gus hadn't moved, and his eyes hadn't left her face. "I'm sorry I have to say this," he said, his voice rough with emotion. "I know you don't want to hear it. My only defense is that I want you so desperately."

Cleo sucked in her breath. With a few honest words, Gus had charged the atmosphere, and it would never be the same again. The air was now thick with his confession, and, she realized, with her wordless, answering response.

She held his gaze despite the fear snaking through her body. But along with the fear she was aware of a soft center of warmth that spread out from her middle to her fingertips, making her whole body feel suddenly alive, more alive than she'd felt in months. He wanted her. Desperately, he'd said. His coolness, his edginess notwithstanding, he still wanted her.

And she desired him so fiercely it took her breath away. The snow was falling furiously now, and the white light of the sky and the hush of the storm allowed her no escape. There were no shadows, there was no dusky twilight to blur the edges of her desire. She had nowhere to hide, nowhere to go, and when she felt Gus's hands pull her to her feet, then slide up her arms and draw her against him, her stiffness dissolved with the heat of his body.

His voice was husky, gritty. "And you want me, too," he said.

"No," she said, even as he removed his glasses, even as her head tilted back, even as his mouth covered her own. "No."

They kissed; they kissed slowly and deeply, their lips and tongues melding into one sweet, long, pulsating stream of sensation. They couldn't stop kissing, they went on and on, standing there, insatiable for the taste of the other, unwilling to stop. It had been so long. They had wanted it so much.

They broke apart, and in a moment Gus eased her down on the floor in the soft, white light of the storm.

The rug cushioned them as they unleashed buttons and pulled off constricting fabric to find the warm, honey skin of Gus's chest, of Cleo's thigh, of shoulders and arms. Luxuriating in the feeling of skin on skin, they embraced, overcome with their emotions and their ravenous need.

Gus was demanding this time, almost out of control. He kissed her wildly, fiercely, holding her head as if she would turn away from him. He wanted to taste her everywhere, and he did, with such a mixture of feverish possession and exquisite subtlety that she had to cry out. Her body throbbing, her skin and her hair damp with perspiration, she held him to her while her muscles shook with the aftermath of her pleasure.

"Cleo," he said roughly against her dewy, fragrant flesh, "you consume me." He rubbed his lips against her soft stomach and then gently bit her there. "I'll never get enough of you." And then he raised above her and moved against her.

"Never enough," he said. His eyes refused to let go of hers; they were lit with an intensity that added to her arousal, and as she watched him possess her she felt a thunderous heat that built to a pitch she'd never imagined she could feel. She had to bite her lip to keep from shouting with the joy of it. She gave him everything, with no regrets, and never before had she loved him so completely, and so well.

They woke at sunset. The snow had stopped, and downstairs the orange rays would be painting the brick wall a vibrant hue, but the loft bed was dusky with shadows. They had left their clothes on the floor and come upstairs to make love again, and then had fallen asleep locked in each other's arms. Gus had kept her within his embrace, capturing her sleepily if she strayed, out of habit, to her own side of the bed.

His fingers danced down her spine. He kissed her closed eyelid. "You're delicious."

"Speaking of delicious—" Cleo said, opening one eye.

"Mmmmm?" Gus asked, his mouth against her neck.

"I'm hungry. We never did eat lunch. Got any spaghetti?"

"Spaghetti at a time like this? Clee, I'd be the first to admit that you were a woman of great appetites, but I should let you know that this is my least favorite one. You'd rather have pasta than passion?"

She nodded guiltily.

"What would an Italian say? Spaghetti instead of seduction, linguine instead of libido, fettuccine instead of forni—"

"Gus."

"Okay, okay. I think I can rustle up some spaghetti if you still make that great marinara. I might even have some wine."

Cleo hesitated, suddenly unsure. It all seemed too domestic, too familiar, and that was scary. "Actually, Gus, I think I'll—"

He put his finger to her lips. "Don't. Don't say it."

"I was just going to say that I—"

The finger became a hand clamped over her mouth. "Don't say you have to go home. Okay?" He waited until she nodded, then dropped his hand.

Cleo took a deep breath. "I only meant that we—"

His large hand covered her mouth again. "You only meant that we shouldn't rush into anything, we shouldn't draw any conclusions from this afternoon, if we're going to finish this book we should take it easy. Right?"

She nodded.

"Wrong." Gus sighed and dropped his hand to her leg, where he absently ran his fingers along it. "Cleo, I've got a proposition for you."

"Another one?"

He grinned, then said seriously, "For once in our lives, let's not *think*. Let's not analyze, dissect, speculate, second-guess. What happened today is inevitable. Can't we just grab on to it and stop thinking of what the future will bring right now?"

It's not that easy, Gus, Cleo thought sorrowfully. *We've gotten beyond that point; we're married, we have a complicated history of hurts and resentments that we just can't ignore.*

But his fingers stroked her so softly, and her body felt so languidly right next to his. And God, how she loved him. Once they'd been best friends; perhaps, in the end, that friendship could pull them through this. Perhaps they could separate the passion and the work, the love and the friendship. Perhaps they could work together and make love without it all blowing up in their faces again.

And besides, Cleo thought as she looked at Gus's strong profile, so dear, so beautiful to her, how could she possibly hurt more than she had already? Surely all her scar tissue could protect her from yet another inevitable loss.

She laced her fingers through his, and they gripped hers, strong and loving, not letting go.

"Spaghetti, anyone?" she said.

So in the end, she stayed. They had a long and hilarious meal, and afterward Cleo stood up hesitantly and carried her dish to the sink. If there was a time to leave, this would be it. The thought of sleeping with Gus tonight made her nervous. It was too much like being married.

"Would you stop worrying?" Gus demanded, following behind her.

"I'm sorry. I can't help it."

Gus enveloped her in a huge bear hug, and she leaned against him gratefully, feeling the tension fade from her body.

"Cleo," Gus said, his voice rumbling by her ear, "let's go to bed. We don't have to make love if you don't want to. In fact, I don't think that *I* want to. I'm exhausted."

Cleo allowed herself to be led to the bathroom. They brushed their teeth together silently. *This is exactly what I was afraid of,* Cleo thought. *Intimacy is more than lovemaking; real intimacy is spitting together in the same sink.*

She trailed after Gus up to the loft. She slipped into his T-shirt and a pair of his socks. When she climbed into bed, Gus drew her into his arms and rested his chin on the top of her head.

"This feels so nice," he said. "It feels right."

It did feel right. It felt wonderful. Cleo snuggled closer and threw one leg over his. She pressed against him and ran her hand down his deliciously warm stomach.

"Uh, Cleo—"

"Mmmmm?" Drowsily, she watched her hand explore his skin, its smoothness and warmth so like its honey-gold tone.

His arms tightened around her. "When I said I was too exhausted—"

A giggle started deep in her chest, and she tried to choke it down. Her hand strayed lower. "Yes?"

He groaned. "I might have been a bit premature."

Her mouth began to explore the same territory her hands had marked out. "Oh?" she asked mildly, her lips against his skin.

In a sudden deft movement, Gus rolled over, and she found herself pinned beneath him. They were both breathless, laughter mingling with desire.

"Now," he said, smiling down at her, "let me show you how awake I am." Riding the crest of their laughter and tenderness, they made love with a sweet passion. Afterward, they smiled into each other's eyes, wrapped their arms around each other, and slid gently into sleep.

Cleo was dreaming of a white house with a wide green lawn. In the distance was a blue, blue sea. She skimmed lightly over the ground as she approached the house, feeling peaceful and happy. The door opened at her approach, and she sailed through the empty rooms, finally discovering a couple leaning over a white wicker bassinet. She peeked into the bassinet, and a baby smiled up at her in that trustful, giddy way that only babies have. When she turned to congratulate the parents, she saw that the couple was herself and Gus. It wasn't strange at all in the dream; in fact, it seemed very natural to approve of herself in these surroundings. Then suddenly a fire bell began to clang. Gus ran out of the room immediately, and Cleo suddenly became herself in the dream, watching him dash away. Panicked, heartbroken, she reached for the baby to discover that it, too, had disappeared. The bell went on clanging, and Cleo spun around like a top, unable to make a move after her husband or to find her baby. She put her hands over her ears to shut out the insistent, terrifying warning of the bell.

She woke up with a start to find that Gus was there, his hand possessively around her waist, and the phone was ringing. It took a minute for her head to clear. Then she allowed herself one quick nuzzle into his warm neck and kissed him awake.

"Telephone," she murmured.

"Phone," Gus said thickly, and kissed her swiftly before reaching over for the receiver, knocking over the alarm clock on his way.

She smiled as he ran a hand through his tousled hair and brought her against him. *This is the way it used to be,* she thought. The sun streaming through the skylight, both of them warm and naked in bed, replete from the night before.

"Yes?" Gus's morning voice was none too welcoming.

She heard the voice, urgent, compelling, on the other end, but couldn't make out the words. She felt Gus's body stiffen, and his hand stopped its caressing motion on her shoulder.

Instantly, alarm was like a hard fist in her stomach. She lay quietly against him, her eyes trained on his face. Something was wrong, she knew; Gus's face had the tightly controlled lines of shock. Cleo counted the beats of her tripping heart and waited for him to hang up.

So far Gus had only uttered "Yes," and "No," and "Of course." Now he said, "Thank you for calling," looked at the receiver for a blank moment as if he didn't know quite what to do with it, and hung it up gently.

"Gus, what is it? Who was that?" Her voice was taut with anxiety.

He sounded dazed. "That was Ellison." He took a deep breath. "I've been nominated for an Academy Award," he said.

Chapter Nine

The calls didn't stop. Cleo barely had time to recover from her shock and congratulate Gus before the phone rang again. It was a correspondent from *Dateline: Entertainment* asking if Gus could tape an interview that afternoon. As soon as he'd agreed and hung up, the phone rang again with another request. It continued all through breakfast.

They tried to work, but it was impossible. Ellison called every few minutes with another piece of business, and insisted he take them both out to lunch to celebrate. Cleo rushed home to change, feeling happy but bewildered.

The feeling persisted throughout the day and into the evening. Gus's apartment was chaos, and she pitched in to help answer the phone and keep track of the various requests that were pouring in. They didn't have more than a minute to talk.

Dusk had insinuated soft shadows up in the loft, making it a quiet haven, as Cleo sat on the bedroom extension, listening to her parents say how wonderful it all was. She absently massaged the back of her neck. She felt exhausted and overloaded by the events of the past twelve hours.

Her body still felt the aftereffects of the tumultuous lovemaking of the night before. She'd barely had time to absorb the enormity of it all before they'd been shocked awake by the news this morning. She couldn't even begin to wonder what would happen to Gus now.

She said goodbye to her parents and hung up, then sat for a moment on the bed, trying to pinpoint the source of her unease. They had managed to block out the world yesterday during the snowstorm. In a strange kind of way, they had come to each other naively; their passion had been all-important, and reality had seemed very far away. And then today the world had crashed back into their lives. Somehow, that had changed things. She didn't know if she was capable of giving herself so completely again, so soon.

The knowledge made her sad; it also told her that she needed some breathing room. She needed some time to think.

She heard Gus's step on the stairs, and she turned. He stood, almost hesitantly it seemed, on the top step.

"I took the phone off the hook."

"Good idea."

He came over to the bed and sat next to her. Sighing, he took her in his arms. "I'm sorry," he said. He lifted her hair off the side of her neck and kissed her there.

"What about?"

"I wanted things to go differently the day after we made love. I wanted to bring you breakfast in bed, and flowers. I wanted us to go to the park. I wanted to talk."

She drew away slightly to gaze at him. "It's all right. Gus, I'm so proud of you. I'm so happy for you. Don't you know that?"

He nodded. "But I'm still sorry I didn't get to spend time alone with you today. It all happened so fast." He groaned and flopped back onto the bed. Pulling her down next to him, he said, "But there's always tomorrow. Let's order in a pizza and go to bed early."

Cleo stroked his hair thoughtfully. "Gus, I have to ask you a favor."

"Anything."

She took a deep breath. "I'd like it if we put our relationship on hold for a little while. Last night was overwhelming for me. It was scary. And your life is changing—"

"Cleo, I—"

"No, don't tell me the Oscar nomination doesn't matter. It does. With that, and finishing the book, we're under so much pressure. I don't want to add to it."

"Making love will add to it?"

"For me it will."

Gus took a deep breath. "How long do you expect me to wait, Cleo?"

She sat up. "Do we have to put a time limit on it?"

"Maybe."

"You're not being very receptive."

"For God's sake, what do you expect me to be!" Gus got up off the bed and stood up, struggling for control. "We made love last night. I didn't take that lightly. It overwhelmed me, too. I thought it was the beginning of something."

"It can still be the beginning of something," Cleo said softly. "I just don't think that it's a good time to make decisions about our marriage. I'm asking for a little time. We can work together without sleeping together."

"Speak for yourself," Gus growled.

She put her hand on his arm. "Please."

She waited long seconds for his response. Finally, she felt his muscles relax.

"All right. Let me put you in a cab. I have to remove myself from temptation," he said.

They walked downstairs in silence. It was still snowing lightly, and they walked out into a hushed, dusky twilight. Blue shadows smudged the still pristine snow. The magic of the evening stole over them slowly as they walked toward Eighth Avenue, their footsteps making pleasant scrunching sounds in the snow. Tentatively, they reached for each other's gloved hand.

Gus squeezed her hand tightly. "God, you are an infuriating woman."

"I know."

"Now listen. We have a month before the Oscars, and we should be finished the book by then. That's all the time I'll give you. After that," he said, narrowing his eyes and squinting at her, "I attack."

They stopped on the avenue and faced each other. "Fair enough," Cleo said. "Now, will you call me a cab?"

"Okay, you're a—"

She punched him amiably. "With dialogue like that, I can see why you're an Oscar-nominated screenwriter."

He reached out to touch a snowflake that sparkled in the lamplight in her midnight-black hair. It disintegrated with the touch of his woolen finger. "I'll miss you tonight," he said simply. "I'll miss you more than you could ever know."

An ache constricted her throat. "I wish I could stay."

Gus lifted his hand to hail a cab, and it pulled over to the curb. He opened the door for her and helped her inside. Closing the door firmly, he leaned in the window and said, "Don't worry, Clee. Someday you will."

"Tell me, Gus, has the nomination changed your life in any way?" The bright blond head of the television interviewer moved closer to Gus, eagerly awaiting his response.

He grinned. "Well, I got a good table at John's Pizzeria last night," he said.

"Good answer," Cleo told Gus's image on the television screen. Gus was being charming and funny and relaxed on the interview, and she would have been on the edge of her seat if she hadn't seen at least a dozen similar interviews in the last month. It was a wonder she still turned on the television or picked up a magazine when she saw his name, but she couldn't help it. She was always dying to see how he did, even though he never asked her if she'd watched him.

They'd spent the last month in an uneasy truce. The work was often interrupted by Gus's new busy schedule, and they hadn't progressed as far as they should have on the book. Their camaraderie was a little stilted, but it was better than the stiff politeness of the winter. And they still scrupulously avoided any physical contact. Gus had respected her wishes to the letter.

But one thing Cleo hadn't counted on was the lack of true intimacy her withdrawal had created. She was an adult woman, she knew that sexual intimacy can often enhance emotional intimacy, the closeness of the nights spilling over into the days. What she hadn't counted on was that taking that step toward intimacy and then repudiating it would somehow put an even more awkward distance between them, a distance that couldn't be bridged by the daily contact of work.

Each evening she wearily climbed into a cab and shot back up the dark empty streets to Central Park West. Gus never said another word about it, but his eyes spoke volumes. He would slip into his jacket, walk her downstairs, and see her safely into the cab. Night after night, she watched him dwindle in the distance as she stared out the rear window at him standing by the curb watching her speed uptown.

She knew he hated her going. She hated it, too, but she couldn't stop it. As soon as the day's work was done, she would get up immediately, afraid if she lingered she wouldn't be able to leave, afraid of what would happen if she stayed. Her fear was involuntary, she couldn't stop it, and she had to obey it. She had to flee.

Her fear had been growing as the days counted down to Oscar night. Her genuine pride in Gus had begun to be tainted by a tiny shadow that had grown steadily longer and more threatening as the weeks went on, darkening her unformed hopes for the future, making her uneasy.

She could see so clearly the end of her time with Gus. Hollywood had returned to reclaim him. It was all too familiar, too sad, to even mourn for. The offers were already pouring in for Gus, and that same light of excitement was in his eyes once more.

Cleo glanced at her watch. The interview was almost over. "And will you be at the awards presentation?" the interviewer asked Gus.

"Are you kidding? I wouldn't miss it. I'm leaving for L.A. this morning, as a matter of fact."

"And will your wife be attending with you?"

Gus hesitated, and for the first time there was a crack in that smooth, cocky demeanor. "If she finds something to wear," he said, then covered up his discomfort with a grin.

Cleo switched off the television and went to brew a pot of coffee. "If I find something to wear!" she muttered under her breath.

The interviewer had hit the nail on the head with that question. Cleo had hung suspended, like the audience, for an answer. Was Cleo Delaney attending the awards? She still didn't know. Gus had adroitly sidestepped the issue during the interview, just as he had with her for weeks now. Cleo had been both relieved and hurt that he'd avoided the subject. Somehow she didn't think she could face going to the glittering affair on Gus's arm. She would feel as though she was once again condemning her marriage to failure. But not wanting to go and not being asked were two very different things. Why didn't he want her there? Why hadn't he asked her to go with him?

She sat at the computer terminal with her coffee, staring blankly at the screen. They were at the very end of the book, at the climactic scene in divorce court with Sophie and Max, where their private battles and the pressures of the murder case have heartbreakingly led them. The material had been too difficult for either Cleo or Gus to face head on. Instead, they had continued to disagree on how the scene would end. Cleo was still holding out for a sudden dramatic reconciliation between Sophie and Max right in the courtroom; Gus thought that would be corny. He wanted the divorce to be granted.

Twenty minutes later, she was still sitting at the terminal, her thoughts a tangle of Max and Sophie, Cleo and Gus, when Gus barreled through the door.

"Hi," he said. "I'm glad you're still here."

Cleo spun around in the chair. "Where would I be—out shopping for a gown?"

"Oh, sorry about that. I was stuck for an answer."

"That's okay. I don't mind all of America thinking that I'm the flighty, frivolous type."

Gus laughed and threw his overcoat on top of his already packed suitcases, which were waiting by the door. He headed for the kitchen to pour himself a cup of coffee. "Oh, come on—they knew I was kidding." He walked back into the living room. "Anyway," he said, sipping his coffee, "*are* you coming to the awards?" His voice was casual.

Cleo kept her eyes on the screen. "Are you asking me to?"

"Well, I figured I'd better, since I'm leaving today. You've headed me off at the pass for the past couple of weeks—"

"I have not."

"Of course you have. And I've avoided the subject, too, I admit. I feel like I'm asking you to the prom. Will you come, Cleo?" Gus stood directly behind her chair. He could tell by the back of her neck, the regal position of her head, that she was upset. But he had to find out now; Ellison was coming to pick him up for the airport in fifteen minutes. "We can look at all the movie stars together."

"If I can't see Gary Cooper, what's the use?"

"Maybe you'll see Jimmy Stewart. Will you come?"

An agonized confusion spread over Cleo, making her hands shake. She put them firmly on the arms of her chair. Now that Gus had asked her, she suddenly knew with a dreadful certainty that she would have to say no.

"Look," Gus said, "you have a week to decide. I'll be busy with interviews, and—"

"No, Gus."

"No what?"

"No."

"No? You won't come to L.A.?"

Tears squeezed out of her eyelids. "I can't."

"You *can't*? You have a date or something? You can't tear yourself away from New York and be with me on the most important night of my life?"

It's the most important night of his life, Cleo repeated numbly to herself. *It's the culmination of every dream he's had since he was a boy. How can you refuse him?*

She gripped the arms of the chair tighter. *Because those dreams took you away from me once, Gus, my darling. Because if they do it again it will tear me apart.*

"You waited until the last minute to ask me, didn't you?" she forced out. With one last spasm, she gripped the chair and shut her eyes tightly. She felt that if she didn't consciously exert her most intense effort, she would simply break apart. She struggled to contain her emotions while Gus waited behind her chair. She could feel behind her his incredulity and his pain. A car honk sounded, and she opened her eyes again.

"Cleo, we both know that I wanted you to be there with me. You knew that it was a difficult issue. You knew all the things that Hollywood would bring up for us so that I would feel nervous about asking. A month ago you made love to me all night and then told me you couldn't anymore. Why do you keep pushing me away? How long do you expect me to wait?" The honk sounded again. "That's Ellison," Gus said in a flat tone. "We have to catch the twelve-thirty flight."

Cleo stood up. Finally, she turned around and faced him. Her eyes were dry, her face composed. "I don't want to push you away, Gus," she said softly. "I'll be here when you get back, and I wish you all the luck in the world. You deserve to win."

He nodded shortly. "Thank you." Anger was set in every line of his face, the way he moved stiffly to pick up his bag. He paused with his back to her when he'd opened the front door. She thought he would turn and say something, something conciliatory, something glib, to lighten the tension. But he didn't turn. He walked through the door, not looking back.

Cleo stood in the empty room, fighting the urge to run down five flights of stairs after him. She stood rigid, afraid that if she moved one muscle she would give in to her impulse. It wasn't until she heard the cab door slam and the cab roar away that she stiffly walked over and gently shut the door.

"And now, for the last piece in my collection." Molly held up a black silk strapless sheath with a deep sweetheart neckline, then draped black satin elbow-length gloves with eighteen pearl buttons over the hanger.

"So, does it scream stunning?" she asked.

"It's gorgeous."

"Thanks, Mom. Cleo?"

"It's very nice."

"*Nice?* Cleo, I don't want you to go overboard here. It's only the most important piece in my new collection. I only looked for the perfect silk for months. Restrain yourself, will you?"

"Sure, Moll," Cleo said absently. She picked at her spinach salad.

Molly and Kit Delaney exchanged a significant look. Then Molly sighed and carefully draped the shimmer of black silk over the breakfast counter. She dropped into a chair across from Cleo, then leaned over and impatiently snatched the fork out of her hand.

"I think you've played with that long enough. I admit I'm not much of a cook, but when I invite you over for lunch you could at least make an effort."

"I'm not very hungry. Sorry." Cleo looked down into her glass of chardonnay. Molly and her mother were alternately peering at her and shooting each other exasperated glances, and she knew what was coming. When Molly had invited her down to her SoHo loft to view some of the dresses in the upcoming collection in her small and struggling line, Cleo had agreed just as much for a diversion as anything else. When she'd found her mother there as well, she still didn't suspect anything. But when they'd plied her with gorgeous dresses and her favorite white wine, she knew something was up.

She'd tried to rouse herself to show some enthusiasm, but it was difficult when her thoughts were three thousand miles away. The Academy Awards were tomorrow night, and she hadn't heard from Gus since he'd left.

Kit and Molly must have suspected something was wrong earlier in the week, after she'd informed them she wasn't attending the awards with Gus. It must have been a clue to how upset she was when Molly had dropped by her apartment unexpectedly and caught her demolishing an entire pint of mint chocolate-chip ice cream. She knew they had put their heads together and cooked up this lunch to try and worm out what was bothering her. She was surprised her sister Andie hadn't flown up from Philadelphia for the occasion.

Now they were getting impatient for her to bring up the subject, she knew. Any minute now they would start dancing around the topic of the Academy Awards, probably with some transparent speculation on who was going to win Best Actor or Best Short Subject.

Molly stopped toying with the fork and leaned forward. "Cleo, go."

"Go?" There was no need to ask where. Cleo should have known better than to expect her sister to be subtle.

"Go," Molly repeated. "I don't want to butt in or anything, but go."

"I can't," Cleo said miserably. "I can't explain why not."

"Oh, for heaven's sake," Molly said briskly, "you don't need to. We all know why. You've got this thing in your head that Gus is going to be seduced by the bright lights of L.A., and he'll get a tan and never come back again, just like last time. And you can't bear to be there and see it. It doesn't take Einstein to figure that out."

"Well, then you know why I can't—"

"I didn't say it made *sense*, you jerk," Molly said. "Of course, I may be overstepping my bounds, and you can tell me to butt out—"

"Molly, you're overstepping your bounds, so butt—"

"Cleo," Kit cut in smoothly, "we don't know what's going on with you and Gus, obviously, and perhaps we aren't in a position to give advice—"

"Not that it's ever stopped us before," Molly broke in.

"But it's also obvious that you're miserable. You said that Gus asked you to be there, and well, frankly, you just might be a bit selfish by refusing."

"Selfish?" Cleo sat up, stunned.

Kit and Molly nodded. "Afraid so," Molly said.

Hot tears stung Cleo's eyes. "How can you say that?" she whispered. "I'm just trying to keep myself together through all this. Whose side are you on, anyway? He left me once—"

"We're on your side, and he didn't leave you," Molly said flatly. "He went to the West Coast for work, and the distance and the pressures made you both go crazy for a little while. Then instead of talking it over, you pulled your typical number and withdrew so you wouldn't get hurt. Not that it's any of my business, or anything, so you can tell me to mind my own bus—"

"My typical number?"

"Remember in high school when you ran for president of the Yearbook Club?"

"Barely."

"Don't lie; you remember it very well. Sissy Cranwell campaigned, too, and she threw a big party on top of the World Trade Center and had a live band and invited half the school. You knew you were going to lose, so you dropped out of the race and talked all the best writers into doing a yearbook parody, remember? Sissy never got over it—the parody sold better than the yearbook. She didn't invite you to her graduation party at the Four Seasons."

"Molly, is there a point to all this?"

Molly nodded vigorously. "Of course there is, and you know it. You're so afraid of rejection that you have to reject first, and act like you never wanted whatever it was in the first place. It's a very successful pose—fooled me for years. But when you start pulling this act when it comes to your marriage, I feel honor bound, as your sister, to step in. This isn't the yearbook committee we're talking about here. This is you and Gus, two people I personally happen to adore. You're giving up before the first round even starts. You're not going to L.A., because that way, if he moves out there again, it will have nothing to do with you." She gave a mirthless snort. "Ha."

"Cleo." Kit said her name gently; Cleo knew she was trying to assuage Molly's bluntness. She must have seen the tears standing in Cleo's eyes. "You think your heart is fragile, but it's not. You can get through anything. You're still Gus's wife, and he needs you. Now you have to be the best woman you can be and go be a friend to your husband. Why do you think you're feeling so miserable now? You feel guilty." Kit put her hand on Cleo's arm. "Because you know that whatever the two of you have been through together, whatever's in your future, you should be at his side tomorrow night, win or lose."

"Maybe it's time to take a gamble, even if you end up losing," Molly said quietly. "If you still love him, that is."

Cleo could think of nothing to say. She looked down at her mother's hand, strong and square-tipped and so like her own. She gained comfort from seeing it there, just resting on her arm, letting her know with a touch that Kit was there, that she was hurting for her. Then she looked up into Molly's serious eyes, dark, almost black like her own, and she could read her expression like a child's first primer. Love was in her sister's eyes, in her mother's hands, and suddenly strength filled her limbs, and purpose.

Perhaps for the first time in her life, Cleo saw clearly that such a basis of love could serve as a catapult as well as a haven. It could send her to Gus. Those tight bands of steel she had forged to keep her desperate heart intact fell away. Somehow she didn't need them anymore.

She had learned in Connecticut to let go of her competitiveness with Gus, to not let that taint their relationship anymore. Then she had let go of her restraint just enough to be able to argue with him again instead of keeping up a false polite wall. She had come to make love with him fully and completely, taking and giving as much as she was able, but she had been frightened by her own intensity and had withdrawn. But maybe now she could learn to trust him again, just a little bit. To advance rather than withdraw. Going to L.A. would be a baby step in terms of how far she needed to go. But it was a step.

She put her hand over her mother's and smiled into Molly's eyes.

"Will you butt in some more and help me find something to wear?"

Molly threw back her head and roared with relieved laughter. She sprang out of her chair and ran to the black silk dress. Snatching it up, she ran back to Cleo and pulled her to her feet.

"Try it on, and I'll make it fit that perfect body like it was made for you. Why do you think I brought out the damn thing in the first place? If you'd been paying attention over the past winter, you'd know I already showed my new collection." She pushed the delighted Cleo in the direction of the bedroom. "And try on the stockings and shoes in there, too!" she yelled after her.

Cleo stuck her head out of the doorway a moment later, her hands full of dress, stockings, and a pair of high-heeled black satin pumps. "Are you going to pilot the plane to California too?"

"I might, just to make sure you get there. But once you're in L.A., kiddo, you're on your own."

* * *

"You're on your own, kiddo," Cleo said. She stared in the mirror. "Smile," she told herself. A weak turning up at the corners resulted. "Heaven help me," she said, closing her eyes.

For the thousandth time, she tugged at the deep neckline of the black silk gown. It dipped between her breasts rather alarmingly, exposing just a bit more of her flesh than she was comfortable with. The red satin gown Molly had sent up to Connecticut had been flashy and exciting, but this dress managed to be much more devastating in a subtle, knock-them-dead kind of way. Molly had spent the entire afternoon yesterday tailoring it to her body, pushing aside her protests with the argument that Cleo would be a walking advertisement for Molly Delaney fashions. Her clothes had never been on national television before, so Cleo had better stand where she'd be photographed. Cleo had to admit that the result of all that work was pretty spectacular. She was beginning to see why rich women had custom-tailored clothing.

As she looked at herself in the mirror, a tiny pleased smile began to grow into a grin. She just might enjoy herself tonight, after all. She had had her share of fame as an author, she had done talk shows and interviews, but literary fame in Manhattan had little of the razzle-dazzle of the Hollywood variety. This was glamour. This was…Hollywood. And thanks to Molly, she was dressed for it.

She glanced at the clock. Gus should be here in the limousine in five minutes. Molly had urged her yesterday to call him—or at least she had tried to urge with a mouth filled with straight pins as she altered the dress—but in the end, Cleo had chickened out. Too afraid to hear him tell her he'd found another date, she had telegrammed, "Still need a date for the prom? I'm available." Gus had telegrammed back a terse "Suite reserved for you at Beverly Hills Hotel. Pick you up at four-thirty."

She had spent the plane ride in a complete fog; she'd watched an entire half of the movie before she realized her headset was on the wrong channel. She'd given up and leafed through a magazine, but pictures of the Oscar contenders only made her nervous, so she'd sat unmoving, her hands in her lap, for the remainder of the flight.

She'd barely noticed the beautiful suite Gus had arranged for her, and she had dressed in the same state of tension, jumping when her cold hands came into contact with her skin. It was too much for one woman to handle—would her estranged husband win an Oscar? If he did, would success take him away from her again?

Now all the days and evenings she'd spent with Gus over the past months—that night of lovemaking, the head cold they'd passed back and forth, the meals, the cups of coffee, the words spinning out between them as they constructed a plot—built up into a crashing wave of emotion that threatened to sweep her away. And it told her just how much she'd been fooling herself.

Holding herself off from making love to him again hadn't guarded her against loving him again. Making the decision to come out and be with him, plus a five-hour flight with nothing to do but think, had forced her to confront the fact that her love for Gus was the most potent force in her life. The terror of losing him had only increased with the new relationship they'd tentatively forged over the past months, the relationship that she had so laughably imagined was devoid of intimacy or commitment on her part. Tonight could be a turning point, for love, naked and vulnerable, was shining out of her eyes. If it was so potent that she was unable to quench it, she knew Gus would recognize it in a flash. Or perhaps he'd be too nervous to notice anything tonight.

And somehow it was fitting that tonight Gus was being honored for translating Sophie and Max to film. The couple had brought them together in the first place; each stage of Cleo and Gus's relationship could be marked by what was happening with Sophie and Max. They were their most loved creations, and they would always bind them together, like proud parents with a growing child.

The phone buzzed, and she crossed the room quickly.

"Ms. Delaney, your car is here."

"Thank you. I'll be right down."

This was it, then. Cleo wiggled her fingers into the long gloves, picked up her bag and the floor-length full white satin coat Molly had loaned her, took a deep breath, and swept out the door to meet Gus.

Chapter Ten

She was so damned poised. She stood there in the lobby, calm and regal, waiting for someone to show her which limousine she should enter. Not a trace of nerves or agitation showed.

Next to that black silk gown her beautiful creamy skin glowed, its luminous paleness making her look more feminine and alluring than any bronzed starlet ever had. The white skin, dark brows and wild hair, the black clinging gown with the white satin evening coat, all combined into a stunning celebration of simplicity and an impression of absolute, confident beauty.

His nerves had been stretched taut, humming like a wire over the evening to come, but they suddenly relaxed in a rush of pure gratitude and, he might as well admit it, old-fashioned masculine pride. This was his woman, and her beauty was unique and perfect and exhilarating.

Strength and intelligence were in her face, her carriage, her expression. She was magnificent.

And she had come when he needed her. His anger at her hesitation in New York vanished in an instant. He just had been so damned afraid she wouldn't come, and so stupidly reluctant about the possibility of losing in front of her. For Cleo, he would always want to be a winner. Suddenly the truth homed in on Gus and made him suck in his breath. He had put off asking her, he had waited until the last possible moment, because *he had wanted her to refuse.* He had set himself up so that he wouldn't have to be a sore loser in front of His Woman. What an idiot he was. He didn't deserve her.

But somehow, miraculously, she was here.

He stepped forward, and she saw him immediately. Her smile was lush and inviting, touchingly pleased to see him.

He crossed the distance and stood in front of her. "I'm glad you came."

"I had to."

"You'll be the most beautiful woman there, Cleo."

Her grin was impish. "Molly dressed me."

"You fill it all out nicely." He couldn't help but glance at the discreetly but suggestively revealed breasts, and Cleo blushed. It pleased Gus enormously. She may have looked poised and sophisticated, but Cleo had an innocent streak that he discovered at the most surprising times.

He took her arm and led her to the black limousine at the curb and helped her in. When they'd settled in the plush back seat, she turned to him, concern in her dark eyes.

"Are you terror-stricken about tonight?"

Gus smiled. "I was. But the sight of you in that dress knocked every other thought out of my head except making love to you. Remember, I told you I'd only give you a month. It's been four weeks to the day, you know."

"Well, that's subtle. You want to skip the awards and go watch it on TV?"

"Believe me, I'd love to. But I'm paying a fortune for this limousine. Care for some champagne?" He leaned forward and opened the bar, then selected two champagne flutes. He pulled out a bottle of Taittinger and showed her the label. "For luck."

"You don't need it."

"Everybody needs luck." Gus popped the cork and poured out two glasses. They clinked.

"Here's to luck, then." Cleo sipped her champagne and studied the bar and television in front of them. "I could definitely get used to this. Gus, remember when we sold *Fast Moves* to the movies, and we got that suite at the Waldorf to celebrate—"

"And we took the subway to get there. We didn't even spring for a taxi. Old habits die hard."

"This is incredible. It's a color TV. We *could* just watch the ceremonies instead of going. Got any popcorn?" She ran her hand along on the seat. "And this back seat is as big as a bed."

Gus looked at her in mock alarm. "Surely you're not suggesting—"

"Of course not. I just meant—"

"Because if you are, I assure you I would never take advantage of a lady in a limousine before the Academy Awards, no matter how sexy and alluring she might be—"

"Gus—"

"And no matter how much I wanted to. No matter," he continued, "how much I was dying to. No matter that we'll be stuck in traffic for at least thirty minutes before we get there. No matter that this back seat is, as you so demurely put it, as big as a bed."

"Gus, I don't believe this. You can't be suggesting—"

"Of course not. It would be so—tacky." Finally Gus gave in to irresistible temptation. He leaned forward and kissed the spot where the dress dipped between her breasts. He felt her quick intake of breath against his mouth.

"Gus—" Her voice held that throaty quality he loved.

His lips trailed against her skin, following the line of the dress. Cleo's head fell back, and she sighed. Slowly, Gus eased her satin glove down her arm, trailing his mouth down her forearm, her wrist, kissing each of her fingers, one by one.

All of her resistance from the past month was gone in a flash. All that was important to her now was to show Gus how much she loved him. But in a limousine?

"Gus, we can't do this . . ."

"Mmmmm. I know."

"You should stop."

"Mmmmm."

"Gus?"

"Mmmmm?"

"Don't stop . . . quite yet."

The excited fans on the bleachers hooted with approval, and the announcer let them quiet down before he spoke into the microphone again. "Thank you, Derek Wilde and Shannon Souci—soon to be seen in *Fraternity Vacation, Part Two*—maybe next year we'll be seeing you as the nominees."

The painstakingly moussed head of Derek Wilde leaned forward toward the mike. "Hope so, Roger."

The blond couple waved at the crowd again and headed for the doors of the Dorothy Chandler Pavilion.

The announcer turned toward the curb again. "Ah, another limousine is approaching. Which star will be arriving now? Could it be one of the nominees?"

The crowd waited expectantly. The limousine rolled to a stop, then sat indolently by the curb.

"I'm sure they'll be coming out any time now," the announcer boomed into the microphone. But the limousine still sat.

"Uh, an exciting evening here in Los Angeles, and soon we'll be talking to another bright star in the Hollywood firmament." Another long pause followed. "And we'll have exclusive interviews with all the stars tonight." The announcer signaled frantically to his assistants to bring up another limousine, and fast, but just then the doors opened.

The crowd shifted forward expectantly, then sat back, disappointed.

The announcer leaned backward to catch the frantic prompting of his assistant. "It's the nominee for best screenplay, Gus Creighton, and uh, his date," he said, relieved. His voice picked up energy when he looked beyond Cleo and Gus. "And right behind him is Opal Gardenhire, the beautiful blonde of *Alien Contact, Part Three*. Come on over here, Opal, and talk with us a minute."

The crowd roared its approval. Cleo kept a smile on her face as they passed the bleachers, but there was no need to—all the attention was focused on Opal Gardenhire.

"Do I look okay? Anything missing?" she asked Gus through her strained smile.

"Perfect."

"Good."

"Tell me something though, Cleo. Is it the style now to only wear one stocking?"

"What?" Cleo looked down. It was true; one leg was bare. She opened her purse and searched frantically through it. "Oh gosh, it must be in the limo," she hissed to Gus. "This is all your fault."

"I'll gladly take the blame. At least I'm not nervous anymore."

"So what does that make me, a tranquilizer?"

"I wouldn't say that. You're a definite . . . stimulant. You definitely keep me up at night . . . and morning, and afternoon, and early evening—whoops." Gus finished by pulling the end of a sheer black stocking out of the pocket of his tuxedo.

"Thank heaven." Cleo grabbed it and hastily stuffed it in her purse. "I think I'd better go put this on. Where's the ladies' room?"

"Behind that door marked 'Ladies,' I'll bet. Need some help?"

"Not your brand of assistance, thanks. I'll be right back."

Her leg appropriately sheathed in black silk hose, she returned to take Gus's arm and find their seats. As soon as they sat, he grasped her hand, hard.

"Nervous now?" she asked.

"Paralyzed. You?"

"Are you kidding? I'm so nervous I'm practically levitating."

"If you start to rise, take me with you, will you?"

For the next hour, they were star-struck as they discreetly peeked around heads and sneaked looks at various stars in the monitors. They poked each other and pointed people out with discreet nods and private glances that spoke of their secret thrill at being there.

After the first hour had passed, Cleo discovered that the main action in the auditorium seemed to be people's leaving their seats to go congregate in the lobby bar. She longed to do the same, but she and Gus were rooted to their seats in an agony of nerves. Though they knew approximately when the nominees for Best Screenplay would be announced, they didn't want to miss any part of the proceedings.

It seemed like years before Opal Gardenhire, the actress who had made such a splash in *Alien Contact, Part Three*, slithered to the podium with an actor who'd achieved fame playing a robot on a television situation comedy. She read a short homage to screenwriters, then, stumbling over several of the names and peering nearsightedly at the prompter, she slowly read the names of the nominees.

Cleo and Gus's entwined hands were slick with sweat, and they gripped each other even harder while desperately trying to maintain a neutral expression for the ubiquitous cameras.

What if I lose? That damn camera will be trained on my face, I know it. I wish I could win, for Cleo. Hell, I just wish I could win. Gus ran his other hand down the leg of his pants to dry it. It would be just his luck to win and then drop the damn statue in front of millions of viewers, including his grandmother in Nashville.

What if he wins? He'll have offers pouring in like Niagara Falls in the wet season. He'll forget all about writing detective novels that hardly make any money anyway.

Cleo watched as Opal Gardenhire fumbled with the envelope. She barely heard the crackle of the stiff paper over her thundering heart.

And as she counted those agonizing seconds while the actress struggled to tear open the envelope, she knew with absolute certainty that in her heart she wanted Gus to win more than anything. He was so talented; she was so proud of him. She brought her other hand over to add a reassuring pressure. *Please win, Gus. If our marriage works out, it will work out no matter what happens to our careers. I can't keep being afraid of your success. Please win....*

"How do you feel?"

"Wonderful. Pretty spectacular."

"That's good. Gus?"

"Yes?"

"Can I ask you something?"

"Sure."

"Why do you feel spectacular when you lost?"

"I didn't lose."

"Oh? I must have missed something then. How was your acceptance speech?"

Gus laughed and turned to her, his eyes lit with excitement. "I am only going to say this to you, because it's such a cliché I can't believe it's going to come out of my mouth."

"Don't worry about it, sweetie; I write with you, remember?"

"Talk about kicking a man when he's down—"

She squeezed his arm in repentance. "Sorry. You sure don't look down, though—that's the problem. So what's this cliché you want to let loose?"

"Incredible as it may seem, I can say with complete sincerity that it was an honor being nominated."

"Come on. Look around, Gus. We're the only ones in the limo. We've already made sure that the driver can't see us or hear us."

"I'm serious. Cleo, it was the strangest thing. After that actress announced the winner, I had a brief flash of agony, and then it just disappeared. All of a sudden I was just so happy to be there, at the Oscar ceremonies. Me, Gus Creighton, of Nashville, Tennessee. I was up against Jeffrey L. Lax, who wrote *One Man's Story* back in the fifties—one of my favorite movies. I was really happy to see him go up and get my Oscar. He deserved it. Corny, I admit. But there it is."

Cleo looked out the window at the limousines stranded with them in bumper-to-bumper freeway traffic. She grinned and turned back to Gus. "It's funny, but I know what you mean. I'm getting a kick out of being stalled in traffic next to Gregory Peck. I guess we should feel very depressed, but I don't. I feel pretty wonderful. I keep thinking of us making the rounds of all those agents in New York five years ago. And now they'll all be calling you."

"No, they'll all be calling Jeffrey Lax."

"Oh, right. But I'll bet they'll be calling you, too."

"And even more powerful people that I won't recognize will be at this party, if we ever get there. Hey, I think we just moved six inches. I wonder if the other losers will be going."

"You're not a loser, remember?"

"Well, not in my own eyes. But what about other eyes?"

"Not in mine."

His hand grasped hers. "Then that's all that matters."

They settled back, strangely content, for the ride. The limousine crawled almost the entire way, but it did manage to reach the movie mogul's mansion where the party was being held. They glided up the long drive to the huge Spanish-style mansion. People Cleo had no trouble recognizing were getting out of limousines and greeting one another with hugs of congratulation or sympathy as they went up the stairs.

"Now I'm really nervous. What am I going to say to these people?" Cleo asked, peering out the window.

"It's very easy, Clee. Just forget about any words except for adjectives. Keep saying things like 'Marvelous.' 'Fabulous.' 'Incredible.' When you're really stuck, roll out a throaty 'Magnificent.'"

"Gotcha."

They walked up the steps together and into a long high-ceilinged entryway done entirely in pink marble.

"What do you think?" Gus asked, surveying the room.

"Magnificent," Cleo drawled on cue.

Giggling like teenaged party crashers, they moved through the crowd unobserved. Cleo noticed that though the majority of guests were deep in conversation, their eyes rarely stayed on the face of the other speaker, but roamed around the room, flitting back to the other person courteously before roaming again. They looked Cleo and Gus up and down, their minds ticking over the mystery of who they could be. Then they turned back to their conversation as though nothing had occurred.

"How come nobody knows you, Gus?" Cleo whispered out of the corner of her mouth. "I thought you'd know everybody."

"Are you serious? I don't know anybody in Hollywood."

"But you lived here for almost a year."

"I was working around the clock. I never went to parties."

"Oh," Cleo said. So all her imaginings of Gus on the town in Hollywood were just that—imaginings.

"Let's find a quiet corner and have a drink before plunging into this madness," Gus suggested.

"Sounds *fabulous*."

"Watch it, there, Cleo, you used a verb. Follow me."

Gus prowled around discreetly until he found a pair of French doors off an empty library filled with video-cassette boxes in the bookshelves. He pushed the doors open to reveal a small terrace lit by moonlight. It overlooked a black-bottomed pool that had been landscaped to look like a naturally occurring pond.

"This is lovely," Cleo said, gazing at the shimmering water. "If only it were real."

"You mean you'd rather have a stagnant pond than a clean, filtered, chlorinated pool?"

"I sure would. I know that's hard for a city boy to understand."

"What do you mean? I grew up in Tennessee, remember?"

She laughed. "Gus, except for the purposes of seduction or charm, you've managed to bleach all that Tennessee grit out of your bones."

Cleo was surprised to see Gus's eyes turn moody at her words. He stared out at the pool.

"Maybe you're right," he said. He looked over at her. "Do you miss that part of me?"

His troubled eyes forced her to be honest. "Sometimes. But I like the Manhattan part of you, too—the ambition, the drive, even the wisecracks. But sometimes I think you're afraid to let the Tennessee back in, afraid you'll lose something by it, that it will diminish you in some way. I guess I'd like to see both parts of you more balanced."

"You want me to move back to Tennessee?" Gus asked lightly.

"No. But maybe it wouldn't hurt you to get out of the city more often. You used to hyperventilate if we had to go to my parents' house."

"I did not."

"You did. And remember when I talked about moving? You promptly fell down the stairs and sprained your ankle, just to prove that if it happened in the country you could have been stranded for hours."

"I didn't deliberately sprain my ankle, for crying out loud."

"Well, it was awfully suspicious."

Gus turned around and leaned against the railing so he could watch her face. "So you want to live in a house with a stagnant pond?" he asked teasingly.

"I want to live in a house near the ocean," Cleo said firmly, and was surprised to discover how much it was true. The dream she'd had about the white house, the green lawn and the blue sea had haunted her days. She had blocked out the lost infant, the husband who had disappeared, and concentrated on the peace she'd felt skimming through the rooms.

"I want to live in a big old white house with a wide green lawn and lots of space," she went on softly. "I want it to be in a town where people come in the summertime to get away from the city, and then is silent and slow in winter. That way I'll have the best of both worlds. I'll have a sophisticated village and a small-town atmosphere. The winter will be for clean snow and hard work and reading and getting to know the neighbors. Then I'll have the warm months for a bustling town and lots of houseguests and swimming and picnics—"

"By your stagnant pond."

"By my beautiful, shimmering blue pool."

Gus's eyes narrowed, thinking. "Good restaurants in the area?"

"Of course—for all the tourists in the summertime."

"A good bookstore?"

"Naturally. And a great deli."

"Chinese food as good as Fourth Street Szechuan?"

"Well, there'll have to be a few compromises."

Gus shook his head. "Forget it. The city still wins hands down. Who can live without good Chinese food?"

Cleo laughed. "I know you'll never leave West Twelfth Street, Gus." The words were spoken without rancor. She put her hand on his. "I know how important a sense of place is to you, of home. I guess I'd always hoped I could give that to you, But now I know everyone has to find their own security themselves. Or at least independent people like you."

"I guess I find security in a slightly bigger village than most." Gus spoke lightly, but the words didn't ring true for some reason. A moment before he had felt warmed by Cleo's vision, by her soft voice conjuring up a rhythm of life that suited him. It was surprising; he'd never imagined living anywhere but New York City, unless it was Los Angeles for periods of work. He remembered the towns at the end of Long Island, the wide, quiet streets, the lush, leafy trees. The blue-gray Atlantic was only blocks away, stretching to the horizon behind rolling dunes with sea oats waving in a breeze that held the tang of salt and the ease of contentment.

Could it be that he was changing? He had been a loser tonight, and he didn't care. He was at a Hollywood party with every star and every producer he'd ever admired, and he preferred a quiet talk with his wife. He'd always thought that the pulse of Manhattan beat in his veins, yet he was being seduced by a vision of a vastly different life. Perhaps he *was* changing, all at once but gracefully, without trauma, like time-lapse photography of an opening flower. Perhaps this magical, extraordinary night could make miracles.

And with that knowledge came a soft, barely felt tremor of fear. It brushed against his face like a feathery leaf, and Gus mentally waved it away. He looked over at Cleo.

The expression in her dark eyes was far away as she breathed in the night air and continued to look at the pool. A wisp of black hair stroked one creamy cheek.

Gus reached out to capture it. He felt resolve flood through him. "Let's go."

"Go? We just got here."

"So what? Let's take the red-eye back to New York and drive out to East Hampton. We can stay at that old inn—"

"You must be crazy!"

"Why? I think it's a great idea."

"You can't just leave the party."

"Who's going to notice? Cleo, you're more important to me than any party. We need to be alone. We need to make love properly and wake up together. We need to talk, to tell each other how we feel. It's time for us to leave."

She looked at him, her eyes soft, yearning. "You really want to?"

"I really want to. Right now. So let's—"

"Gus! Yoo-hoo! Gus! Over here!"

Gus felt Cleo stiffen even as his own muscles tensed. Even if he hadn't recognized that husky voice, he should have known that that woman would show up just when she was least wanted.

"Over here! On the other balcony!"

Stifling a curse, Gus turned around. On his right was the terrace off the living room. Wendee, in a one-shouldered red satin dress that looked very much like the one Cleo had worn in Connecticut, was waving at him frantically. A man in a tuxedo was by her side.

"What are you doing over there?" she called.

Gus stepped away so that Cleo was revealed. "I'm talking to my wife," he said pointedly.

Wendee's face dropped for a minute, but she recovered and waved gaily at Cleo. "Hi, Cleo!"

"Hello, Wendee."

Wendee backed away from the railing. "Don't move, you two. Gus, you're just the person I've been dying to see. Look who's here with me!" The man stepped out into the moonlight, and Gus saw with a spurt of surprise that it was Denton Ballard.

Wendee giggled at their surprise and took Denton's arm. "We'll be right over," she said. "Denton has a wonderful proposition for you. We're going to get you back to Hollywood, Oscar loser or not!"

Chapter Eleven

Cleo and Gus waited in uncomfortable silence for Wendee and Denton. Her last words still rang in the air over the subdued party noises from the other rooms.

"This shouldn't take too long," Gus said.

"Fine."

"I just don't think we should be rude to them."

"Of course not," Cleo answered. "I'm very fond of Denton."

"Do you think they're...together?"

"It looks like it." Somewhere a demon rose in Cleo's throat, prompted by her fury at Wendee's showing up at that moment, dressed in a copy of Cleo's—or rather Molly's—red satin gown. "I do hope that doesn't bother you," she said, her voice sharper than it should have been.

Gus gave her a furious look. "I haven't heard from Wendee since the weekend in Connecticut," he said icily. "I would infer that I was dropped like a hot potato for something far more promising, like the Ballard billions."

"No! By that shy, insecure soul searching for love?"

The iciness faded as quickly as it appeared, and Gus grinned. "What can I say? You were right about Wendee."

"I never said anything bad about Wendee."

"Sweetheart, with a face like yours you don't have to say a word. A lift of your eyebrow holds more information than a novel."

Cleo's eyebrows lifted involuntarily at his words, and she tried to disguise it by immediately furrowing her brow. Gus choked on his champagne, and Wendee and Denton walked in.

"However did you find this cozy little terrace? We've been looking all over for a quiet place to just *be*, haven't we, darling?" Wendee asked Denton. Without waiting for his reply, she continued, "It's so tiresome to have to stand around and be nice to producers. I hate it. So nice to see good friends here that we can really *talk* to, you know?"

Both Cleo and Gus smiled politely but made no reply, each deciding it might be dangerous.

"Hi, Cleo. Hi, Gus." Denton finally was able to greet them. They shook hands with real warmth.

Cleo eyed Wendee's dress. It seemed to be an exact copy of the one she'd worn that night. She couldn't resist making note of it. "That's a beautiful dress," she said.

"Thank you," Wendee answered, unperturbed. "I love yours, too. Did you get it in L.A.? I haven't seen it anywhere."

"I got it in New York, but I'm sure you'll be able to find it if you want."

Wendee paused for an instant, then turned to Denton. "Doesn't Cleo look marvelous? That New York winter pallor is so, well, *exotic* next to all these tans. But, Cleo, if you should want to get some color while you're here, let me give you the name of my tanning salon. It's the best in Hollywood. I mean, look at Denton, doesn't he look terrific? Oh, silly me, I'm sure you know a good one in New York."

"Wendee," Gus broke in quickly, "it's nice to see you, but we were actually on our way out—"

"Oh, don't go yet, please. I really was looking forward to seeing you here. I have the most incredible news."

"Yes?"

"Denton has decided to become a producer! Can you believe it?"

"No!" Gus said politely.

"Yes! And we've been talking about something that just might interest you. Denton wants to set up an independent production company for television shows. And the property he's interested in is—"

"Fast Moves," Cleo said.

"Now, how did you know?"

"Lucky guess." Cleo took a long sip of champagne.

"And he's dying for you to come aboard as executive producer and head writer, Gus. That is, if you decide to give up the rights to the film. I happen to know that the studio wouldn't object at all. On the contrary."

"Cleo owns quite a piece of it, too," Gus pointed out. "And Cleo, too, of course."

"Have you thought about casting at all?" Cleo asked offhandedly.

Wendee giggled. "Well, Denton absolutely insists on a certain actress for Sophie—"

"A talented actress," Denton said, beaming at Wendee.

"Not you?" Gus asked in a surprised tone that he supposed was a bit impolite. But surely she couldn't be serious. Wendee had been hinting about the project for a while, but he'd never paid any attention. Now Gus guessed how those false rumors about his interest in doing a series had gotten started.

Wendee nodded. "Well, Denton seems to think I'd be perfect."

Cleo kept a smile on her face, but she was genuinely incredulous. It would be a spectacular feat of miscasting for a twenty-three-year-old fragile blond actress to play the sophisticated, dark, aggressive, sardonic Sophie, who was well into her thirties. She waited for Gus to withdraw politely.

Gus shifted uneasily. How could he respond to such a preposterous suggestion? "Sounds interesting," he hedged. He knew enough about Hollywood to be noncommittal rather than dismiss them. Lots of projects got talked about at parties; few ever got off the ground.

"The series could make you a very rich man, Gus," Denton said. "With the success of *Fast Moves*, we're guaranteed to have a lot of interest at the networks. And you'd have a piece of the show as executive producer, of course. You could be pulling in a substantial amount from syndication eventually. Plus licensing—there's no limit to where we could go. You could conceivably make a tidy sum. A very tidy sum."

When a Ballard referred to a tidy sum, it certainly wasn't chicken feed, Gus thought dazedly. He wondered what Cleo was thinking. Both of them newcomers to success, they were a little naive about money. He'd never been overly concerned with it; he was happy as a clam in his studio apartment in the West Village of Manhattan—a little too happy, according to Cleo. But this evening he'd had a vision of the kind of life Cleo wanted, the kind of life she deserved. A big white house by the ocean. No worrying about down payments and mortgages. Maybe he and Cleo should simply take the money and run, straight into a life of leisure and contentment. Maybe he could get the series off the ground and then go back and taste a new life with Cleo.

And it was in his hands to give that to her. Wouldn't that make up for all the heartache he'd caused her when he made the film in the first place? *Fast Moves* could give something precious to Cleo; it could give her freedom. Still lost in the dream he had glimpsed of a new life, Gus thought it wouldn't hurt them to hear just a bit more.

"What exactly do you have in mind, Denton?" he asked.

Cleo couldn't believe her ears. What was he doing? "Gus," she began, but Wendee cut her off smoothly by taking her arm.

"Gus, I'm going to hijack Cleo and take her to the ladies' room. You've got to see it, Cleo, you won't believe it. All done in stainless steel and marble."

"Okay, Cleo?" Gus asked.

"Fine," she said, tight-lipped. She followed Wendee through the library, down a long hall and into a deserted bathroom, its slick surface of steel and full-length mirrors reflecting the two of them, black and red, over and over again.

Wendee immediately headed for the mirror to check her makeup. She leaned closer to scrutinize her face from all angles, then spun around.

"Cleo, I have to say something. I'm so embarrassed." She actually sounded sincere. "What is it, Wendee?"

"The dress, of course. I'm a rat, I know, to wear it after I saw you in it. But I just thought it was smashing, and I honestly didn't know you'd be here tonight. I didn't even think Gus would be. He never goes to parties."

Cleo found herself smiling at this unexpected confession. When sincere, Wendee did have a little-girl honesty that was rather endearing. "Don't worry about it, Wendee."

"I want you to know that it's from your sister's collection, at least. I didn't copy it. Gus had mentioned once that she was a designer, and I put two and two together and figured it was hers. So I found out what shop carries her dresses, and I had it fitted. Really, I feel terrible."

"Wendee, don't worry about it, really. I don't mind at all. It wasn't my dress, anyway. It was Molly's."

Wendee giggled in relief. "You don't understand—here in Hollywood, I committed a capital offense. You probably could have murdered me tonight and a jury of Hollywood women wouldn't have convicted you."

Cleo laughed along with her. *Holy cow,* she marveled, *I actually kind of like her.* Aloud, she said, "Let's just consider the subject closed. Unless, of course, you want to wear this dress next year."

Wendee tilted her head and looked at the dress. "I wouldn't dare. I'd never look as good in it as you do."

Taken off guard, Cleo managed to stammer out, "Well, thank you, Wendee."

"Anyway, I don't want to alienate you any more than I have already. We could all be partners in this new project."

Rather than answer, Cleo stalled for time and searched through her purse for lipstick she didn't want.

Wendee turned back to the mirror and opened her makeup case. "I hope you're not upset about Gus losing tonight. It really isn't too important. I mean, it's his first film and nobody really expected him to win. It was enough that he was nominated." She carefully squeezed out a drop of bronzer on the tip of her finger and smoothed it down the center of her nose, then blended it in. "Of course, he's got to act fast now. He really should have been out here for the past month, lining up projects." She shrugged while she scrutinized her face for places in need of repair. "But the iron's still warm. Sophie and Max Fast are still a hot property. Very hot. If there's one thing Hollywood loves, it's a known quantity." With the tip of a pinky, she smoothed bronze shadow above her eyelids. "Gus can be naive about things like that." She dusted more pink blusher high on her cheekbones and in the center of her chin. "He doesn't realize how short Hollywood's memory can be. He just might put off making decisions and go back to his little apartment and write for another six months." She quickly twirled a small brush on the tip of a bright pink lipstick. "Then, when he feels like emerging again," she said, pausing to paint her mouth, "there might not be any interest in Sophie and Max anymore. Especially if the next book isn't the success that *Fast Moves* was." Wendee surveyed the effect and took out a feathery brush. As she finished off her face, she met Cleo's eyes in the mirror. "Imagine me giving you a lecture about all this," she said. "You'd think I was a film professor at U.C.L.A."

The words were light, but her pale blue eyes were serious. Cleo could only lean against the sink. She'd been barely listening throughout the first part of Wendee's speech; she'd been too fascinated by Wendee's expert application of cosmetics, which had demonstrated to Cleo how far removed her own swipes with lipstick and mascara were from the real art of makeup.

But she had started to pay attention once she'd realized what Wendee was leading toward. Like any good actress, Wendee had saved the big punch for last. It had been an expert performance, from the initial softening of the atmosphere with a humorous apology, to the seeming casualness of the lecture, to the last frankly serious look in the mirror. And now Wendee had disappeared into a marble stall, leaving her to think.

And she had to think hard. She had to be careful. She knew Wendee was telling her that she could hold Gus back, that this was the time for him to push his advantage and solidify his career. But somehow Cleo had to be objective; she had to ignore Wendee's double-dealing and her own hurts and fears and concentrate on what was really important: Gus. What did he want?

And would getting what he wanted be hampered by her presence? Cleo loved the movies, she was even a fan of television detective shows, but she wasn't kidding herself that she was like a fish out of water at this party. Gus was visually oriented; she was literary-minded. It was another one of the differences that sparked their collaboration. She would always write books; that was her love, what she was good at. But Gus's first love was the visual medium, and it would always tug at him.

Cleo knew with the unerring instinct of a wife that he would be pulled in conflicting directions if she were present at this meeting. Simply put, Gus would feel torn between New York and Hollywood. And she also knew that holding him back could be disastrous for any future they could have together.

She supposed that if they both followed their natural inclinations, their marriage would end up to be an unconventional one, with residences on both Coasts and a good deal of transcontinental flying back and forth. She could handle that, she supposed; what she couldn't handle was a life without Gus at all. But even worse would be a life with a Gus who had regrets that he'd never seized this opportunity.

Since she was being honest, she might as well admit to herself that she was hurt by Gus's interest in the proposal. The series would demand his residence in Los Angeles and take all his time for a year, perhaps longer. But how could she argue with that, when they had made no commitments? Why should she be involved in the decision at all? She was the one who had drawn back a month ago, when they had first formed their fragile, magical connection.

Her thoughts in a tangle, Cleo rested her forehead against the cool mirror. She didn't know what to do. All she knew was that she had absolutely no interest in Wendee and Denton's project. All she knew was that she needed to give Gus room to maneuver. All she knew was that she needed just a little time to think.

Wendee emerged from the stall and looked expectantly at Cleo. "Ready to go back?" she asked brightly.

"Wendee, could you do me a favor?"

"Of course."

"Could you tell Gus that I've gone back to the hotel? I'm awfully tired. He can call me after he's finished his business with Denton. Or just come by my hotel. It shouldn't take too long, should it?"

"Oh, no. There isn't much to discuss at this stage. Of course, Cleo. I'll tell him."

They walked down the hall together, two glamorous women who to all appearances were delighted to be in each other's company. Wendee pecked her cheek as she left Cleo to head toward the library, and Cleo threaded her way through the party and found the limousine with relief.

It was only a few minutes to her hotel, and she sent the driver back to the party with misgivings. Gus would probably be annoyed when he found out that she'd left the party. He would probably leave and come after her. Was that why she'd done it? Cleo forced herself to be honest but concluded that wasn't so. She didn't need proof of Gus's love anymore. The situation wasn't that simple. She'd just wanted him to be able to discuss the project without worrying about her negative reactions. At any rate, if she knew Gus, he should be here very soon. Then they could talk. It was time they did.

Conversation with Denton was always agreeable, but Gus was beginning to get restless. Wendee and Cleo had been gone for twenty minutes, at least. With his more accurate perception of Wendee's true character, this made him very, very nervous.

He broke into Denton's recounting of literary gossip with a brusque, "Where the hell are they, anyway?"

Denton looked taken aback but, the true gentleman, said mildly, "Probably girl talk. You know how women are in powder rooms."

Gus nodded shortly, but he knew better. Cleo certainly wasn't about to chatter away to Wendee as she did with her women friends, and if Wendee was chattering away to Cleo, it could be dangerous or, at the very least, dull. He waited another ten minutes, during which some friends of Denton joined them, and then finally gave up.

"Excuse me, I'm going to search for my wife," he said, and left the group.

"Send Wendee back if you find her!" Denton called after him.

"Gladly." Gus searched through rooms filled with people, looking for the shimmer of red or black and embarrassing himself by tapping a few strange bare shoulders. Fifteen minutes passed and he was beginning to get testy. What could they be doing?

He was recognized occasionally and was stopped to be told that it was a shame that he lost, but Gus was barely listening. He shook hands cordially, stood for a minute, then excused himself and moved on.

He killed some time standing by the large Ming vase in the main room, telling himself his foreboding was ridiculous. Cleo was simply enjoying herself at the party. She was probably talking to some handsome sex-symbol movie actor at this very moment. Gus knew he was worried when he realized that, at this point, that wouldn't bother him in the least.

Finally, after he'd searched all the rooms again, he noticed a couple heading down a long hallway. Abandoning all social graces and any pretense to subtle detecting technique, he blatantly followed them. They ambled down one corridor after another and around a bend and came to a pair of French doors. They pushed them open and disappeared. Gus followed and found about fifty people enjoying the night in a landscaped English garden. Wendee was off behind a rhododendron, talking earnestly to a silver-haired producer Gus vaguely recognized.

Gus approached them and suffered through a lengthy introduction before he was able to ask Wendee where Cleo was.

"Oh, she told me to tell you she went back to the hotel."

"She *what*? When did she leave?"

"Don't panic, darling, it wasn't too long ago. Let's see now—it was after we went off together, and I was on my way to tell you when I was waylaid by Sheldon here—"

"This isn't exactly on the way to the library," Gus pointed out tersely.

"Oh, I always get lost in these houses. After all, I'm a struggling actress; I live in a three-room condo. What do I know about mansions?" She smiled at her silver-haired companion.

"Wendee," Gus bit out, "when-did-Cleo-leave?"

"Well, I guess it's been about an hour or so," Wendee admitted.

"An *hour*?" Gus made a great effort not to seize Wendee by her thin, muscular arms and shake her. "Did she say anything about my coming by or calling?" he asked evenly.

"I don't think so." Wendee looked prettily confused. "She said she was awfully tired."

Gus cursed, roundly and effectively. He turned away.

As he stormed out of the garden, he heard Wendee's voice piping, "Those New Yorkers are *so* touchy about their spouses, aren't they?"

Cleo carefully folded the black gown. It had been silly to keep it on for so long, anyway. She'd been reluctant to change out of it; it was the most becoming dress she'd ever worn. She'd thought that any moment Gus would be arriving, and in her foolish, feminine heart, she hadn't wanted to be wearing her usual sweater and pants, or her cotton robe.

But it had been well over an hour, and it was beginning to be apparent that Gus wasn't coming. She pressed her hands against her eyes, trying to stem the tears that kept leaking out from the corners. He was talking business with Denton, or some other producer. It would be idiotic for him to leave the most important party in Hollywood on Oscar night, in a town where social gatherings were really business meetings with hors d'oeuvres.

He would call her tomorrow morning. Perhaps he'd suggest breakfast, or brunch. They would meet to discuss how they could fit in finishing the book before his Hollywood commitments began. Isn't that what she'd wanted?

Suddenly Cleo couldn't face the suite any longer, the white roses Gus had sent to her room, the glamour and promise of her black silk dress. She rammed it into her suitcase, ruining her careful folding, and tossed in the few items she'd used that afternoon. She slipped into the knit dress she'd brought to travel in and then called the airport. There was space on the midnight flight to New York. She'd have to fly first class, but at least there was a seat.

Her heart pounding, she hauled the suitcase down to the lobby. She needed to cool off from the unreasonable anger that had arisen just because he'd stayed late at the party. She had some big decisions to make, and like any smart general, she wanted to be on her own turf when she discussed the terms of surrender. Cleo headed for the front desk to check out.

He tried to find a phone. That was his first mistake. He searched through all the downstairs rooms, but the phones must have been hiding in closed cabinets or enameled boxes; Gus supposed it must be terribly déclassé to have something so pedestrian as a phone in the hall.

When he finally poked his head into a study and saw a telephone sitting on a desk, he almost wept for joy. Gus was in the room before he realized that the receiver was off the hook, and when he followed the cord with his eyes, he saw that someone was sitting in the enormous swivel chair with his back to Gus. He just caught the words "No problem, we could get him for ten mill now that he lost," before he hurried out again.

This time he didn't hesitate. He went straight to the front drive and looked for his limousine. The only problem was that he was faced with twenty other black limousines lined up along the curving drive. Gus went from one to the other, desperately hoping to see the familiar face of his driver, Wally, who had earlier confided with a freckled-face grin that he was a struggling actor. Gus prayed Wally hadn't decided to try his luck inside. But finally he found him playing a desultory game of gin with another driver. The look in Gus's eyes made Wally drop his hand, and the tone in his voice as he directed him to the Beverly Hills Hotel made him peel out of the driveway with a skill that would have gotten him hired as a stuntman. But even Wally couldn't bypass the traffic jam that suddenly materialized in front of them.

When he was finally able to inch forward enough to make a fast right turn and bring them to the hotel by a circuitous route, Gus began to relax. The limo screeched to a stop in front, and Gus leaped out, dashed through the lobby, and asked the front-desk clerk to ring Cleo's room.

But Cleo had already checked out.

Cleo swung her bag over her shoulder and left the ladies' room in the lobby. She bypassed a black limousine at the curb and stepped into the hotel limousine for the ride to the airport. Everywhere you turned in L.A. there was a limo, she thought incredulously, and she was certainly riding in her share of them. Then she remembered the ride earlier in the evening, when she and Gus had shut out the world as they'd crawled through traffic to the Oscar ceremonies. She almost asked the driver to turn around ... but she didn't.

The traffic was surprisingly light, and they made it to the airport quickly. Her flight was already being announced as she checked in, and she was able to board immediately. Cleo tucked the blanket the flight attendant gave her around her and closed her eyes. She knew she wouldn't sleep a wink on the plane, but she didn't want to be disturbed. She was relieved when the lights were dimmed after takeoff, and the rest of the passengers slept.

Five and a half hours was a long time to stare out a dark window. Cleo thought all the way back to New

York. She thought as hard as she ever had about her marriage, her love for Gus, and her own failures. She thought about Molly's words and her mother's, and she thought about what she wanted from her life and what she had done with it. She thought without self-pity and, she hoped, without rancor. And by the time the plane had touched down at Kennedy Airport, she knew what she had to do.

Gus rubbed red-rimmed eyes. He asked the bartender for another Bloody Mary. He'd reached the gate just as the midnight flight was taking off, and he'd stood there like a fool watching the red blinking lights head for New York. The next flight didn't leave until eight o'clock, but he'd known that he wouldn't be able to sleep, so he'd had Wally drive him back to the hotel, where he'd crammed his clothes into a suitcase. Then they'd driven right back, and he'd dismissed the exhausted driver with an extravagant tip and a promise to keep him in mind for future projects.

He'd been filled with fury and some kind of nameless terror when he'd found out that Cleo had returned to New York. On the one hand, he was angry that she would rush back without a word, but then, he was the one who'd kept her waiting for an hour and a half after telling her that she was his first priority. She must have been terribly upset.

He supposed he should be planning what he was going to say to her, but he was too exhausted to think. The strain of the evening had finally taken its toll, but he was too keyed up with frustration to sleep. Perhaps if he had enough Bloody Marys, he could manage it on the flight. Then he could take a cab straight to Cleo's apartment.

And I'm sure you'll be fresh as a daisy when you get there, buddy boy, Gus told himself sardonically. *You'll be in terrific shape to talk to her.* He grimaced and swallowed the rest of his drink in a gulp.

"Attention, passengers. Please fasten seat belts and bring chairs to their full upright position. We'll be landing at John F. Kennedy International Airport in approximately twenty-five minutes."

Gus awoke with a start. How could he be back in New York? He'd just gotten on the plane.

Cold water splashed on his face in the tiny rest room helped to revive him a bit. He stared at himself in the bright mirror. He wasn't exactly looking his best, but what the hell.

Gus returned to his seat to watch the approach to the airport. The first sight of Manhattan Island never failed to thrill him. It looked so magnificent from the air, a gray and green expanse with slender bridges spiderwebbing over blue-gray ribbons of river to the larger, flat-textured land masses next to them. If he was lucky and the weather was clear as it was this afternoon, he could see details, even picking out the major streets. He marveled at the impossibly large green rectangle of Central Park, and he loved how the march of the tall skyscrapers of midtown gradually slowed and gave way to the smaller buildings of downtown, making that area look so strangely placid from the air. It was the only perspective that reminded him of why his part of town was called a village.

Despite his exhaustion and his tension, Gus felt, as he always felt approaching Manhattan from the air, incurably, incredibly optimistic. There was courage down there, there was opportunity and chance, there was energy, there was heart. And there was Cleo.

She was down amid those gray buildings bordering the west side of Central Park. She was there. He could talk to her, he could touch her, he could be with her. He could make everything work out.

He hadn't checked his bag, so he was out of the airport and into a cab quickly. After a second's hesitation, he gave the driver his address. He would shower and change before he went to see her; she'd seen him at his worst before, but there was no sense pushing things.

By virtue of the time change, they had to struggle through evening rush-hour traffic to get into the city. By the time Gus reached his apartment, he had forgotten his earlier affectionate paean to New York and now cursed it as a foul, dirty, abominable place with too many vehicles clogging the streets.

The telephone was ringing as he opened his door and he sprang for it, hoping it was Cleo to explain her strange behavior. As he picked up the receiver, he wondered how long he would let her apologize before he forgave her.

"Hello," he barked, just to let her know what a bad mood he was in.

"What's the matter with you? I know you lost, but if you'd get off your behind and start working on a script, you'll get nominated for another one."

"Hi, Ellison."

"You sound distinctly underwhelmed to hear from me."

"Sorry. I just got back from the airport. What's up?"

"That's what I'm calling to ask you. What's going on with you and Cleo?"

"What are you talking about?" Gus asked cautiously.

Ellison gave a snort of disgust. "I'm not going to get any satisfaction from this quarter either, I can tell. Cleo called me this morning. She said she wants to sign over the rights to Sophie and Max to you as soon as possible."

"She *what*?" Gus sank into the living-room couch. He'd slept through lunch on the plane and his head was pounding from the three Bloody Marys. He'd fought traffic in two different cities and in the air, and he'd lost both the Oscar and his wife in one night. Needless to say, he was in no mood for surprises.

"Not only for some television series she says you're interested in, but all subsequent rights for further books, films, et cetera."

"She must be crazy."

"Exactly what I said. Did you two have another one of your famous battles?"

"No."

"That's what she said. I don't know why I find it hard to believe." Ellison sighed. "One of these days I'm going to represent some normal clients for a change. Do you know if Francis the Talking Mule wants to make a comeback?"

"Did she give you any reason?"

"Nope. Said she'd talk to you about it if you want, though."

"That's big of her."

"I don't know why you're so testy. Seems to me you make out well on the deal."

"What about the book we're working on now?"

"Naturally she'll retain her financial interest in that. But she says you're almost finished, and that you can write that last chapter. Said you'd disagreed about it anyway, so she'll concede.''

"Holy cow. Cleo said that? She said she'd *concede*?''

"That she did. I couldn't believe it either.''

"She can't do this.''

"What are you talking about? First of all, she can, and second of all, it's a great deal for you.''

"I won't let her get away with it.''

"Gus, she's *giving* you Sophie and Max, not taking them away. Did you hear me correctly?''

"I heard you. She can't do this. Listen, Ellison, thanks for calling. I've got to go.''

"Okay, but what's all this about a television series? Not that it's my business. I'm only your agent.''

"Tell you later. Bye.'' Gus hung up and immediately began to dial Cleo's number. Then he slammed down the phone again.

He wasn't going to go off half-cocked, not this time. He was going to sit here and coolly figure out what the hell was going on. Gus settled into the couch to think.

The hell he was. Gus grabbed his keys off the coffee table and headed for the door.

Chapter Twelve

Cleo remembered about the cheese sandwich she'd put in the microwave just a few minutes too late. She opened the door to the oven and discovered a pile of an oleaginous yellow substance, once resembling Vermont cheddar, running off a wet limp slice of rye bread.

She removed it gingerly. "I wasn't really hungry, anyway," she said aloud, then shook her head. She was starting to talk to herself again, which was annoying. It reminded her too much of the early days of her separation from Gus, when he'd been in Hollywood and she'd bumped around her apartment, trying to convince herself that all her solitude was good for her work.

Today the argument had rung hollow, however. As much as she tried to concentrate on notes for a new, tricky plot for Sister Mary Claire, her thoughts kept returning to last night. Between jet lag and fatigue, puzzlement and anger, she was practically bouncing off the walls.

She had to be honest with herself and admit that she was furious with Gus for considering the proposal without even testing the waters where she was concerned. And then he'd stayed at the party so long. It wasn't fair of her to be angry or hurt, but there it was. She was angry, and she was hurt. *You're more important to me than any party,* he had said. *We need to be alone.* But then Denton's proposal had turned out to be more important after all.

"Grow up, Cleo," she murmured. Gus would have arrived eventually. But by that time she would have been pacing the suite, hurt and angry. Better to leave when her mind was still cool and she could figure out what she wanted to do.

Giving up Sophie and Max had hurt. She had had to let go of her fantasy about her and Gus. They would have their own projects—she would write other books, as would Gus, and he would make other films—but their alter egos would bind them, hold them together, and they would continue writing Max and Sophie's story as long as anyone was willing to read it.

But last night Cleo had faced truths about herself. She had unfairly used Sophie and Max as a tie to Gus. She was sentimentally tied to them beyond what was proper; she couldn't even bear to have them divorce.

But Sophie and Max were only two characters they'd created. They weren't flesh and blood, they weren't a living, breathing, hurting couple who were fighting to keep their marriage alive. She couldn't confuse them with Gus and her any longer. She had to let them go and give her marriage a chance. She had to give Gus room. Her tie to him was like a leash, anchoring him to a career he probably wasn't suited for.

Once, in Connecticut, she had been willing to give him Sophie and Max. That decision had been based on a simple unwillingness to fight any longer. But this time, fighting for Gus meant standing still and letting him go. This time, she had given him Sophie and Max out of love.

She dumped the bread and cheese in the garbage and heard the unpleasant rasp of the buzzer. Cleo pressed the intercom button.

"Yes?"

"Mr. Creighton to see you."

She paused for a split second. Gus was back in New York already? Perhaps he'd heard from Ellison and was coming to thank her. "Send him up."

She was able to pace across the living room exactly seventeen times before her front bell rang. Cleo opened it and Gus strode in past her.

"Just what the hell do you think you're doing, anyway!"

"Hello, Gus. Nice of you to drop by." Cleo shut the door and followed him into the living room. She sat down in one of the matching oyster-white leather couches she'd bought in a burst of independence when she'd moved back to the apartment. She watched Gus pace across the living room furiously. He needed many fewer steps than she had.

"Well?" he demanded.

She looked at him blankly.

"Sophie and Max!" he supplied.

"Oh. I'm sorry I'm so slow on the uptake, Gus, but I couldn't figure out why you'd be so angry if we were talking about the rights to Sophie and Max. I didn't think Ellison would call you so fast, either.''

"He couldn't wait to call—this is a bit important, don't you think? What are you doing? What scheme is in that head of yours?'' He paused and looked around for the first time. "And when did you get those couches?''

Cleo blinked and had to smile at the ending to such a beginning, but she answered composedly. "Last summer.''

"The whole place looks different,'' Gus said, looking around.

"I got a few new pieces, but everything else is the same.''

"It's nice.'' Gus continued to study the apartment. Cleo had positioned the furniture with an eye toward the spectacular view of Central Park and the gracious buildings on the Upper East Side across it. The park was just beginning to show the subtle colors of early spring, and somehow the freshness of the scene seemed part of the room itself. The pale walls and bleached hardwood floors gave a light, spacious feeling to the apartment. Cleo had a good eye for antique pine furniture with simple spare lines and good fabrics in unusual colors. A deep purple-blue rug was on the floor; it was a striking choice that worked. And though she'd only been back for an afternoon, there was a huge bouquet of spring flowers in a crystal vase. "It's very nice,'' Gus said again, and wondered why the comfortable apartment bothered him so.

"Thank you,'' Cleo said. What was the matter with Gus? He was acting as though he'd never seen her apartment before. As she watched his face, he shook his head as if to clear it.

"Wouldn't you say it's slightly startling news?" he barked in a complete change of tone.

"Not really. Isn't it what you've wanted all along?"

He looked at her carefully. "Is it what you want?"

She met his gaze steadily. "Yes." Her voice sounded sure, but Cleo was aware of her heart's yearning as she looked at Gus; she wasn't sure in the least, really, but there was no turning back now.

"Gus, with both of us owning Sophie and Max you'll never get to do what you want—it's obvious even over the past month that we don't agree anymore on what direction to go in. It's the next logical step in our careers. I have Sister Mary Claire to work on now; my publisher is interested in another book."

He felt as though his heart were being torn out, and she was talking about logic. "What about the book we're working on? You're just going to abandon that?"

"You can finish it. Or if you want me to work on it, I will. We don't have a contract, but—"

"Of course, a contract," Gus said witheringly. "What an oversight that was. Sorry I didn't have one drawn up at the time, but I figured that since we'd been working together for about five years, you might trust me a bit."

"That's not what I meant. If you want me to finish the book with you, I will. But all we've been doing is arguing about the ending. This way you could do what you wanted with it. You can end the scene with the divorce being granted. No corny reconciliation. Isn't that what you wanted?"

"Your name is going to be on it. Don't you care how it ends?"

This wasn't as easy as Cleo thought it would be. She'd imagined that Gus would be delighted to have sole control of the couple. "Of course. But I'm involved in my next book already. I know you'll do well with the final chapter. I trust your judgment."

"Glad to hear it," Gus said shortly. He jammed his hands in his pockets and swiveled around so his back was to her. He needed to think without those perceptive eyes on him.

"Want some coffee?" Cleo asked hesitantly, afraid of a rebuff. It appeared as though the large, furious man in her living room could turn on her at any time.

"I'd kill for a cup," he said gruffly. "Thank you." He glowered and stared at the park while he listened to Cleo grind coffee beans in the kitchen. He was being a fool. Why was he arguing about this? It wasn't going to change things. It was just that he felt so . . . deserted, so bereft.

She had always fought tooth and nail for Max and Sophie. Hell, she couldn't even face the prospect of them divorcing. He had been using them as a gauge for her continuing affection for him, and now that she was giving them up, he couldn't help but think that she was giving him up as well.

He hadn't even discussed the money with Ellison, although Ellison would have told him, he supposed, if the price was too steep. The Fast team had a very lucrative future, though, and it was puzzling that she would give that up . . .

He spun around just as Cleo returned to the living room. He was almost choked with love and grief as he watched her sit back gracefully on the couch and tuck her legs up underneath her.

"The coffee will be ready in a minute," she said faintly.

"Thanks." Gus was suddenly fed up with trying to figure her out. Why was he so bent on refusing what she was offering? "Cleo, I suppose you're right. You should work on your new Sister Mary Claire book. And this way I can take Denton up on his offer to do the series."

"Fine." Cleo's heart sank. She had hoped Gus would do something different with Max and Sophie. A sequel to *Fast Moves*, perhaps. Not a television series with Wendee Tolliver floundering about as Sophie Fast.

"That means I'll be living in Hollywood again. For a while."

"Obviously."

"But that doesn't mean we can't continue working on our marriage."

"Do you really think so?" Cleo asked evenly. Their eyes met across the room. Gus's expression was puzzled.

"If we want to enough," he said. "It's obvious that you don't feel that way."

"I'm not sure how I feel," Cleo said. "I just know that you're going away again."

This remote Cleo, blunt and cool, was disconcerting. He'd rather she be yelling at him and throwing things. Anything was better than this.

The buzzer rasped, punctuating the stillness of the room. Cleo sighed and rose to answer it.

"Yes?"

"Your parents are here, Ms. Delaney." Cleo heard some disturbance on the other end, and then heard Molly's voice. "And your sister, so let us up!"

Cleo smiled. "Send them up." Kit had already warned her that afternoon that they'd be in town and might stop by. They were all dying for a firsthand report on the Oscar ceremonies.

She turned to Gus. "I know this is a lousy time, but they want to hear all about last night. Can you stay?"

"No," Gus said in a polite tone. "Please tell them I said hello, though. I have to go."

"What about your coffee?"

"Thanks, anyway. Goodbye, Clee." Gus headed for the door.

It was no surprise that Gus was fleeing before her family could see him. Disappointment flooded through her. He could love them and yet still feel constricted by that love. Love wasn't a liberating force for Gus; it pinned him down. Because of that, they were always leaving each other in a cloud of misunderstanding and hurt. They were never able to finish an argument; one of them was always leaving. Their love was made up of grief and tension, and they were locked in the same circle of fate that bound them together, destined to battle, to love and to part, and to keep on loving.

How stupid she'd been to think that severing ties with Gus professionally would somehow bring them together again. Gus was still the same; he hadn't changed a bit. He still thought that they could live three thousand miles apart and work on their marriage.

Well, Cleo finally realized that she was tired of talking about working on her marriage, and she was especially tired of pretending she could work on her marriage long-distance. They'd already made that mistake. She had a feeling that the best marriages didn't require too much work at all.

But she and Gus would never have that kind of marriage. And the kind of marriage they did have was tearing her apart. She couldn't bear yet another parting.

The force of the revelation almost knocked her to the floor. *She wasn't strong enough to handle this again.* This was the last time she'd be able to watch Gus disappear out a door while she longed to run after him, while her heart was torn with terror. Her fear of last year when he'd left for Hollywood was nothing like this. This was her soul, as well as her heart, being rent right down the middle, torn, tattered, ripped to shreds. An ache so huge it made her eyes smart lodged in her throat.

It was like being trapped in a nightmare. Again, they had argued stiffly; again, Gus had told her of his decision to take on a major project across the country; again, she could make no move to stop him. They'd said nothing of parting forever, nothing of their marriage being over, and while once Cleo would have clung to that like a straw in the wind of her emotion, now she saw it for what it was. It was futile to think that, because they never said the final words, their marriage had any chance of surviving.

She and Gus were shadowboxers, flailing away at problems they couldn't ever connect with. They were worthy opponents, their individual demons so perfectly matched that they would dance around each other forever. *Oh my God, Gus,* she told him silently as she followed behind him to the door, *It's finally happened. I can't bear any more. It's over.*

He turned to say something to her at the door, but the words died on his lips. He stared at her, color draining from his face.

He knows. Cleo gripped the doorknob so hard her knuckles strained white. The brass was cold and slick, and she held on to it as the only anchor in a spinning world.

"Goodbye, Gus," she said.

The door shut behind him with an unpleasant finality. *What the hell is going on?* Gus wondered angrily. The past twenty-four hours had been a nightmare, and he couldn't figure any of it out. Had he imagined the whole long day?

He moved mechanically down the hall, heading for the elevator. There was one thing he hadn't imagined, and that was the look on Cleo's face as he left. He couldn't say exactly what it was; it was full of sorrow and something undefinable, something shuttered and frightening. Her face was suddenly closed to him; it was as though her heart and her soul had folded into themselves protectively, and no matter how he could batter at them or cajole them, they would remain closed to him forever.

Gus shook his head. Was that really what he had seen? The thought panicked him. So forget that look you thought you saw on her face, Gus told himself. Go home and pack. Go back to Hollywood. Get the series off the ground, give her a percentage whether she wants it or not, and show her how much you care.

The elevator arrived and it was full of chattering Delaneys. He was instantly enveloped in bear hugs from Molly, Kit, and Cleo's father, David.

"Gus! Gosh, you're a sight for sore eyes," Molly said as she finally released him. "Where are you going? Did you just see Cleo? Can't you stay?" Her eyes, dark gray like Cleo's, grew wide as she took in his appearance. Gus remembered belatedly that he was rumpled and unshaven. He probably also looked as if he'd just gotten his guts kicked in. He had.

"You look awful," Molly said bluntly. "Don't worry, you're still a winner in my book."

"What?" Gus asked blankly.

"The Oscar, Gus. You lost, remember?"

Kit looked at her husband, and Gus saw the flash of concern pass from her eyes to his. She took Molly's arm firmly. "Molly, let's go."

"But I want to—" Molly stopped. She looked at Gus again. "I think I'd better see how Cleo is doing," she said in a subdued voice. She kissed Gus on the cheek and squeezed his hand. "Bye."

Cleo's father patted him on the shoulder and went after Molly. Kit didn't follow. She wrapped him in a surprisingly fierce hug. "We're here for you, Gus, always, and don't forget that," she said in his ear. "I love you." She let him go and quickly went off down the hall.

Gus stepped into the elevator and rode down to the lobby. It wasn't until the doorman looked at him oddly that he realized that there was a wet trail of tears on his cheeks. He quickly dashed them away.

But that doesn't mean we can't continue working on our marriage.

Do you really think so?

The words had revolved over and over in his head as his cab sped downtown. He'd climbed the five flights to his apartment heavily. Then, when he unlocked the door and stepped in, all he saw was Cleo.

Cleo, stretched out on the floor, improvising dialogue. Cleo, making tea at four o'clock. Cleo, trembling as he finally broke down and kissed her last February. Cleo, her body white and beautiful against the rug, holding him to her, grasping his shoulders, winding her legs around his waist. Cleo, snow sparkling in her dark hair as he hailed a cab for her on Eighth Avenue. Cleo, holding the door open for him to walk out of her life.

Do you really think so?

Gus pulled open a closet door and methodically began to pack. His blue shirt, his gray tie. His tweed jacket—no, his lighter one, California would be warmer than New York. His sweatshirt, his black cotton sweater. He tossed them into the soft leather suitcase Cleo had bought for him before he'd gone to Hollywood.

Hollywood. Why was he going, again? To work on a television series. With Wendee Tolliver as Sophie Fast.

Gus stopped with a pair of socks in his hand.

To work on a television series? With Wendee Tolliver as Sophie Fast?

Was he crazy? When had he decided that?

He had decided it standing in her living room, when he'd finally accepted the fact that Cleo wanted to give up Max and Sophie. He had made the decision because he had wanted to tell her then and there that he'd be going to Hollywood again. He had wanted to hurt her as she had hurt him, because he was afraid he no longer had the ability to hurt her.

Gus sat down. A colossal feeling of shame swept over him. He was acting like a child—a spoiled, hurt little boy. He deserved no better description than that.

The phone shrilled, and Gus snatched it up. "What?"

"I am never calling you again unless you learn your manners," Ellison said.

"I'm not having the best day, Ellison. What is it?"

"You sounded so terrible before, I thought you might want to have dinner. Now I'm not so sure I want to."

Gus chuckled weakly. "I don't think you should. I can't anyway. I'm packing. I guess."

"You're packing? You guess?"

"Yeah. Hey, Ellison, you didn't tell me before. What's the deal with Cleo signing over Sophie and Max? Do we pay her a lump sum, or what?"

"We don't pay her anything. When I told you she was giving you Sophie and Max, I meant it."

"Nothing?"

"Nope. I almost resigned as her agent. Then I figured I'd still make out on the deal since you're my client, too. Listen, where are you packing for, anyway? Not that it's any of my business. I'm only your agent."

"L.A.," Gus answered mechanically.

"Oh. For the television series you're going to produce that I know nothing about."

"Right. Talk to you later," Gus said, and hung up.

Why did she do it? Money had never been too much of an issue between them; it was only lately, when Hollywood had entered the picture, that it had become important, only by virtue of the fact that there was a bit more of it. But Gus and Cleo had both left the financial details of their entwined lives to Ellison and a very capable accountant.

But that didn't mean she was foolish about it. Once they'd separated, the rights to Max and Sophie had become crucial. By giving him her half instead of selling it, Cleo had effectively given up a substantial portion of her income.

The point, Gus realized, was that Cleo's decision had been sentimental, not financial. For some reason, she had wanted him to have sole control so much that she wouldn't even approach it in a practical way.

But why?

She gave you enough rope to hang yourself, and you went right ahead and did it.

She had given him Sophie and Max as a gift of love. She had given it because she believed in him. Maybe she had had the crazy notion that, for once in his life, he'd be able to balance his ambition and his love for his work with his love for his wife. For once, he would be able to put first things first, to see how things really were. And he had failed.

Gus looked at his packed suitcase and remembered this time last year, when he'd left to take over the direction of *Fast Moves*. He had told her that the weeks apart would be good for their marriage. He had said that they could use the time to think about their problems.

And Cleo had said, with the same bluntness he had heard today, "I don't know what problems we have except that you feel you have to get away from me."

How he had protested. He had accused her of not wanting him to take the job at all, when what was so painfully obvious was that she had simply wanted to be included in his decision. He had been shocked, hurt that the woman he loved so deeply could make such a charge. It was just as he'd been shocked today when she'd looked at him with those beautiful, intelligent eyes and said flatly, "I just know that you're going away again."

Could it be that he was afraid of his own wife?

And could it be possible that he could be such a colossal fool as to make the same mistake twice? Could he be so intent on his petty insistence to prove himself a success without her, to prove that he could provide for a woman who was supremely capable of providing for herself, that he would risk losing her? And if he *were* that colossal fool, what dark forces were driving him to it?

Gus thought with heart-wrenching clarity of how he had bungled this afternoon, storming into her apartment. He'd never really asked her what her true reasons were, and suddenly he realized that he'd never explained about not coming to the hotel last night. How could he have forgotten to explain about Wendee's deception? Did his own hurts cancel out Cleo's?

Last night Cleo had confronted the fact that it appeared his deals were more important than his promise to leave the party early with her. But then she had reached down into her heart and given him the most treasured gift she could, the gift he had claimed so falsely that he had wanted. How ironic that he had used Sophie and Max simply as a ploy to stay with her, and all his words about how important they were to him were a sham. All he wanted was to be close to Cleo, and as usual he had used deception and wisecracks to get there. He had never even considered using honesty with the woman whose integrity shone out in every word she wrote, in the way she spoke and moved and thought.

His mind touched on a thousand things, a thousand ways he had failed her. When he'd gone so angrily to her apartment, the spaciousness and comfort of it had shocked him so much he hadn't been able to gather his thoughts. Now Gus realized why he had felt so strangely resentful, so angry, at Cleo's couches and her flowers and her view of the park. It was because he had never really looked at the apartment before. They had gotten married, and he had never even considered living there.

Gus slowly looked around his apartment. He had lived in it, clung to it for ten years without really seeing it. His books. His pictures. The sofa he bought in the East Village five years ago and the coffee table he'd built himself. The desk he'd found in an antique store on Madison.

The amazing thing was that the apartment looked exactly the same when Cleo had moved in and during their marriage. Had he ever really made a home with her? She had brought a few things and he had made room, but mostly everything had been his. "Ours," he had said, even while clinging to them.

He had forcefully "suggested" they live in his apartment, though hers was undeniably larger. He had built a loft bed with a great deal of show to prove to her that he was making a home. But had he, really?

Gus got up to pace as realization after realization thumped through his brain. He had been lucky enough to find an extraordinary woman. He loved her and worked with her and depended on her. Her family had embraced him as their own, and finally, in his thirties, he had been shown what security was. He had found love that would be there tomorrow and tomorrow and tomorrow, it would never diminish, it would never disappear. After losing his family and being brought up by grandparents he'd always been afraid would die, he'd never thought he could feel that again.

He'd had to create his own sense of security. He had never been able to rely on someone else for it. He'd never been able to give himself to a woman, had never felt the need to. And then Cleo had come into his life and everything had changed. He had mellowed and thawed through her love, through the sense of family, of place, that she had given him, but then his heart had failed him. Instead of taking the gift of her abundance and her generosity and her exuberance, he had held back, held out, for the only sense of home he had managed to create—a ragtag assemblage of furniture, a cherished library of books. The apartment had been only one symbol of his need to keep a part of himself back from Cleo. Hollywood was another.

Things had been such a mess on the set of *Fast Moves*, and he thought he had been being brave keeping that from her. He had been a coward, all the way down the line. What a ridiculous notion, to think that he could separate himself from her and be free of any dependence on her. That Oscar nomination had belonged as much to her as it did to him; her talent had created the characters, her love had kept him going. Why hadn't he told her that?

Even his attempt to win Cleo back at the murder weekend had been ill-conceived, pure foolish blindness to the real difficulties of his marriage. If he'd really been serious about changing, he would simply have discussed the solution of the murder as equals. He wouldn't have sat in a coffee shop, warmed by the fatuous knowledge that he was "letting" her win as his grand secret gesture. How could he have been such an unbelievable prig?

Now Gus knew that the expression he'd seen on Cleo's face today had been the knowledge that she just could not stand any more. No wonder months ago she had been afraid to sleep with him. How could she have entered back into a marriage with a man who had never grasped the simple art of loving?

It was over. He had riddled his marriage with lies, and it was dead.

The knowledge sent him reeling. His legs gave way and he sank to the floor. Tears coursed down his cheeks. He had been such a fool all along. He thought of his banter and his wisecracks, and they sickened him. They had made him sidestep every issue, and they had helped him pretend it could all work out without forcing him to really look at what was wrong. He had failed the people who loved him, and that, in anyone's view of the world, constituted a most grievous sin.

Gus dropped his head in his hands for long, agonizing minutes, unwilling and unable to face the apartment that mocked him with all the evidence of his folly. He saw slow tears drip through his fingers, and he thought he'd never known what despair was until this moment.

He didn't know how much time had passed when suddenly, on his knees on the floor, there came, slowly, like the tiny sliver of silver on the horizon that heralds the promise of a new day, the possibility for his redemption. Gus raised his wet face and felt his strength creep back into his body.

Cleo still loved him. The knowledge was pure and sweet, running down his throat like a cool drink of spring water. He felt it to the bottom of his soul. It was a miracle he didn't deserve, but he would sin again if he didn't fight for that love.

And by God, he'd fight every day of his life to deserve it in the future. If he could just have a chance to tell Cleo how much he could change, had already changed, would keep on changing to love her the best way she could be loved. If it wasn't too late.

He had to show her how vulnerable he had become, a terrifying vulnerability he hadn't felt since he was twelve years old—a vulnerability he now welcomed with every cell in his body. It told him he was a member of the human race. It told him that he loved.

He thought about calling her, he thought about going over, but Gus knew with a sickening certainty that she wouldn't believe him. Words were so inadequate; how could he possibly convey to her how shattering the realizations he'd had were, how deeply they had marked him? It would be impossible. He wasn't sure himself. He felt as weak as a baby with the force of his emotion. He needed to show her these things, not tell her.

Gus knew he needed help, and for once he wasn't going to be ashamed to ask for it. For once, he was going to lean on the people who loved him. He looked at his open suitcase and smiled for the first time that day. Perhaps there was a way, after all.

Chapter Thirteen

Cleo fumbled for change for her coffee as the crackling loudspeaker announced what track her train would be departing on in three minutes. She deposited the coins on the counter, hitched her bag on her shoulder, hugged a bulky envelope to her chest, and ran.

She dashed onto the train with seconds to spare. Since it was a weekday and she was going opposite the commuter flow, there were plenty of seats. In fact, the train was practically deserted. She settled into a window seat and carefully tore a small hole in the rim of the plastic lid of her Styrofoam cup. Sipping at her coffee, she regarded the manuscript in her lap. She'd brought it along for company on the ride out to her parents' house, but she wasn't exactly dying to read it. It was Gus's last chapter to their book, *Jump Street*.

She'd spent three days alternating between listlessly staring at notes for her new book, going for brisk walks to toughen herself up, and crying herself to sleep. Finally, her mother had put her foot down. When Kit had called that morning and heard Cleo's flat tone once again, she'd demanded that Cleo come out for a visit. Immediately.

After Cleo had agreed and hung up, Ellison had called with the news that Gus had sent him the chapter and wanted her to read it as soon as possible. He'd messengered it over to her so she'd be able to read it that day.

Cleo slipped the pages out of the envelope. Ellison had already told her that Gus had handwritten the chapter. He hadn't used the computer, Ellison had told her, because Gus wasn't in Manhattan. He must be in Hollywood, then, she figured, and had probably scribbled these last pages in his hotel room.

She looked at the first page. Gus's handwriting, bold and black, sent a shock wave of recognition through her. It was almost as though his strong personality had entered the train, taken her by the lapels, and announced itself.

She had to admit that she had been disturbed at first to discover that Gus had chosen to go through Ellison about the final chapter rather than send it to her directly. But she was being silly, she knew. From now on, all their necessary communication would most likely be through lawyers or their agent. It was easier all around. Taking a sip of coffee, she started to read.

The chapter began in Max's voice, apparently in the stand at divorce court, and Cleo could see by scanning ahead that almost the entire piece was a monologue. That was strange.

"Yes, I've worked with my wife, Sophie, for six years now. We've been married for four years. We've always had a—a complicated relationship. But now you ask me what forces have led me to be sitting in court with her. And I have no answer. I am bewildered.

"I say bewildered because I have no idea how one person could be such a fool as to be afraid of love. I am bewildered at how a thirty-six-year-old man could be so childish for so long. And I am bewildered as to how such a man could be so slow to realize these things, and lose the most extraordinary woman he'd ever known."

Max was thirty-nine, not thirty-six, Cleo grumbled, and made a note in the margin. As the train sped through the towns of Long Island, she kept on reading as Max traced his marriage with Sophie. Tears came to her eyes with the eloquence and simplicity of the language. It was some of the best writing Gus had ever done, touching something in him she'd never seen before. These weren't the slick sentences and clever wordplay she was used to. Here Gus seemed to be speaking from the heart.

From the heart...

Cleo went back to the beginning. Everything in these pages could just as well apply to their marriage, she saw. She shook her head. Impossible.

She took another sip of coffee and read on. Max's voice had always been distinct, but now she noticed that there were jarring elements in the speech that she couldn't reconcile with his usual pattern or with Max and Sophie's story. He sounded, she realized, like Gus.

Impossible. But it was with a swiftly beating heart that she read the concluding paragraph.

"There are so many different kinds of love. There's the best kind of love, the exuberant, generous kind, the kind that gives and keeps on giving with joy. And then there's the kind that loves while running from a shadow at the shoulder. But all the while it clings to that shadow because it has the power to diminish love—because the threat that lies at the heart of love is its most specific nature. It can never be guaranteed. Some people are cowards; they are afraid to face the truth which others already know—that the fragility at the heart of love only makes the people who embrace it stronger. And then they know what it means to be alive."

Max rose and walked to Sophie. He stood in front of her. Tears stood in his eyes, but his voice was steady. "Teach me how to love," he said.

The pages blurred before her eyes. Could it possibly be that these were Gus's words—to her? Cleo put down her cold coffee and stared out the window at the trees rushing by. The pages sat in her lap with a taunting question she couldn't answer. She turned back to the beginning and started to read it again.

She was concentrating so hard on the words she was reading that she almost missed her station. The closing doors nipped at her jacket as she jumped out, cradling her weekend bag and the slightly mangled envelope in her arms.

A honk directed her to the parking lot and her mother. "I'm going to ask how you are," Kit said without preliminaries out the window as she approached, "but if you say 'fine,' I'm going to drive away."

"I'm not so great," Cleo admitted.

"Okay, you can get in."

Cleo slipped into the front seat and tossed her bag in the back. She kept the envelope in her lap. "Thanks for making me come out today. I need a dose of home."

"Honey, I hate to see you going through this. I know this is an awful thing to say, but it will get better. I promise."

Cleo sighed. "Mom, I'm not a little girl anymore. And I'm not kidding myself about my marriage anymore either. It's over, and it would be better if you helped me accept that."

"I'll do that when I believe it, too."

"Mom, please. There isn't anything you can say to change my mind. There's a part of Gus that will always have to hold back for some reason, and there's a part of me that can't push him. And I just can't have a marriage like that."

"But, Cleo—"

"Mom," Cleo said gently, "don't you think it's a little late for you to give me advice?"

"First of all, you haven't allowed me to say a word, let alone give you advice. And second of all, it's never too late. For anything. Or hardly ever never."

"Hardly ever never what?"

"Too late."

"Oh. That sounds positive. Where are you going, by the way? You just missed the turnoff."

"I thought you might appreciate a little drive to remind yourself that spring has arrived, life goes on and all that."

"That sounds nice," Cleo said. Kit was a great believer in the recuperative power of nature, and it would do no good to argue that she'd just been on a train for an hour and would prefer to be stationary for a time.

Kit let her alone and didn't speak much as she drove. This was a relief to Cleo; her whole being was concentrated on the pages she'd read on the train. She cursed the hope winging through her heart as foolish. And even if Gus had written those pages for her, what did that mean? They were just words. As a writer, she knew how inadequate words could be.

Spring was beginning out here on the Island. The azaleas had already bloomed, and the sight of the frothy pinks and reds and violets was lushly promising. Cleo rolled down the window and took a deep breath. The smells of growing things and wet earth were rich and heady, filling her senses. She fought the intoxicating feeling. She desperately needed to be rational today.

It was better to face it: it was all too easy for Gus to write such a thing. But actions spoke louder than words, and where was he? In California. If one were going to make a passionate declaration, wouldn't it be polite to at least be in the same vicinity? One could talk beautifully about the strength of love and the foolishness of cowards, but how much did it mean if one were busy getting a tan at the time? Once again, Gus was making a tiny step forward while actually committing nothing, and she'd almost fallen for it.

Cleo had been so intent on her own thoughts that she hadn't noticed how far they'd been driving. "Is this going to be a *long* drive?" she asked her mother carefully.

"I told you I wanted to take some photographs today," Kit said. "You said you'd come with me."

"But where are we going?"

"To the beach."

"What beach?"

"I thought I'd drive until I found someplace I liked. I also thought," Kit said, "that it would be good therapy for you. You always loved the beaches toward the end of the Island. The ocean relaxes you, remember?"

"Okay," Cleo said agreeably. "I guess I'm game."

"Good. We can stop for lunch later. My treat."

"This *is* an occasion."

"Don't be impolite. Enjoy the scenery. I know it's hard for you to appreciate anything that's not gray and a hundred stories high, but do your best."

Cleo did her best. It really was a marvelous day, with the sky a perfect cerulean blue and the scent of spring wafting softly in the windows. She wished her heart wasn't so heavy, and that tears weren't so close. She was grateful to her mother for trying to help her, but she just couldn't relax. She tossed the envelope into the back seat but it still mocked her.

She was beginning to get sleepy and cross when Kit finally turned off the main road and meandered around one of the small towns. She drove through blocks of houses with long green lawns and budding azaleas.

"Pretty neighborhood," Kit said.

Cleo yawned. "All it needs is a restaurant. I'm hungry, aren't you?"

"As a matter of fact, yes. You know, your father and I were out here a while ago and found the most delightful place for lunch. It was near the beach. Let me see if I can find it again."

Kit drove around and around the wide leafy streets until Cleo got dizzy. Finally, she pulled over.

"I know it's around here somewhere," she mused. "I just know it."

Cleo lifted her head from her hand and looked at her. "You may know it, but my stomach's still empty."

"You're awfully testy."

"Why don't we drive back into town and go somewhere else?"

"Oh, I don't want to drive all the way back. The beach is right here. I've got an idea. Let me look at the map, and you go ask directions from that house up there."

"Mom, I can't just ring a strange person's doorbell and ask them where the 'delightful lunch place' is."

"Of course you can. This is a small town. They'd love to help. Go on, stop being so cranky. I'm going to treat, remember?"

Sighing, Cleo got out of the car. She started up the wide green lawn toward the house. Her footsteps faltered.

It was her dream. The house wasn't white, it was bluegray with white shutters, but it looked the same otherwise—big, solid, with plenty of bedrooms and a long porch along the front and one side. The lawn seemed to stretch forever, deep green and lush, the sky that same shade of brilliant blue. And the air—Cleo filled her lungs with it—was bracing, tangy with the salty scent of the sea.

She walked slowly up the lawn to the front door. She felt unreal, as if her footsteps weren't touching the ground at all. Cleo enjoyed the sensation and prolonged the dreamy sense of peace she felt, because she knew that in a moment she would knock on the door and a stranger would answer. She would have to ask about a cute lunch place near the beach...

She walked up the porch stairs. When she knocked, she noticed that her hand was trembling slightly. There was no answer, and she knocked more firmly. The door swung open.

Cleo stepped inside hesitantly. The hallway was completely empty, and when she heard the echo of her footsteps she knew that the whole house was empty as well. There was no one living here.

A long staircase beckoned but she turned to the right and found herself in a long white room that stretched the width of the house with double French doors at the end. They opened out onto a lawn that sloped down toward the dunes. The blue Atlantic, whitecaps ruffling its waters, was visible beyond the sand.

She walked a few steps into the room and her feet hit something. Looking down, she saw a blue-green Oriental carpet. It looked familiar somehow.

Cleo stared down at the intricate design, the deep colors. Her mind felt muddled and confused. Surely it couldn't be—

"Hello, Clee."

The voice echoed in the empty room. Her back stiffened, and the hairs on the back of her neck rose. She turned around slowly. He was standing in the entrance to the room, dressed in a black cotton sweater and black jeans. Tension was in the lines of his muscular body; his face looked strained.

Her voice was hoarse, faltering, holding a question. "Gus."

"I asked your mother to bring you here. Don't be angry with her."

"I—I'm not. But what—"

"You described a life to me the other night. A life that I wanted to share with you. I never got a chance to tell you that. I thought I'd show you." Gus took a step into the room. "I've been so wrong," he said. "I've been so wrapped up in winning you again I never looked at the reasons I lost you in the first place. I lost you because I loved you too much. I couldn't accept that dependency on one person for my happiness. It scared me."

"It scares me, too."

"But you go on." He took another step. "That's the thing about you, Cleo—you go on. I've been such a coward. I knew that night at the party that I was changing, that I was beginning to realize how many mistakes I'd made. I wanted to let you know, and then Wendee didn't tell me you went back to the hotel until later—"

"She didn't?"

He nodded. "I should have told you that the other day, but I was too busy flying off the handle because I thought your giving me Sophie and Max meant you didn't love me anymore."

"That's not why I gave them to you."

"I know that. It took me a while. I can be awfully slow."

"Gus," Cleo said hesitantly, "did you write Max's monologue for me?"

He nodded. "I've been busy. I holed myself up for three days, thinking about my entire life, and you, and finally wrote it out. I broke your parent's typewriter on the first draft from banging on it out of frustration, but they already thought I was crazy."

She paused. "My parents?"

"I needed somewhere to go," Gus said.

The pause spun out a silence with rivers of elation coursing through Cleo. She couldn't speak. Tears sprang to her eyes and ran down her cheeks. "Gus," she whispered. She couldn't say any more.

Gus walked all the way past her into the room and looked out at the ocean. "When I wasn't writing, I was driving around here. I would look at the houses, walk on the beach. One day I saw this place from the beach. You can't tell from here, but the entire back of the house is all windows. I couldn't believe it when I climbed over the dunes and saw it was empty. I prowled around and looked it over, then called the realtor. I didn't even have to see the inside; it was just a formality."

He turned around to her. "It's not white, but we can paint it. It doesn't have a pond, but we can put in a pool. And it's got a study downstairs and even a barn in back I can turn into an office so we can both have one. Plus guest rooms for all those summer visitors. A huge kitchen—I've been thinking about learning to cook. And I hear we have a good school district."

"You planning to go back?"

He grinned. "I'm talking about starting a family, Cleo," he said gently. "It's a good place to raise kids."

Her heartbeat seemed to slow, and stop. She could barely breathe. "Kids?"

"Not right away. I want to spend some time alone with my wife first. If she'll have me again."

Cleo felt rooted to the carpet. Her expression was watchful and uncertain. "Are you sure?"

Gus crossed the distance between them in two long strides. He grabbed her fiercely. "I can't bear it when I see that look on your face. I can't bear that I made you look that way. I never want to see it again. I want to make it go away forever." He drew her to him and cradled her against him, finally giving in to his need to touch her. He felt her tremble, and he caressed her back, her arms, her shoulders, her hair, her face.

When he spoke his breath was warm, sending fire through her, stopping her shivers. "Teach me how to love, Cleo," he whispered.

She touched his cool cheeks with trembling fingertips. "I don't have to," she said, smiling through her tears. "You're doing just fine."

"I guess I've just proposed to you." He took a deep breath. "Will you have me, then?"

"Yes," she said. "Oh, yes."

She reached up and brought his head down to hers. Their kiss must have been one of more than a thousand kisses, but this time it had the force of all their love and all their pain behind it, and the strength of their renewed commitment. It rocked them, and when they finally were able to pull away, there were tears on both their cheeks. They wiped each other's faces gently, smiling.

"So," Cleo said, "how did we afford this place, anyway?"

"First of all, I want you to know that I just put down a deposit. We can still back out if you don't love the place. I'll show you all over it in a minute. We can always look for another house together. This one seemed so much like the place you described I couldn't resist. And I wanted to show you I was ready for a commitment. A real commitment. You and me, forever. No holding back. I thought I needed a big statement. You know, something theatrical."

Cleo looked around. "I'd say you made it."

"I've also been busy on the phone these past few days. We can sell the rights to *Jump Street*, if you'd like, and they want me to direct. I described the plot on the phone, and they leaped at it.''

A chill ran through Cleo. ''You'd have to go to Hollywood?''

''Just for a couple of meetings,'' he said, watching her face. ''The movie will be filmed on location in Manhattan and Long Island. What do you think?''

Relief flooded through her. ''I think it's wonderful.''

''Staying in the area was a condition of my employment. And from now on, it always will be. Other directors do it; so can I. My family is my first priority. There's just one thing, Cleo—''

''What?''

''We might have to do some rewriting on the book. I don't think our hearts were in it.''

''Is it awful?''

''No. But we've been better.''

''Mmmm,'' Cleo said. She ran her hands up his chest slowly. ''I guess we were a bit distracted. All that tension.''

''You said it.'' Gus brought her up against him. ''We'll have to be sure and avoid that in the future.''

She slipped her arms around him and brought him even more snugly against her. ''How will we do that?''

Slowly, he lowered himself down on the rug, taking her with him. ''I seem to remember a technique we tried on this very same rug. Why don't we see if we can—''

Cleo sat up. ''Gus!'' she hissed.

''What?''

''We can't! My mother!''

He grinned. ''I haven't heard that in quite a while.''

''I mean she's outside, you dope.''

"No, she's not. She just dropped you off and went home."

She relaxed and leaned back against him. "You were pretty confident."

"No, *she* was confident. I was terrified."

"It's hardly ever never too late," Cleo said, laughing. "That sounds fairly confident, doesn't it?"

"Enough talking," Gus said sternly. "Come down on this rug with me, woman. We've got a lot of time to make up for. You're a hard woman to win back. I thought I could do it in a weekend, and it's taken six months of time, effort, and excruciating self-analysis."

Cleo laughed as she went back into Gus's arms. Then she sat up again. "Gus—"

"What now?"

"I have something to confess. From the murder weekend."

"Can you come back down here, please?" Gus pulled her into his arms again. "Thank you. Now, what were you saying?" he asked, nipping at her ear.

"I solved the murder but didn't tell Denton because I wanted you to win."

He sat up abruptly, and Cleo's head slapped down on the carpet.

"Hey!" she said, rubbing the back of her head.

"Sorry. I did the same thing, Cleo. I thought I would let you win, and I never could figure out how Sidney Clott got ahead of you." He threw back his head and laughed. "What a ridiculous couple we are."

"Come back here," Cleo ordered him. Gus obediently stretched out next to her. They kissed. "So we're the Silliest Detectives in the World instead of the Smartest," she murmured. "My only regret is that we lost that trip on the Orient Express."

"No more regrets allowed," Gus said.

Epilogue

A shrill whistle blew as fog swirled around the dark, cavernous train station. A man in a trench coat leaned out of the train, looked down the deserted track, and pulled his head in again. The whistle blew once more, the train gave a hiss and a squeal, and started.

Inside, the man headed down the narrow corridor quickly and silently, despite the jolting movement of the train. When he reached a large compartment, he knocked three times. Then he quickly twisted the brass knob and, with a final look around, slipped inside.

"I got them," he said tersely.

"Good," the woman replied.

The man reached slowly inside the trench coat's deep pocket. He held his hand poised over the turned-down bed. Then he dropped an assortment of candy bars and crackers onto it.

"Thank goodness," Cleo said. "I'm starving."

"Me too," Gus said. "I'll open the champagne." He slipped out of his coat.

Cleo eyed his bare chest and silk pajama bottoms. "I hate to tell you this, but you forgot your top. Not that I'm complaining, or anything. But it's cold out there."

"I was in a hurry," Gus said, wrestling with the cork. "Besides, I was hoping to impress you with my fabulous physique. It's all that gardening I've been doing." The cork popped and the champagne foamed out the top. Cleo reached out to catch the bubbling liquid in two glasses. She handed one to Gus.

"Here's to our honeymoon on the Orient Express," she toasted, raising her glass. "I had to wait a few years, but it was worth it."

"Hmmm—we'll see. I'll let you know tomorrow morning," he said, grinning. They drank.

Cleo pushed aside the candy and stretched out languorously on the bed. She sighed in contentment. Bending over, Gus kissed her ankle and then stretched out next to her to capture her mouth. They kissed for a long time, spilling a little champagne on the blanket.

Gus reached over and took Cleo's glass from her hand. "What do you say," he suggested, "that we forgo the chocolate and celebrate by recreating our wedding night? Just in the interest of total accuracy, of course."

"That sounds like a very good idea," Cleo said. "But then," she continued softly, reaching behind him to switch off the overhead light, "I'm not surprised. You were always so good with proposals at midnight."

Silhouette Special Edition

COMING NEXT MONTH

#391 SOME WARM HUNGER—Bay Matthews
Once, Jessie Harper had put her career first and had turned down
Bodie Lattimer's marriage offer. Years later, she was a first-rate horse trainer, a
loving mother, yet an unfulfilled woman. Then Bodie came back to town....

#392 ALL THINGS CONSIDERED—Debbie Macomber
When her long-absent husband reappeared, Lanni Matthiessen was
understandably wary. Judd soon proved mature, manly, worthy of her love. But
with the fates—and his father—against them, could she keep Judd by her side?

#393 CHASE THE WIND—Rebecca Swan
Suffocated by urban life, Justine Fleming fled to rural Washington. Though
high-powered Blair Sutherland needed her country comforts, his fast-track
moves were taking her breath away!

#394 SNOWBOUND—Lisa Jackson
As teacher Bethany Mills reluctantly helped private eye Brett Hanson track
down her criminal ex-husband, they forged a most uneasy alliance—until a
blizzard trapped them in an avalanche of desire.

#395 TREASURES OF THE HEART—Anne Lacey
Lane Hartleigh wouldn't stand by and watch brawny demolitions expert
Graham Randall destroy her beloved ancestral home. Against all odds she'd
defend her treasure, but against Graham, could she defend her heart?

#396 CARVED IN STONE—Kathleen Eagle
Weary of being typecast, actor Sky Hunter retreated to the Rockies. Battling the
elements, he had his chance to play hero to novelist Elaina Delacourte. But he
soon learned that truth is far less predictable than fiction!

AVAILABLE NOW:

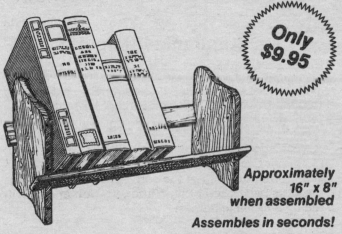

FREE!

Never Before Published

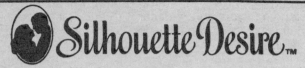

by
Stephanie James!

This title *Saxon's Lady* will be available exclusively through this offer. This book will not be sold through retail stores.

A year ago she left for the city. Now he's come to claim her back. Read about it in *Saxon's Lady*, a sensual, romantic story of the same excellent quality as the over two dozen other Silhouette romances written by Stephanie James.

To participate in this exciting offer, collect three proof-of-purchase coupons from the back pages of July and August Desire titles. Mail in the three coupons plus $1.00 for postage and handling ($1.25 in Canada) to reserve your copy of this unique book. This special offer expires October 31st, 1987.

Look for details in July & August Silhouette Desire titles!

Doff-A-1